The Earring

By

James Alan Vincent

Copyright © 2020 James Alan Vincent

ISBN: 9798642191217

All rights reserved, including the right to reproduce this book, or portions thereof in any form. No part of this text may be reproduced, transmitted, downloaded, decompiled, reverse engineered, or stored, in any form or introduced into any information storage and retrieval system, in any form or by any means, whether electronic or mechanical without the express written permission of the author.

This is a work of fiction. Names and characters are the product of the author's imagination and any resemblance to actual persons, living or dead, is entirely coincidental.

www.publishnation.co.uk

CHAPTER ONE

The three drunken women were staggering around looking for somewhere to sit. Each had a bottle of wine in their hands as they stopped to light up their cigarettes. Their ages ranged from about forty years to about sixty, but it was difficult to tell in this light. Yet sadly all of them were dressed as young women. Their skirts were far too short their heels too high and they all had their boobs virtually hanging out. The pub garden was still very busy even at this time of the night there were hardly any tables left. It had been a beautiful day and the evening was still very warm. It had been a freak burst of summer for this time of year in early May.

Alan Reed was sitting outside the Old Barge pub and restaurant by the side of the Manchester canal not far from the city centre. Having just enjoyed a meal of steak and chips with a cold beer he felt good. It made a nice change after the long miserable winter to be able to sit outside again and to eat. Dressed casually he was wearing dark blue cargo trousers, with a white shirt, a navy blue ribbed jumper and a pair of dark blue kickers which he'd just bought that day to cheer himself up. However, the last hour had been pleasant enough after a very frustrating day. There again you can't have it good all the time that was his thinking. So he thought after all he had nothing to complain about. The meal was excellent and the beer was good. Now he felt totally relaxed as he gazed around the large pub garden with various people all enjoying themselves. The garden lights were lighting up the area like it was a summers evening which would not be long in coming. The moon was now popping in and out as the clouds became a lot thinner in the night sky turning the later evening a little chillier.

Suddenly and without warning the women unfortunately sat down at the table next to him. Looking at them, he thought they were what he called a trio of slappers. All three of them were drinking and laughing loudly, but that wasn't the problem they were being very obnoxious with it. There was one in particular who was shrieking her head off in a ghastly way. This woman's voice seemed to foghorn over everyone else's, apparently she was called Wendy. He couldn't help hearing the other two calling her that. She was doing most of the talking, yet very loudly. And she was also making gestures towards all the men walking by who were certainly a lot younger than themselves. Surprisingly, or perhaps not, all the women had wedding rings on their fingers. Looking at his watch he noticed the time was ten minutes past eleven. Suddenly, two of them got up they were walking towards two younger men who beckoned them over they obviously knew the two men. One of them was called Rita she stopped and turned back then shouted to Wendy. 'Sorry Wend but we've pulled. Look I'll see you tomorrow you have fun and don't fall in the cut,' she screamed with laughter. She wobbled off with her mate called Sue to where the two much younger grinning men were waiting. Both of the men had a cigarette in their hand as one of them flicked his lighter on they both lit up. They looked like a pair of cheap idiots trying to look like gangsters. Then off they swaggered laughing with the two slappers Rita and Sue. The age difference was so obvious to see. The quartet was well pissed by now and nothing would distract them as the evening promised a session of debauchery. After all the two men Kevin and Steve shared a flat together where they had all been there before. The flat was in a side street just off the main street near to the taxi rank. It was handy for all the clubs too, and a place to have sex without being disturbed and where they all shared each other by swopping over and with different men and women they brought back with them from the clubs.

Alan watched all of this. Yet he was thinking later on they would probably spread something nasty to their unsuspecting husbands. This made him feel disgusted and angry. Why should it bother him, well it did bringing back horrible memories from his childhood. This type of filthy behaviour from women of that age made him sick to his stomach. It also reminded him of his long ago dead mother.

Wendy suddenly found herself on her own, and now she was feeling fed up because her two mouthy friends had each pulled a young man, yet she hadn't. On her own she decided to make a move for home. She'd been the loudest of the three but she always was with her horrible shrieking cackling laugh. She looked at her glass of wine, stood up and almost threw the full glass of red wine down her throat. She was angry now. Then she wiped her mouth with the back of her hand just like a drunken pirate. Now watching her two drunken mates wobbling off with the two younger men she was getting annoyed because she could still hear them screeching with laughter. They were all going off to some night club or other first she thought. Wendy shouted after them 'oh never mind me then,' the quartet looked back and waved then turned away to explore the night clubs. Her moans fell on deaf ears.

Turning towards Alan who she spotted at the next table she smiled a come on smile, she thought wow he's a bit of all right, but he turned his head away in utter disgust. She thought, oh bollocks to him. Angrily grabbing the almost full bottle of Merlot from the table Wendy wobbled off, but a little dangerously while hopefully heading for her home which shouldn't take her long.

Her blue skirt was far too short, yet it would have been even for a younger girl. Her heels were four inches high and her white blouse was very low cut revealing her heavy ample breasts.

The evening had now become a little chilly. As she walked along she pulled a light blue cardigan over her shoulders to keep the chill out. Her hair had recently been cut short. It was a mix of blond and pink with touches of green and blue, but it looked nice and it suited her really well, taking years off her. But she was still very annoyed at being left out. She felt let down, and after all it was far too soon to be going home on a Friday night.

Alan Reed could also see her large gold hoop earrings shining in the half light on her way home. She turned her head to see if anyone was following her, there wasn't.

Stopping to take a swig from her bottle of wine Wendy was still pissed off. She was usually the one the young guys wanted she was always ready to oblige, that's why her large breasts were on show like a man magnet, and it usually worked.

Once again she was starting to wobble off but slowly in the opposite direction along the towpath. She'd decided to go home this way because the canal was a short cut to the city centre where the taxis waited in line like a small herd of hippos. Taking a taxi home would be easy and it would take just about ten minutes to her council house in West Gorton. She knew she had to get home to take her small dog Toby out as her husband was away on some engineering job up in London. Wobbling on she pulled her cardigan once again closer around her shoulders then continued to head for home.

Alan Reed had watched her leave her table. When she was about twelve metres away he slowly stood up to look around to see if anyone was watching him there wasn't. Cautiously he left his table to follow her, but keeping well back hidden in the shadows. The moon was now giving off quite a lot of light as it broke out from the cloud curtains surrounding it turning the canal into silver.

He was ever hopeful she would make a mistake when suddenly she obliged him by stopping under a small dim light under a road bridge spanning the canal. The canal was snaking underneath where it curved round a bend and then it disappeared out of sight again.

Wendy was looking around and the only thing she saw was the gang of moths all fluttering around the dim light emitting from a lamp attached to the bridge. The old lamp was covered in cobwebs with all kinds of insects caught in the webs. They made her shudder; she had always hated insects and especially moths. Angrily she told them in a loud voice, 'go on all of you, fuck off I haven't got any bread.' Bending forward she screamed with laughter at the thought of a moth with some bread. In her inebriated state she found this hilarious. She was holding on to the bridge wall as she screamed out loud her thunderous laughter. Now she was using both arms to steady herself from falling over with her bag hanging from her elbow.

You could clearly hear her words, 'I hate moths, the little fluttering bastards.'

Drunkenly she placed her bottle of wine by her feet then searched in her bag for cigarettes and her lighter. Having found her cigarettes she was now fumbling furiously for her lighter whilst moaning very loudly, but finally she managed to find her lighter. Slowly she put a crumpled cigarette into her mouth and then lit up. She leant on the wall of the bridge with one hand then took a long pull on the cigarette and blew out a lungful of smoke then she let out a long sigh of pleasure.

Now she turned around to lean her back against the wall. Defying gravity she was standing there with one leg raised and her foot leaning on the bridge wall, the other leg straight. She bent down and picked up her bottle which was in one hand, but hanging loose, and now with the other hand she took another drag on her cigarette. Under the yellowish light of the bridge she looked just like a Parisian prostitute waiting for a client as she dragged on her fag completely lost in pleasurable thoughts.

Alan stood there in the shadows quietly watching her. That view of her would make a brilliant painting. He thought if he could only paint he would paint her standing like that. Yet considering her age she managed to somehow in the light still look elegant and sexy at the same time.

Looking both ways in case some piss head was behind her and now satisfied there was nobody following her she turned to head for home. Again she carried on wobbling in a dangerous manner. You could hear the echo of her clip clopping shoes loudly as she walked under the road bridge and she could clearly hear the traffic thundering by overhead as the vibrations went through her.

Moths seemed to be everywhere they seemed to be in gangs. She was sick of them ganging up on her, and now she was yelling at them again to fuck off as she slowly wobbled along.

Wendy was seemingly oblivious to Alan who was still carefully following her in the shadows. The parachute regiment had taught him well on how to stalk his prey at night.

Stopping once again to take a long pull on her bottle of wine, she almost fell backwards into the canal. Turning around to take a look she shouted 'oops.' Once again Wendy bent forward screaming with laughter. Alan didn't know why, but then she wobbled off for home again.

He thought of his mother again and felt the usual hurt and fear grip his very soul which happened every time he thought of her. He realized it was Wendy who had made him remember. Alan had an overwhelming urge to kill Wendy the moment he saw her, and more so when heard her. His thoughts were throwing her into the canal would be the easiest option then watch her drown. This urge was so bad he was having trouble controlling himself, like something was stuck in his throat. These thoughts he'd had before, but this time he needed to gain some sort of satisfaction. He needed to control his urges. However, he was very quickly losing the battle. The reason he was in Manchester was because he had applied for a job as a paramedic for a private firm. Alan had been taught his considerable skills in the Parachute medical section, the 16th Med Regiment. He used to be a top Paramedic. Because of circumstances today he was beaten to the job by another younger man. He thought what the hell that's life, you can't win them all. Unfortunately due to heavy traffic and a breakdown on the M6 he was two hours late. When he finally arrived for the interview the person doing the interviews had long gone home. His secretary told him she was sorry, but the position had already been filled.

As it was a Friday evening Alan decided to make the most of it and see some of the sights. He did a little shopping then walked around various shops and one treat for him was the pair of kickers he bought and was now wearing. His small garden was a little bare so he bought some plants and a bag of garden ties plus some gaffer tape because one of his fences had broken. When he got back home he would tape the fence temporarily. All of these were still in his man bag back at the Motel except the plants which he had secured in the boot of his car. When he went out he'd forgotten he had some garden ties in his cargo trousers, not realising they would come in useful later on that evening

Wendy was still walking in a manner only known to those who had drunk far too much. Her mind was somewhere else as she trundled along in her high heels and now paying no heed whatsoever to whom or what was behind her. Stopping for another cigarette she lit up, but this time without any problem. Looking up she saw there were the lights from the town now glowing and making it look very welcoming, yet not far away, or so it seemed.

Wendy could see the reflection of the moon in the water again. The reflection looked lovely and it was the sort of night you wished someone was walking with you holding your hand. That was never going to happen with her husband Derrick, not after twenty seven years of marriage and arguments on a daily basis. But now she hadn't far to go home and anyway her dog Toby loved her, even if nobody else did!

She started to feel a little hungry her tummy was beginning to rumble. She wondered what she had at home, but quickly decided she would have a kebab in the town which in any case was near the taxi rank. Yes she thought a lamb kebab would go down a treat with garlic mayo. Normally she couldn't finish a kebab as there was too much there, but her small dog Toby would soon make short work of it. She liked to give him a treat now and then.

Feeling excited, nervous and now very angry, Alan suddenly found himself directly behind her. She half turned to flick away her stub of the cigarette into the canal, or the cut as the locals called it. While watching it arc through the darkness she saw it hit the water making a fizzing noise as it went out. Then with her eyes closed in anticipation she took another long pull on her bottle of wine. She thought this is a good wine then she took another long pull on the bottle. Now she felt it smoothly hitting her empty stomach it felt so good.

Suddenly and violently Alan grabbed her around the neck where he held her in a strong vice like grip. His strong left forearm was held against her windpipe whilst pushing hard with his right hand onto her head which was now stopping the air from getting into her lungs. She dropped the bottle which clunked onto the towpath and rolled away. He held her like this until she fainted which was a move he had learned in the Parachute regiment, 3 Para. Quickly looking around and kicking the wine bottle into the canal, he dragged her behind some thick bushes where he laid her down gently on the grass. Suddenly he heard voices as three young men obviously the worse for drink were heading in his direction. They were laughing and swearing as they got nearer and then just before they reached Alan one said 'Christ I need a slash.' One of his mates decided he needed one as well. The two men stopped to take a slash as Alan lay there hidden. Then they were gone laughing and swearing as they walked on towards town, oblivious of what was happening almost next to their feet.

Quickly tying Wendy's wrists together with the garden ties from his pocket, but not before he took her bracelet first. Then he did the same to her ankles until she was trussed up like a pig.

Suddenly she started to come round and soon Wendy was almost fully awake. Her windpipe was really hurting. Suddenly she began to realise what was going on. A look of terror now spread across her face. She was absolutely petrified and she began to pee herself, suddenly there was a flood as she somehow knew she was about to die. When she realised what he'd done to her she panicked and started to try to get up and run. He'd used her light blue jumper from her shoulders to stuff into her mouth then tied the rest around her mouth and head, she was sadly going nowhere. It was hard to describe the terror it seemed to be wrapped around her like a shroud.

He looked at her struggling. Desperation had crept in. She wanted to talk with him but was unable to speak. As she was trying, thick mucus had started to run through her nose, and her throat was feeling cloggy and tight. She couldn't clear her throat now it felt as though her eardrums were bursting the pain was severe. A cold had been with her for the last two weeks, she had been trying to get over it. She couldn't quite understand what was going on and desperately wanted it to stop. She was still peeing herself through fear. Then she heard his voice, it was actually a nice soft calming voice, a hypnotic voice, a sexy voice. It was a cultured voice which was now whispering into her ear.

'Look Wendy, all you have to do is stay calm. I'm not going to rape you or hurt you, but I do have to put you in the canal. It will be cold at first but it won't take long. I do like your earrings and would like to keep them please? I'll keep them as a souvenir of our meeting, they're really rather lovely, oh and look, I do like your bracelet as well which I have taken. I hope you don't mind.'

Carefully he took her earrings out. 'Thanks for these Wendy, hey they dangle really well and they did suit you. Anyway, here I am rambling on. Listen Wendy, the plus side to all this is you can look forward to a lovely journey to the next world I wish I could come with you, I really do. The trouble is I have so much work to do on this side. Anyway you will be on the other side soon. They tell me that apparently, it's a lovely place to be or so I've heard, so here we go my dear.'

Wendy was so terrified she started to urinate again, and then inside of her it seemed her stomach exploded. Her mouth became free of the jumper as she managed to spit it out. 'Please, please let me go, I have to get home. My little dog Toby has to go out he needs feeding. Please don't hurt me, please! Let me go and I won't say anything to anyone, honestly I won't.' Suddenly sober she could hear him and see him listening to her, but she realised the end was very near. 'Look I'll do anything you want me to, please my dog needs me. He has to go out for his walk and he'll miss me. I'm also about to be a grandmother anytime soon. Please I beg you, please let me go. Oh please my arms are hurting me so much can I go home please, oh please let me go I won't say a thing honestly.'

Alan listened to her, but said nothing, he'd heard enough. So he stuffed her mouth with her jumper once again, but this time he did it a lot tighter. Then she felt herself being dragged along the towpath as one shoe fell off followed by the other one.

Alan dragged her the ten yards to the side of the canal without saying a word. Then he quickly slid her head first into the canal. Her head went into the freezing cold water. Gasping at the coldness of the water she couldn't breathe out, she was unable to breathe at all. In her panic she tried to kick out to get out of the water, but it was futile, her ankles were bound together and now her head felt frozen. Struggling like mad, she saw lots of lights flashing on and off she saw lots of things from her past life from many years ago. She was suffocating yet it seemed to go on for hours, but then unexpectedly there was darkness, her heart had stopped. Suddenly there was no pain. There were no more lights, there was nothing. Suddenly a door opened letting in light it was so bright and so warm, so wonderful and so different it was real. She felt as though she was filled with the colours of the rainbow. There were lots of people calling out to her with their arms open as she walked towards them. Yet all of them were happy to see her, including her long dead parents and her dead sister plus the two dogs Sammy and Judy who had died many years ago both of them wagging their tails like crazy, so happy to see her again. She was in a place of wonderful enlightenment.

Alan had held her feet up so she drowned in about seven minutes. When he finally let her go she bobbed up to the surface again. She was very dead. Her handbag was a Gucci fake which he threw into the canal. Taking some money from her bag and also some perfume with her mobile phone which was just a very cheap one someone had given to her he put it back in her bag. The money amounted to a miserable £30 and some lose change. Still it was a good half decent meal out somewhere. Filling her bag with canal water he threw the bag into the middle of the canal where it sank with a glugging sound, and then a few bubbles appeared for a few seconds and then all was still.

After checking that nobody else was about, he saw some branches nearby from an old bush he quickly broke some off. He managed to pull her body a little closer to the side with the help of a long branch. After collecting a few more broken branches he used them to cover up her face. That would give him time to get back to his car and his Motel. First thing in the morning he would drive back to London. On the walk back he came across nobody, so no-one could associate him with the killing. When he finally got back to his Motel he made himself a cup of coffee. Sitting in the one chair in his room he held her earrings in his hand also her cheap bracelet and her perfume, they so reminded him of his dead mother. Putting them safely in his pocket he turned his bedside light off, and then he lay with his head on the pillow and fell asleep. He'd had a hard day, but he thought this would be the start of a new chapter in his life. The strange thing was he slept like a baby, yet he hadn't been sleeping well for many months.

When he did wake up he felt utter elation. He felt beautiful and happy, clean and refreshed from years of turmoil which came from his terrible past. In some way he did get some retribution, however it would soon consume him, taking over his life completely.

Knowing he had made some mistakes whilst killing Wendy he had to plan the next one with precision, but at least this was not on his doorstep so to speak and he would, he reckoned get away with it, and the next time too for there was definitely going to be a next time and time after that. As he was taught in the Para's it's all about preparation at all times, that's if you have the time to plan things out. So using this as his mantra he would prepare for the next kill because now he had the urge. It had strangely made him peaceful again. Now there was a real purpose in his sad lonely life.

When he arrived back home he invented a killing kit. There were syringes with the date rape drug Rohypnol in them also Ketamine. He had also obtained two stun guns from Germany, some garden ties and lots of gaffer tape from on line. Yet he was pleased about the earrings, he also had his dead mother's old earrings. That was all he wanted when he had found her body, so this reminded him about her death which as far as he was concerned was the best day of his miserable life. Her earrings were his trophy to keep. Thinking about what he'd done, he'd realised the body had shot back up to the surface. It wasn't so much that, but the fact her face had appeared. The next time he would place a plastic supermarket bag with a couple of railway sleeper bolts into the bag which would weigh the head down. There were plenty of slappers around he would soon be looking for another woman to kill. Changing his style would be good. So he decided to use dating sites to find his victims. After going on the sites he thought a lot of the women just wanted a cushy life they would go with anyone if they had money. After giving it some thought he realised it would be easy to reinvent himself. One way he thought of he decided to pose as a Doctor who had lost his wife in a terrible drowning accident in Portugal. His story would work well. Who would call a doctor a liar?

Alan's main job at the moment was working part time as a middle aged male model. Yet he was now aged forty eight, but he only looked about thirty four. Being a very good looking man it hadn't really done him any favours because he was actually unable to have a sex life. Having had a good pension from the army he retired when he was thirty eight. He had been retired early with mental problems. With his gratuity and his savings and even after purchasing his small house which was paid for he lived very well, up until now he had no vices. Only drinking an occasional glass of wine and he never smoked. There were lots of opportunities to take women out because he found they threw themselves at him, also some men too. He always said he was married or almost married to a French woman who lived in Paris he said she was an artist. However, he did speak excellent French which corroborated his story. He wore a wedding ring, but no-one it seems these days gave a toss about that any more. There was only one reason for that; it was women, he decided they had no respect for anyone only what they could get mostly by lifting their skirts to virtually anyone.

For him going to Paris was one of life's pleasures. Being able to speak fluent French and very good Spanish too, was a big help. Having been taught languages whilst in the Parachute regiment he found it came in useful when he was in war zones during his twenty one years in the service of his country. Alan had thought seriously about living in France, next year he had pencilled in to move there. It had to be Paris though, but the trouble with that was the cost of an apartment. It would be possible to purchase one but that would leave him far too short for enjoying himself so where was the fun in that? It was far better to go over whenever he wanted and have a good time, but only when he could afford it which was about six or seven times a year. That way he would not be counting the pennies because if you have no money in Paris, or indeed anywhere it would be pointless. You had to have money in Paris as good restaurants were his favourite haunts while he was there. Food was one of life's pleasures and the French knew how to cook food. He always tipped well and the waiters soon fell over themselves to serve him. They also enjoyed the fact he could speak French like a native, while most British people could not. It seemed the waiters despised anyone who could not order from the Menu's after all they thought of themselves as special and had no time for idiots who could not order, they had no time to teach ignorant people the secrets of a French menu.

He'd often fantasised about killing a prostitute in Paris, but he did not want to spoil any chance of enjoying himself and besides he thought the French women were not as slutty as the English women. The last thing he needed was to bring any attention to himself. That would spoil his little dreams of living in Paris. Killing a French prostitute would be an easy target, yet somehow that's what made Paris as it is today they were all part and parcel of the way of life in the capital. To him there seemed to be an air of romance about them. He would love to have a woman by his side to love and to make love to. Walking hand in hand with a lady was something he had never done he could not bring himself to visualize it either. To walk by the River Seine holding hands was just a dream, but it was never going to happen. Having been with a few women in the past, but sadly he could not or did not want to perform sex with them, because the very thought made him feel unwell.

CHAPTER TWO

Katie Parish was the Ealing Parks Surgery's Practise Nurse Manager. At this time of the mornings she was usually standing at the small kitchen sink washing up all the coffee mugs from the day before. Again she had replaced the large jar of coffee and made sure there was enough milk in the fridge for the next two days. The tea had needed replenishing and the biscuit barrel was empty. Nothing new about that so she filled it up with rich tea biscuits, although by tomorrow she knew they would all be gone again. She blamed this on the doctors who she thought were incredibly greedy. They were fond of saying to patients they need to cut out biscuits and cake, and yet they were always eating the very same. She laughed, talk about the pot calling the kettle black. Katie was a no-nonsense nurse five feet five inches tall and tubby but still attractive with a nice round face and short dark hair. But she did not suffer fools easily

The sound of the doctors and receptionists were now buzzing in her ears as the place was coming to life after her busy weekend and now the phones were ringing. A couple of doctors were laughing at a joke the other nurse Silvia was telling them. By the sound of it, it was obviously a dirty joke, you could tell by the sound of the laughter. She must remember to ask the nurse Silvia what the joke was all about.

By now she had already made two mugs of coffee ready to go, one for herself and one for Helen Burk the district nurse who was due in at any second. A mug was always ready for her to start her busy day. Glancing out of the surgery's kitchen window she watched as Helen pulled into her parking slot at the back of the neat modern surgery while confidently parking as usual her bright red Mini Cooper into her allocated parking space which was next to Katie's. She noticed how clean and sparkly Helen's car was compared to her own which was to say the least, rather grubby. That was thanks to taking her three kids to various rugby venues and her daughter's riding lessons. Yet every time she saw her white Ford Focus she said she would get it cleaned inside and out but she always forgot. Helen's car made her feel embarrassed.

Helen was the only district nurse the surgery had at the moment, but they really needed another one as the surgery was getting incredibly busy. There was talk about building an extension to take on a couple more doctors and two more nurses as there was plenty of space. However, these things cost a lot of money, and it isn't easy to recruit district nurses or even Doctors these days due to shortages.

It was not a large surgery but a very friendly one where the staff morale was good. The same members of staff had been there for the past nine or ten years. Helen was busy gathering her medical bag there were some things that needed replacing from the surgery. She made sure she locked up her car even though it was at the back of the surgery as there had been thefts from their cars before. They had to be diligent. It was after all in a deprived area right on the edge of an industrial estate. A canal was running parallel with the back of the surgery. There were always a few down and outs who were wandering about looking for the quick opportunity to steal something medical, and sometimes they did get lucky.

As Helen started to walk to the surgery's back door she caught a waft of bacon butties being cooked from the catering van about fifty yards away which was run by two sisters Mavis and Joan Squires. There was always a queue of working lads at this time of the morning. She wished it wasn't there because it always made her hungry especially at that time of the morning, well any time you smelt bacon cooking usually drove you mad and made you drool. The two sisters had been in their catering van in the same spot for the whole ten years the industrial site had been there. The sisters were definitely a class act and local legends in the area.

Helen was just approaching the back door when she noticed the blinds moving. Laughing to herself because she instantly knew it was Katie looking through the slats at her. She knew she was going to find herself in a Spanish style inquisition regarding her date last Friday. She was still so excited about it, and anyway she wouldn't be able to keep anything to herself because if she didn't tell someone she was going to burst. She was still in wonderland.

It was a beautiful glorious spring day in May. However she felt lucky, very lucky as she turned to look at the trees and the shrubs. Daffodils were fully out along with the glorious primroses which were her favourite little flower, not forgetting the swathes of bluebells which would soon to appear in the far undergrowth. All the flowers were out in force, the leaves on the trees had started to thicken up and the buds had started to burst through. There was different coloured blossom everywhere. She noticed the grass had been cut around the edge of the surgery again and like most people she loved the smell of freshly cut grass. God she felt so good, and so alive. With a smile she was walking into the surgery with a spring in her step and seeing Katie she had the biggest grin on her attractive face.

'Well, you're looking pleased with yourself Mrs Helen Burk. So come on, how did your date go on Friday night and don't you dare leave anything out, and that's including all the juicy bits. I want to hear all of it if you don't mind young lady. So leave nothing out, and I mean *nothing* out.'

'Katie Parish, I knew you would be standing there looking. I saw your large nose poking out from behind the blinds, that nose of yours is so hard to hide' she laughed, 'you're so nosey. Oh but Katie, he was lovely, he's a doctor and he's not a poor one either. He was driving a Mercedes 4x4, a top of the Range. It was dark blue one, it had cream leather seats, pure heaven, and I do love the smell of leather.'

'Yes I bet you do especially if the guy is trying his luck with you.'

'It wasn't like that at all' she laughed 'trust you to say that. He took me to that posh expensive Italian Restaurant in Knightsbridge called Marcos, you know, the one that is always on the telly. We had a lovely amazing time and I got in a little late, and then he kissed me goodnight. OMG I don't know where to start, he's so nice. Guess what Kate.'

'What! What tell me for god's sake?'

'He mentioned casually like he does it every day, that he's only just gone and bought a house in Notting hill in Blenheim

Crescent I think he said number sixty seven. That must have cost a fortune Kate.'

'Look Helen here's a street map on the surgery wall did you say Blenheim Crescent. OMG look that's about the best you can get and it's a huge house too by the looks of all the houses in that area. Girl you may have hit the jackpot here. You said he kissed you goodnight, where did he kiss you?'

'It was only on the cheek unfortunately, but we have arranged to meet again though.'

'When are you meeting him again?'

'Later tonight, God I do hope he turns up. Today is going to drag on and on. I don't think I can stand the wait, I really can't.'

'Hey you're keen. Didn't he even try anything on, has he a problem down below' laughed Katie.

'No silly, well anyway how would I know about that? Oh trust you to think of that, but no he didn't try anything on, and don't be so rude! He was a perfect gentleman and so very dishy, quiet and shy but much better in the flesh. I have to say if he had tried to seduce me I wouldn't have said no, maybe tonight though.'

'HELEN,' Katie said in mock surprise. 'What sort of a doctor is he anyway, general, GP, surgeon, a shrink, what is he?'

'He's in private medicine in Harley Street and all that nonsense. He's a psychiatrist, but he only sees posh people or those show business types, oh and lottery winners' she laughed. 'He wouldn't talk about his clients though, not ever, which is quite right because it wouldn't be ethical would it? Anyway I wouldn't dream of asking him anything, you of all people should know that.'

'Well then, that lets you out, you're just a common district nurse' laughed Katie.

'Let's have less of the common please Katie, if you don't mind.'

'Hey check you out lady muck, you must be really keen.' Katie was secretly a little jealous.

'Katie, the weekend was like a year. OMG didn't it just drag along? I couldn't sleep for thinking about him. I washed my car twice and went to bed early to hurry up the weekend but that didn't work either. Anyway tonight he's taking me to the Golden Bird restaurant somewhere in Soho. Apparently it's very expensive and has the best reputation in London so I can't wait to see what it's like and all the show business folks go there.'

'Helen, you're such a jammy lady but you go for it girl, after all you've had a hard five years with Laurence sadly passing away. What with you bringing up the kids on your own and all of that, but now they've flown the nest you have to get on with life and let's face it, it's your time now so use it wisely darling. Go and enjoy yourself, yesterday has gone and today you're a day older.'

'Oh that's charming that is Katie, and it's not about age or sex with everyone. Oh no, now look at the time, I have patients to see all day today and they're situated far and wide. I'm going to have to go but I'll tell you all about it tomorrow.'

'Don't forget your coffee, here drink some, you need something.'

'Yes you're right.' She grabbed her mug and managed to take a few swallows. 'I have to go and I'll tell you all about the date tomorrow Katie.'

'Just make sure that you do and as I said don't you dare leave anything out' she laughed. 'Anyway, today will soon go. Hey is he picking you up or are you meeting him out somewhere again? I suppose it would be nice if he picked you up Helen.'

'Hey he already has' she laughed. 'Doctor Walker I mean. Geoffrey is picking me up at 8pm sharp, he's not into anyone who's late as he has to run a tight ship.'

'Right, but don't you forget to change your sheets young lady.'

'Katie, whatever do you mean' she laughed. 'I've already done that.'

'Live a little darling, now it's your turn for a change so go and enjoy yourself.'

'Anyway, I'm as young as I can be for a forty eight year old Katie.'

'Sweetheart you silly girl you don't look it, and anyway what the hell has age got to do with it? Don't hold back if you want something, you go get it and hold on to it.'

Helen picked up a few more essentials, some gauze, bandages, plasters, medical socks etc. She needed some Metformin and insulin for her diabetic patients, then she shouted 'Katie I have to go, you have a nice day. I'll catch you tomorrow.'

Helen Burk had been a widow for five years. She was 5ft 5in tall with a bobbed blondish hair style and was always smiling. She had kept her figure which for her age was amazing, and she dressed very well. Unfortunately, her late husband Laurence who was a science teacher died of a heart attack aged just forty three, but he left her with a good insurance enabling her to pay off the house. Her children, two boys Peter and Simon had both left to go to university. But now she was feeling lonely and wanted to try internet dating it seemed everyone was encouraging her to go for it, otherwise where else are you going to meet anyone? She had heard horrible things about it, some good but mostly bad. After all where do you go to meet anyone, because after work there was the housework to do, the cooking, shopping and also the large gardens to maintain, and thank god she had no pets! The kids kept saying get a dog mum, it will be good company for you, but she would never have the time to take it out, and in reality her busy day didn't leave a lot of time for meeting anyone socially. The weekends were the worst, because you seem to see couples old and young and you're on your own. She hated weekends especially in the summer on a nice day. As for holidays, well forget them. Who the hell would want to look like a sad person all on your own so she didn't go, there was no point.

There were plenty of offers from friends to pop round for a drink or a meal anytime, but she felt so out of place. Not only that but she felt that husbands of her friends were always a bit too friendly. One of them in particular was always trying to put his mucky hands on her while offering to help her out, but why do men of a certain age think that single women, especially widows were desperate for sex? It defied belief. She dared not mention it to his wife Liz (and he knew she wouldn't) because they had been friends for twenty years and it would have ruined their friendship permanently, so she always tried to keep away. Anyway as far as she was concerned he had ruined the friendship already.

However, this lovely man she met on the dating site was a doctor called Geoffrey Walker. He was a charming and attractive man with immaculate manners. He was also very clean and well dressed, very good looking too although he obviously played that down. He said his age was forty eight but he only looked thirty eight and was yummy and so nice with it too.

She didn't want a male model, just a genuine nice straight guy, but not realising that's what he was.... a part time male model. Being the same age as Helen, they did appear to have a lot in common. She had turned to a dating site called Professional Lonely Singles, PLS for short. She had a lot of interest, but mostly from weirdoes, married idiots and the odd nice man which was a rarity.

Having met a few she was getting very disenchanted with it. For some odd reason men seemed to exaggerate about their height which made her laugh, she wanted a tall man and most of them also lied about their age, but a lot seemed to have photographs on the site taken years ago. However, Alan Reed had more than he could cope with because of one word DOCTOR, it was ridiculous. He only paid for one month and then came off knowing he would get lots of replies because the word Doctor was like a golden magnet, and of course how he looked was a great help to him. The pictures of him looked as though he smacked of money and success what more do the ladies want? But now he had deleted all his photographs. That was his details which were false anyway including his mobile phone number, he also gave a false address to the dating site. To the ladies it looked as though he had it all, or so it seemed. That's the sort of women he wanted to meet so he could rid the world of the greedy money grabbing sloths that they were. His mental condition was now getting rapidly worse, which had

now begun to release the sleeping evil creepy monster hidden inside of him.
They had first met in the White Horse pub car park in Wembley. It was a lovely warm evening, some weeks in April can suddenly turn into a mini summer for a few days and this was one of them. He asked her for a piece of paper so she ripped a piece out of her diary for him. Alan had insisted they use his car, but only after he wrote down his name and address with his car number plate, along with his mobile number on the piece of paper she gave him and left it in her car as a precaution, as he explained it was daft to use two cars to go out in. When she saw him she couldn't believe how nice he looked. She thought what a wonderful gentlemanly thing to do, but it did make her feel very safe. Helen hoped into his Mercedes as he held the door open for her. He smiled at her as they slowly drove off for the night and later he would bring her back to her car.
On the second date he had arranged to pick her up at her home. She had been in a state of flux all day. Alan arrived at 8 pm on time and her next door neighbour watched her as she left her house with Alan, she was pleased about that. It was simply showing off, but she loved it as he held the door open for her again and they after waving to her nosey neighbour Mrs Wilkins, they drove off into the night.

Alan knew about medicine although he didn't dwell on it, after all they were out on a date and not at a medical meeting. The one thing she liked was that he did make her feel very safe and secure. They talked about family, their children and to a certain extent their jobs. They talked about what they were both hoping to find in a relationship. Both of them had agreed it wasn't easy and there were a few odd people on the site but you have to have a laugh and try not to take all of them too seriously, but just try to take them with a pinch of salt.
The conversation turned to their children. Alan told Helen that he had three children, two girls aged 24 and 22, and one boy aged 19. Suddenly he found he was a widower because unfortunately his wife had drowned on a weekend break in

Portugal two years ago. He was only just feeling it was time to start dating again because his children had now gone to university. However, they were good kids all of them, and they had also given him lots of encouragement to date again. In fact they insisted he at least try to meet someone so he didn't just work, work, work. You have to have some enjoyment in life they all told him.

So he was now like Helen. He told her he was all alone at night in an empty house, climbing into bed on his own and then waking up on his own was a long term prospect he didn't welcome any more. It was time to get a life again, however it's not easy because work does get in the way which was unavoidable, one had to live.

When she asked him how his wife had drowned, he replied 'Helen, honestly I still can't talk about it because it still hurts, I wasn't there and couldn't save her, and the pair of them were sucked out to sea.'

'Oh my god, that's really terrible Geoffrey.'

'Look Helen, I have to move on so can we please leave it for now. I'm sorry if that sounds rude but I don't wish to be reminded as I have been every day for the last two years. Is that okay with you maybe someday perhaps I will explain? All I can say is I was in England at the time and she was with a friend. They were taken out by a very strong rip tide, but someone had moved the warning flags. Both of them drowned. They found the two bodies eleven days later after the fish and crabs had had a go at them.'

'Oh I'm so sorry I shouldn't have asked, you must think I'm terrible now.'

It was typical he thought to himself, typical bloody woman, go find out what the guy has and milk him.

'All I can say it was not a pleasant sight to see your wife in that condition when before she was so beautiful, vibrant and happy. It just broke my heart, but the sad thing is she only went for a long weekend with Jane our next door neighbour. I had a seminar to arrange so I couldn't go. So if you don't mind can we please leave it at that for now Helen?'

'Oh dear God, again I'm so sorry. I won't ask again you must think I'm so nosey. I'm sorry.'

He patted her knee and said 'let's forget it, let's face it Helen it's only natural to want to find out about someone. I can see that you have to be very careful, so please don't worry about it. Let's have a nice time and see how we get on, and so far I think we're doing okay.' He smiled his devastating smile at her, 'don't you agree?'

'Yes we are, and it's a lovely evening, thank you Geoffrey.' She was well smitten.

His smile made her go weak at the knees. His smile was wonderful, he had dark curly hair with a touch of grey coming in with strong dark eyebrows and his blue eyes held you in their gaze. Alan was 6ft tall with strong hairy arms and broad shoulders. His smile was a killer smile for sure with a row of strong even white teeth. Also he had that tanned look and was dressed in a pair of faded but very expensive Levi blue jeans with a very nice white shirt. There was designer stubble, not too long and his watch was a Rolex. His after shave was a smell she had not encountered before but you could tell it was very expensive. It was a little heavy and musty but the sort that will linger all night, it smelt very sexy which suited his persona perfectly. But he was very sexy she couldn't help being smitten to the core.

She was also dressed in a pair of tight faded blue jeans as she remembered that he told her he liked ladies in jeans. So she wore a really nice pair, but she did have nice legs, but even with Annie Bing jeans you could see that. She wore a nice cream blouse from Top Shop showing off her breasts which were a nice size, not too large but enough to get any man's pulse racing. The small jacket she was wearing was bought from Miss Selfridge. It was a sort of dark red colour which fitted her perfectly. Her hair was just the length of her collar, it was a nice blond colour with silver streaks running through it and she looked stunning. She had made an urgent appointment on the Saturday to get it styled and that alone had cost her £78 but she thought it was worth it. She was also wearing a pair of fashion denim kitten heels by Aldo.

Helen loved his 4x4 Mercedes. It was so comfy the cream leather upholstery was divine, it was pure luxury, and you couldn't hear anything from the outside it was so quiet to drive. They had now arrived at the Golden Bird Chinese restaurant where he had reserved a nice table for two by the window. The whole place was busy with wealthy diners, she saw two BBC News presenters, also members of a well known soap opera, and she told him she felt a little out of place.

'Hey, now you listen to me young lady, please don't say that. Do you know what, you look lovely? Have you any idea how attractive you are, so no more of that please. Good god you beat this lot hands down for looks and personality, otherwise we wouldn't be here would we?' Then he smiled that smile again. Also you have to remember Helen, your job is very important to the public. All you see here are people who are so pretentious and false. Believe me I see a few of them and none of them have an interest in anyone but themselves. So be proud of what you do and who you are. Life is about people, about love and about caring. You have all these wonderful qualities that's what I can see. Qualities this lot have never heard of, trust me I know he smiled at her then he squeezed her hand in a gentle but strong way.

This lot have no conscience, only what they have in the bank. Trust me I see them all the time, the first thing they ask me is how much will it cost me, rich as they are, yet they all want something for nothing. As I just said you outshine all of them in looks, personality and devotion to the public, so be proud of yourself.' He picked her hand up again and then he kissed the back of it.

Helen went red she felt embarrassed, but pleased. She had fallen for him hook line and sinker. To meet someone like Alan was a huge bonus and she was not going to let go of him.

Katie Parish arrived at the Ealing Park Surgery at 8am on Tuesday. The date was April 2nd and again the weather was beautiful, only this time she had paid her 12 year old son to clean her car. She had gone round the Doctor's surgery switching on all the electrical appliances which was her usual morning ritual. She was the main duty nurse. There was one other nurse Brenda, and Helen their district nurse and the two receptionists, also three Doctors. They all turned in at around 8am.

By 9am Helen had not arrived for work. She was the only district nurse at the small tight knit surgery and was never ever late, not in the last nine years had she been late. She was such a conscientious nurse and this didn't feel right to Katie. If she hadn't arrived by 9.30am she would phone her mobile. Her start time was normally 8.30am but perhaps she had been called out by a patient?

By 9.30am she still hadn't arrived or been in touch. Katie was now a little concerned she decided to ring her home number, but no-one answered, then she rang her mobile, again nothing. By 11am the whole surgery was concerned as nobody could get hold of her. At 12 o'clock which was lunch time, Katie drove round to see if she was in. She only lived about fifteen minutes away by car so she soon arrived at Helen's house in Elm Crescent, Ealing. The weather had now started to get very warm giving that summer feeling. The first thing she saw was Helen's car. She drove up behind it, got out of her car and looked inside Helen's, then she knocked on the door after ringing the bell, but no one answered. Peeping through the windows she saw nothing unusual, she went round the back and still there was no one there. Curiously the next door neighbour Mrs Wilkins came out because she had seen the nurses uniform, the dark blue top and skirt with the upside down watch they all wore and said 'hi are you looking for Helen?'

'Yes, have you seen her at all, its Iris isn't it? I'm Katie I work with Helen told me she had a nice neighbour called Iris.'

'Yes that's me, but I haven't seen Helen today, and I never saw her this morning either, I usually do. Look, strangely her car is still in the car port. Last night was the last time that I saw her. She went out with a nice looking man who arrived to pick her up in a posh sort of car at about 8pm. My husband said it was a 4x4 Chelsea Tractor although it didn't look like a tractor to me. Anyway whatever that is, he rang her door bell and she came out looking nice and then she got into his posh car. He was a tall man; very nice looking he looked very professional and very smart. He looked like a star, she called out hello to me, with a nice big smile on her face trying to make me jealous....mind you she did. Then she waved cheerio and that was that, off she went, but I never heard her come back. I'm a very light sleeper unless it was when I was in the loo I can't even remember going in the night, but sometimes I do,' she laughed.

'Well yes that may have happened Iris, you must sleep through some things and knowing Helen she would have crept in like a little mouse so as not to wake you up, she's so considerate.'

'I can tell you now Katie, Jim my husband sleeps like a dead dog and snores like a sailor, mind you he did used to be one.' Now realising what she had said she peeled of a long howling laugh as though it belonged to a mad woman, which wasn't far from the truth.

Helen told Katie lots of times she thought she was a milk bottle short of a full crate, and all the neighbours avoided her like the Black Death, because she never missed anything, yet she heard everything.

'Is there something wrong with Helen? I never heard or saw her leave for work I always do every morning from my kitchen sink at about 8 am she always waves back to me. Anyway look I do have a key to her house as Helen asked me to look in on the house when she was on holiday. I've forgotten to give it back and she hasn't asked for it either so we had better take a look inside then shall we dear?'

'Yes, that's a good idea Iris. We are concerned as she hasn't turned up for work. It's never happened before so we hope she's okay and not laying ill in her bed.'

'Oh my God, do you think she could be ill, lying there all alone without being able to ask for help that would be terrible.'

'Let's find out Iris then we will know for sure, it's best if we take a look to make sure she's not ill, because you never know.'

'Yes you could be right what with all the food poisoning you can get today.'

They thoroughly searched the house and everything seemed to be in order. It was so neat and tidy especially now her children had left home, but there was no sign of Helen. Her bed had not been slept in either.

'Anyway look Iris, thanks for letting me in as that's helped to put my mind at rest about her being ill. I have to go as I'm due back in the next twenty minutes, I'm sure there's a perfectly rash explanation for her absence, well we all hope so.' However, Katie was now getting very worried indeed because this was not at all like Helen and she felt there was something very wrong. She had no information either about this man she had met for the second time. So who was he, where did he come from, where had he gone and where had Helen gone? That's what concerned her the most now. Katie had a dreadful creeping feeling about all this she had a horrible tingling run down her spine into her bottom. Arriving back at the surgery everyone was now concerned. Katie feared the worst as she now had a terrible feeling in the pit of her stomach that something had happened to Helen. Katie had no explanation what or why, she knew it was bad though. It was her intuition which was usually correct now she found it difficult to concentrate on her duties in hand. She did however ring the local hospitals to see if there had been any incidents involving Helen and then she rang the local police station at Notting Hill Police station in Ladbroke Grove.

Sergeant Bob Willis answered the desk phone he gave his name 'Sergeant Willis, he asked what the problem was and could he be of any help.'

She gave her name Katie Parish she said 'look I'm sorry to bother you sergeant. 'I'm enquiring to see if was there was any incident concerning a nurse of ours called Helen Burk. She's the district nurse. I'm the practise nurse from the Ealing Park surgery.'

'She's one of your nurse's you say and now she's missing, how come you think that' asked Sergeant Willis.

'Well she'd been out on a date with this doctor called Geoffrey Walker who was a psychiatrist who worked out of Harley Street, but she had not reported back to work. She was not at home and her car was in the drive. She had been picked up by this man, supposedly a doctor and she had for all intent and purposes simply vanished during, or after the date with him.'

Bob Willis asked Katie to hang on for moment while he would check with a psychiatrist panel in Harley Street which the police used from time to time.

She hung on what seemed like hours, but really it was just for five minutes. It was a long list.

'There was just one who was now aged 77 he worked part time, does that sound like him to you?'

'No it certainly doesn't sound like him,' she asked him 'what if Helen has been abducted?'

'Well it's still best to leave it 48 hours unless you know for certain that she has been, and in this case you're not are you? Please ring us again after 48 hours and I'll get DCI Eric Fletcher to look in on it. We can't do anything before that, because she can turn up at any time, that's how it works. I know you're really concerned. People go missing all the time and honestly they pop up the next day. Anything can happen they meet old friends they haven't seen in years. Some run away sometimes from pressure of family or work. Sometimes even with a new partner. I'll leave a note on DCI Eric Fletcher's desk, that way he will be aware of it if nothing else Katie. I'm afraid that's all I can do at this moment in time. We can't put in a full search operation at this moment in time. But I will keep my ears open for you and I do have your number, my wife is a patience of yours' he laughed.

CHAPTER THREE

Alan Reed had been retired early from 16 Med Regt the Parachute regiment for an unspecified mental condition, alias Doctor Geoffrey Walker. He had been in the Parachute Regiment since he was a seventeen year old. When he was thirty eight he left after being retired early due to his mental condition. The medical team advised him to seek medical treatment without delay. But he was now forty eight years old and his condition was worse than ever.

Having paid for the meal at the Golden Bird, he had left a generous tip then helped Helen on with her jacket and they walked out to his Mercedes 4x4. Opening the passenger door for her as she sat in the passenger seat she felt wonderfully special, but for him the urge to kill was destroying him inside.

Helen said 'OMG that was the best Chinese meal I have ever had Geoffrey, it was superb thank you so much. Hey and you're wonderful company too.' She leant over and kissed him softly on his lips. She felt he slightly recoiled, but maybe he was a little shocked.

'Helen look can you please call me Geoff, it sounds friendlier? Would you like to come back to my place for a coffee, I don't live too far away. I am just renting a house at the moment as I am buying a town house in Notting Hill. In fact I have bought it already, but annoyingly I can't move in for three months unless the tenants decide to move out early. The house is rented out and the tenants have the right to stay for that three months period which is fair enough. A friend of mine has let me have one of his houses for that period. Having about thirty odd houses he rents out, he's well minted. We went to med school together. Anyway, we have to pass my new house on the way so I can show you, but unfortunately only from the outside. The tenant is a German Doctor, a heart surgeon, and his wife is a trauma nurse at the Great Ormond Street Children's Hospital, they're such really lovely people.'

'Oh that's a shame Geoff, but three months will soon go, it's not long now.'

'Yes of course you're absolutely right. You know, I could do with a woman's good eye for decorating, you know like choosing colours and things, someone to take charge like an interior designer. Are you any good at that sort of thing' he laughed 'anyway you must be a lot better than me. I really am useless at things like that, seriously I'm absolutely useless.'

'Yes that sounds lovely. I'd like to see your house and I'm not bad at design either. You'll have to see my house, I did all of that but I can't be late home Geoff as I do have work in the morning, so I can't stay for long.'

'Yes of course Helen, and Geoff sounds a lot better, I won't keep you that long trust me, I'll soon make sure you get plenty of sleep. I know how hard you nurses work and especially district nurses. Some years ago before I got married I dated a district nurse for about two years. She was always on call. Anyway she moved back to Scotland, but she always worked so very hard. I like Notting Hill Helen, its lovely and it has a sort of village atmosphere about it, let's go and I'll show you.'

When they got to Notting Hill he had already picked out a house in Blenheim Crescent it was number sixty seven, which anyone would like to own. The large house had six bedrooms and was a town house, but it was beautiful. 'That's the one there with the flower baskets and the street lights outside it.'

'Oh Geoff, it looks lovely and so large. I do love the steps up to the huge front door and all for you. What happens then if you get lost in it, but it looks wonderful, so clean and well kept? I'm not asking, you understand, but it must have cost a fortune! Just take a look at all the expensive cars and all the lovely cafes, restaurants and the little bars. It looks so nice I've never seen this area lit up at night Geoff, it really is quite gorgeous.'

'Thank you, I was so lucky I had quite a bit of money left to me by an uncle in America some thirty years ago now. I was advised to invest it in a fledgling technical company; you know Sim cards, computer chips and mobile phone stuff. After very expensive advice I made some investments in a company in Silicon Valley California thirty years ago, and do you know the dividends alone have paid for the house, so it cost me nothing in real terms and I still have my original investment, plus a lot of dividend money.'

'It sounds to me like you know what you're doing Geoff, so very well done.'

'Thanks, I know the house is large, but the ground floor will be my practice rooms. I have already let four other rooms on the bottom floor. One is a podiatrist and the other a dentist, then a plastic surgeon and a hair clinic. So that will bring me an income alone of another £150,000 a year and then there's mine too, so all in all it's a good investment and a lovely home. The garden is huge and beautifully kept by a gardener, a lady gardener too. Can you believe that a lady gardener? I've never heard of such a thing!'

'Well don't look so surprised we can do other things you know' she teased him.

'I know, I don't mean to sound so misogynistic, I'm sorry.'

Slowly he cruised past the house he chose, so she could have a good look, she was really impressed and thought she would love to live in a house like that. He saw her look too.

'Look please don't take any notice of the house I rent, it is in Norton Road Wembley. It's very small but as I say it's only temporary and I won't keep you long Helen. I can show you the plans of the house. I think you'll like the look of them, I can't wait to move in, but I do need advice on all new furniture and I know I'll get it wrong. Anyway I have lots of brochures so you can help me look,' he laughed. 'I have a budget of £160,000 for furniture and decorating and things like that, also bedroom furniture and a new kitchen, but I'm far too busy at work to look, you know it's very worrying.'

'Hey, listen I do like that sort of thing Geoff, so let's have a look and see what you have. Getting the curtains right as well is so very important, they have to match the decor and the furniture, you must get it right, or everything else will look out of place, if you don't, it will look like a joke.'

'Oh my lord Helen, I never thought of that. Do you really think the curtains are that important, my wife did all that, I left it all to her as she knew what she was doing which was great? I sold the house because there were far too many memories and the kids didn't mind, and anyway they all wanted to live in the London area, and let's face it Helen, it's where the money is.'

'Where did you live before Geoff, if it wasn't in London?'

'Exeter, I worked for the NHS as a consultant, I was there for seventeen years. I enjoyed it there but at the end of my contract I had a rethink. I was offered a partnership in a practice, I thought about it but there was more money working in the private sector so here I am. There was a good opportunity to work with my mentor from my medical student days, so I accepted and joined the practice, but after only eleven weeks he died in his sleep, so I had to take over the business, now I own it.'

She looked at him and said 'I'm also glad you're here Geoff.' She kissed him again, but she felt again there was not really a positive response. Now he seemed to pull back a little, not a lot but it didn't go unnoticed. She thought he must be shy, what with losing his wife not long ago and in the middle of trying to settle down, it was difficult for him to adjust, but she understood that, after all it had happened to her some five years ago. She knew it took time to settle down to a normal life again. She thought it was sweet.

'That didn't take long Helen and here we are' slowly driving into the car port by the side of the small, but neat looking house. The car port was a long one, at the end there was a garage. Hopping out of the 4x4 he opened the door to the kitchen then he showed Helen in. He put the light on and pressed the switch on the electrical kettle to boil the water for the coffee.

'Oh this is a nice little kitchen Geoff, and very clean too.'

'Well yes it will do until we.... oh sorry. I mean I get the chance to move into Blenheim Crescent. How do you like your coffee, strong, medium or weak?'

Pleasingly she heard the 'we.'

'Oh not too strong, medium will be fine, but not too hot. As I said before I can't stay for long so show me the brochures Geoff, you have really got my interest now' she laughed.

'Let me pour the coffee, you go into the lounge, all the brochures and colour charts are in there on the coffee table. As she got off a kitchen stool to go into the lounge he dropped a large amount of the drug Rohypnol into her coffee, two 5mg tablets. It's tasteless, but a powerful drug and 5mg would have done the job but he wanted to make sure, not that it mattered to him because she was going to die anyway. Stirring her coffee well he took both their coffees into the lounge. It was cool enough to drink without waiting for it to cool any further. Helen was already looking through the colour charts and also the furniture brochures.

'Oh thanks Geoff, hey these are lovely colours you know.' She took a sip of her coffee then a large swallow. 'Oh this is nice, I love this sofa and the curtains to match, take a look. Oh and this would look divine, but this wallpaper is wonderful Geoff.' After ten minutes she said 'oh dear I feel so tired, I haven't felt this tired for years.'

'Really Helen, you must have been overdoing it, are you okay? Look sit back a moment and finish your coffee, it will help to keep you awake' he laughed, 'and then I really must take you back home.'

'Thank you Geoff I will.'

She managed to drink the rest of her coffee before she passed out. Then he tried to arouse her but as expected there was no response. Looking at his watch the time said 1.45am. Tying her wrists together and putting them behind her back, and also her ankles too. Then he wrapped gaffer tape tightly around her mouth then he picked her up and carried her out of the back door to his 4x4 after making sure there was no one else about, but they couldn't see him anyway because it was very dark. Covering her up in the back of his vehicle he wrapped her in a large rug while quietly driving off towards the river Brent in Ruislip Road, East in Hanwell. It took him about twenty five minutes to drive to a small clearing off the main road where he stopped the car. The time was now almost 3.23am. Waiting for a while making sure there was nobody about, he made his move.

Silently, but carefully he carried her sleeping body down the steep bank to the river. All was very quiet and very still, he was about seven yards from the water's edge when he slipped up in the Dewey wet grass and dropped her. She quickly rolled away down the bank, but he managed to stop her at the water's edge. Keeping very still whilst looking around and making sure no-one was looking he picked her up saying 'I'm so sorry Helen that was so clumsy of me.' Carefully he slipped her into the water, but she suddenly became awake. The look in her eyes was of abject terror, they said 'please don't kill me, please!'

Helen wanted to fight back but she was unable to as she was trussed up too tightly. She started to make a squealing noise through her nostrils, but he just smiled at her then he tenderly kissed her forehead. He said in a comforting tone 'please be still Helen, I promise you it will soon be over' then he pushed her out into the water where she sank in the middle hardly making a sound or a ripple.

But now she had fully woken up and was in a blind terror. She felt herself slowly sinking, she began to struggle some more it was to no avail and she slowly sank to the bottom of the river. Suddenly she broke the surface as somehow she kicked off from the muddy bottom of the river then she began to make even more squealing noises through her nostril which made him laugh. Her head had now disappeared again under the water, which was due again to the heavy railway sleeper bolts he had attached to her neck by a supermarket bag and within ten minutes she had drowned.

Pleased she had gone he sat there for another ten minutes just in case she re-appeared again, but there was no sign of her now. The river in this part was only about five feet deep, so he took his time to remove any evidence of his being there while not forgetting the rug he had used to hide her. The false cloned plates on his vehicle he had made himself which came from another 4x4 on a garage forecourt. When he arrived home he switched the correct plates back, it was a simple job to do as they were held on with Velcro tape. The pleasure he got from killing her was enormous and very satisfying. The feeling of elation was wonderful. Now he felt happy but most of all he felt clean.

Looking through her handbag he took her money, her mobile phone door keys and some perfume etc. He had also removed her earrings and a nice little opal ring which he put into a cup in his kitchen cupboard to keep as a memento so now he had three pairs. Now he decided to check her phone, what he found made him angry because somehow she had taken a few pictures of him without him knowing. So he checked and then re-checked that she had not sent any to anyone, she hadn't but he knew she would have done.

This caused him to rethink his profile on the dating site, that's why it was a good idea to take his pictures and details off the site. After all he couldn't afford for anyone to pass his pictures around. However, he had another seventeen women lined up waiting for a date. After drawing a circle around the inner London area he specifically looked for women within about ten miles or nearer to Hyde Park. He wanted to create terror amongst the greedy, promiscuous and loose women in the age range of between 40 and 65. However, he would take his time as he had all the time in the world because this was now his mission in life. Already he had received the mobile and landline numbers from gullible women. After ringing them he had said he was going on holiday for three weeks and would not be on the dating site because he had removed his details he would be ringing them when he got back home. So now he had his work cut out, but he was untraceable and would not be caught, not until he had got rid of a few more women. Getting caught held no fear for him whatsoever.

Helen was the first one from the dating site. The experience, for him was wonderful, also very calming, but he wanted to do it again and as soon as possible. Her body would float away down the River Brent where it merged with the Thames so maybe her body would end up in the River Thames, but he doubted if she would travel that far without being discovered. The water would wash away any evidence of him and now he would also destroy the clothes he was wearing.

His priority was to get rid of her handbag and personnel items, but he would keep her gold earrings, and of course her money which was about £83, not a lot but useful. Taking off his surgical gloves he put them in his garden incinerator to be burned later.

After waking up in the morning he made arrangements to dump her bag in the river weighed down with a brick. Now he felt elated, clean and fresh again, but above all he felt good and he would set out to meet another woman.

His dating site profile had a massive response it read:

Widowed Doctor aged 48 now seeking ladies of similar age, with sense of adventure for a life time of romance and fun. Must have no baggage and must be able to pack a bag when required as I have property in Spain, France and Australia and need to visit them from time to time. Expense is no problem for the right lady. Must also be tactile with a great SOH would be a bonus. If you like sailing I have a sail boat in the South of France. Please, no time wasters and honesty is a must. Must live within ten miles of central London or near.

He had seventeen phone numbers, why, because he figured it was greed, pure greed and his looks. That's women for you he thought, they just wanted the money and the easy life without the work, and someone who looks good on their arm to show off to friends.

To him it just showed what a mercenary lot of bitches were out there, there were always these women who just wanted the money and the property. These women wanted the easy life without working for it so the sooner he got rid of them the better place this world would be. Yes he would now start his well planned campaign. In his own mind he was now on a mission to rid the world of scrounging women and yes the world would be a better, cleaner, fresher place without them so he would start to do his bit. He thought he was not born to kill but his mother had driven him to kill, it was not a problem to him, anyway what's not to like about it? Now he was doing the world and men in general a great big favour, plus of course he liked it which helped enormously. In a way he should be rewarded for his efforts; after all he was cleaning up the dregs of society.

Also, he wasn't that bothered about getting caught, he never had done because in some ways the sooner the better, but in the meantime he was going to make sure he took as many women down as he could. It didn't really matter how many he did because it would never make up for his miserable life, and the memories would always be there to haunt him until he died, of that he would be certain. That was just the way it was and the way it is now. He was fully aware that when he did get caught he would commission someone to write a book about his life. Alan didn't particularly like his life anymore but he liked isolated places.

He got used to them while he was a child so a good prison cell would be fine, and anyway it would have a TV with a video and plenty of books to read he was sure there would be a computer, maybe even a phone, but he would make do.

There was no need of women in his life and anyway he had their earrings which now belonged to him. There would also be stupid women who always wrote to prisoners he would ask them for their earrings. These women got their kicks that way, look at the Yorkshire ripper, what a guy he was! The ripper was somewhat of a hero to him, he got away with his killings for years and years and now he was inundated with mad bitches that sent him more or less what he wanted, whenever he wanted. He thought that was brilliant so that was to him a sort of bonus to look forward to. Someone was bound to want to make a film and write a book about him so he would always be from time to time in the public eye, and that pleased him no end. So as far as he was concerned he was in a win, win situation and he would just carry on until he was caught. He hadn't felt this good in years!!

CHAPTER FOUR

Tom Handley looked at his watch, the time was 5.43am it was a lovely sunny spring morning which promised a good day to come. The early mornings were wonderful as they were so fresh. Always at the same time he walked the same way before he went to work as a mechanic. As usual he was walking his Jack Russell terrier dog Henry by the side of the river Brent. The dog was a pain in the arse, but he loved the little character to bits. Today was looking lovely and already the sky was a clear blue. Henry always walked well ahead of Tom as he was in charge of his own walk. But he was a disobedient, obstinate and petulant dog at the best of times and today was no exception to the rule, Henry's rule.

It had been eight days since the district nurse Helen Burk had disappeared yet no-one had any idea where she had gone. The police had nothing to go on, although they were well aware of her having gone missing in strange circumstances. You have to remember it happens all the time. Every day the police get calls about someone going missing.

But as Tom Handley walked along he noticed his dog Henry was ahead of him about fifteen yards away pawing at the murky water whilst balancing on three of his stubby little legs hanging over the water trying desperately not to fall in. Tom thought *oh no, not another dead smelly fish, or even a water rat.* But now he could see that Henry was frustrated. He was barking and whining whilst looking back at Tom as if to say *get a move on look what I've just found, let's get it out.*

Stopping by his dog who was looking at him and whining with his tail going mad, Tom said 'what have you found Henry, there's a good boy what is it?' Henry looked at the object then back at him and barked. Tom saw what looked like a thick sack, but then noticed it had a dark red jacket wrapped around it. Curious he used his walking stick to push the sack away, but it felt sort of squishy then with the momentum of the push it turned over in the water. Tom stopped perfectly still when he saw the face of Helen Burk slowly turn around in the water towards him, even Henry was startled he quickly backed off and hid behind Tom's legs.

Helen's face was covered in some sort of tape, but he could plainly see she was dead. He quickly used his mobile phone to dial 999 and told the operator what he had seen and where he was and within seventeen minutes the police had arrived, followed by an ambulance.

DCI Eric Fletcher and DC Ronald Buckley were both still in bed as per normal. Then at 6.47am DCI Fletcher had a call to say a body had been found in the River Brent, it was a body of a woman who had by all accounts been in the water for a few days.

Eric rang DC Ron Buckley saying 'get out of bed and wait by your gate for me. I'm on my way, we have a dead woman in the river Brent and I'm betting it was this missing nurse Helen Burk.'

As it was he was right. They were based at Notting Hill Police station in Ladbroke Grove. They quickly found the area the police and an ambulance were already there. They stepped into their white plastic forensic suits which also covered their shoes as in all crime scenes; they were obligated to do so. They sealed the area although they knew immediately whose body it was.

DCI Fletcher was right. It was that of Helen Burk who had been reported missing now for eight days. She was not in a good state as eight days in water does that to a body. She had been tied by her wrists and ankles with garden ties she had been weighted down with a large heavy bolt. It didn't look as though she had been raped because all her clothes were still on her and her tights intact. There was gaffer tape, or what was left of it wrapped around her face except for her nostrils, but it was her eyes that said it all, even though she was very dead.

They threw a cordon around the area, but DCI Fletcher knew there would be no clue at this spot. She had come from further up the river.

DC Buckley said 'Tom have you seen anything or anyone else or anyone at all walking in the other direction or anyone who had passed him on his walk, on this side of the bank or the other side.'

Tom said 'no sorry, oh yes there was just one, a lady jogger. She came past me about ten minutes before I found the body. I see her most days. Oh look here she comes again, she's got great legs.' Then as the lady jogger came ever closer, she turned around having seen the commotion and jogged off in the other direction.

DC Ronald Buckley quickly commandeered a mountain bike from a man who was standing there looking, and then he took off after the young lady jogger.

'Stop please, I'm a police officer. We need to ask you some questions. Can you please stop now' he shouted to the young woman.

She stopped with her hands on her shapely hips while still puffing then she asked him 'what's the problem why had he stopped her. What had she done?'

'Ah nothing, Miss err?'

'Miss Janet Cleaver and no I didn't see anything officer, nothing at all.'

'Was I that obvious then, so you knew I was going to ask you if you had seen anything?'

'Yes I did, I haven't a clue what about though, because that man and his bloody lunatic dog who always has a go at my legs every time I run this way, well he seems to be there grinning at me and his stupid dog called Henry. For god sake who calls a dog Henry? The idiot dog tries to bite my legs every time I pass them, which is most mornings and the owner eggs him on. He knew I had been running this way so he must have told you I may have seen something, about what though I can't imagine. What was I supposed to see officer?' She was looking at her watch and now jogging on the spot to keep her rhythm going. She had a routine and didn't like to be stopped. All joggers and runners would think exactly the same thing.

'We have just found a woman's body in the water and wanted to know if after coming this way on your regular run, jogging trip or whatever you call it, have you seen anything suspicious at all, anything that is not, you know considered as normal?'

'Considered as normal,' she laughed. 'Yes, as a matter of fact I have.'

'OK, can you tell me what you saw, if anything Janet?'

'I certainly can officer, err what's your name and rank. You're not in any uniform, except for the forensic suit which makes you look like a milk bottle it's so ridiculous. Anyway so what and who are you?'

'Sorry Janet, I'm Detective Constable Ronald Buckley.' He showed her his police warrant card 'so what did you see, that's not considered normal?'

'I've just told you. Look to reiterate in case you haven't heard the first time, only this time keep your eyes on me not my body and keep your ears open and listen to me again, and why aren't you wearing a tie? Once again detective, that bloody nut case and his stupid black and white dog with the short arse legs, the little shit always goes for my legs every time I come this way, while the even more stupid owner eggs him on. The guy is one loaf short of a baker's dozen.' Which made DC Buckley, laugh out loud.

'No sorry, I mean did you see anyone acting strangely in the last week by the river at all?'

'Sorry I can't say I have, except that guy's a complete idiot, he always leers at me and now even his dog does it too. Oh Christ, will you look at the time, now you've made me late for work, I do have to go detective Buckley.'

'Okay sorry to have stopped you Janet you can go, but if you do remember anything at all please give me a ring, he gave her one of his cards. Some rotten bastard has murdered this lady, she was a district nurse and all she did was to help people.'

She took his card and said 'Oh look I'm really sorry I was so rude, but the bloke and his dog are a bloody nuisance. If I do remember anything I will ring you DC Buckley. Oh by the way I'm a solicitor, a junior solicitor. I work at Henley and Brooks and we do a lot of work for the CPS' she winked at him, and then jogged off laughing.

'Why didn't you say?' DC Buckley watched her jog off, he thought she did have a nice bum, in fact she was nice all over and he wouldn't mind asking her out, but how unprofessional would that have been! Turning the mountain bike around he rode back to the scene where the body was located. He thought he may just get a bike as it was a good way to exercise. Then he saw the man whose bike he had 'borrowed' and handed it back, but the man was now visibly annoyed.

'Look I'm very sorry about the bike sir, but you have been an immense help, you really have, and thanks to you I have obtained some very important information from that lady.'

'Yes I bet you have, so did you get her phone number? Christ sake you couldn't have made it more obvious, and the way you slobbered all over her, frankly it made me feel ill!' He snatched his bike back and rode off with a moody on.

DC Buckley went red in the face which didn't go unnoticed by his boss DCI Eric Fletcher who stood there shaking his head from side to side, desperately trying not to laugh at his young protégée, but perhaps he would learn to be a little more discreet in future.

'Well Ron, what did you get, apart from your embarrassment? Do you have a lead or any clues and did the nice looking very attractive young lady see anything of any use?'

'No sir, she saw nothing. She just moaned about the guy with the small stubby dog and what shits they both are. Apart from that, I'm sorry but nothing at all, and anyway she has my card.'

'Yes Ron, I can believe that and I bet she marked it too. Anyway, this lady was not put in the river here so let's all look up river. You do one side and I'll do the other because it would be helpful if we can establish where the poor girl was dumped, but I doubt it was this side.'

'Why do you say that sir?'

'Because I reckon whoever did it would have used a car, you can't get a car this side but let's see if I'm right.'

Ron started to walk slowly up the side of the river which was against the flow, while Eric walked the other side which had an embankment. Eric got to the top of the embankment which was quite high and it was running alongside Ruislip Road East.

Starting to walk up the road he was looking for a suitable place to park. There wasn't really an obvious one but then after 35 minutes he did come across a small area where you could get a large car parked. Looking around he walked down to the embankment at the bottom, there was an easy access to the river Brent. All you would have to do would be to simply push a body into the river and walk away. The body would go with the current and end up who knows where, it was anyone's guess, but he was sure this was the place where Helen was put into the river.

DC Buckley had now stopped opposite DCI Fletcher because looking up he could see Fletcher waving at him. Stopping he shrugged his shoulders then Fletcher rang him on his mobile phone. 'Get back over here Ron, I think she was placed in the river here.' He rang forensic to come over to check the spot out.

When DC Buckley arrived he checked out the site for about thirty yards one way, and Fletcher checked thirty yards the other way. They found nothing only the pull in, which was flattened by the use of various cars where some people had stopped, probably to use as a toilet break if the smell was anything to go by.

DC Buckley said 'Sir I think I'll check those houses over the road and see if anyone had seen anything unusual in the last say ten days? Let's face it the guy wouldn't dump her in daylight would he, it would have to be at night and late at night, anyway its best that we check sir.'

'Ok Ron you can do, let's say those ten houses. I'll check these other ten houses, let's go.'

Of the ten houses he had knocked on the doors, DCI Fletcher found only three people in, but at the last house which was more or less opposite the flattened area, he found the occupants were in. DCI Eric Fletcher rang the door bell and an elderly man and a woman called Bill and Mary Bellman answered the door together. The woman had quickly pushed herself forward first and was filling the doorway with the man which presumably was her husband looking over her shoulder. She didn't look very sociable; in fact she looked visibly very annoyed.

'We don't want any today thank you, so can you please go away or I shall be forced to call the policeman who lives next door to remove you' said Mrs Bellman. 'So go away now this minute, you have been told and I won't tell you twice my father is also a policeman. He's a big tough sergeant too.'

'Ah, but I am the police' said DCI Fletcher, 'I need you to help me if at all possible.'

The woman scoffed then she laughed. 'You're not a policeman,' she sneered 'because if so where's your uniform then, and why aren't you wearing black boots, policeman's boots, not those silly slip on brown shoes. Look here young man, are you gay?'

DCI Fletcher just stared at her in utter disbelief.

'Oh my god Billy, look he's a gay policeman. Why that's quite ridiculous, my father was a policeman a very tough one too, he wouldn't stand for this nonsense, not at all. He was also a big burley Sergeant. He wouldn't have gay policemen in his police station let me tell you! His boots were proper boots, proper leather black boots and polished on a daily basis, I should jolly well know because I used to polish them for him, you could see your face reflected in them too.'

DCI Fletcher looked at Mr Bill Bellman who had seen and heard the conversation between him and his wife; he couldn't help but feel a little sympathy for him.

'Ok look sorry about this' said Bill Bellman 'but.......'

'Billy, there's absolutely nothing to be sorry about, why are you apologising? I've already told him I don't want anything, we never buy anything from the doorstep, does anyone ever listen to me? Well do they, good God are you both deaf and utterly stupid?'

'Mary, listen to me. He's my friend, he's come to see us, it's err, what's your name' he whispered.

'Eric Fletcher, Detective Chief Inspector Eric Fletcher,' he quickly stuttered it out.

'Mary you silly girl, it's Eric, DCI Eric Fletcher but he's out of uniform. That's why you didn't recognise him, it's his day off today, and...' he whispered 'there's no policeman next door it's a daft thing she always says. Look Eric we get our fair share of these Jehovah types knocking on our doors around here.'

'Why didn't he say he was a policeman then, he should learn to speak up? Is that because he's gay? He still has brown gay shoes; he's such a silly young man. God what's happening to the world, I really don't know, my dad would not have stood for this nonsense let me tell you, not at all!'

'Can you make us all a lovely cup of tea Mary? Your tea is so wonderful. That's what Eric would like as he often tells me your tea is the best he's ever had, isn't that right Eric?'

'Oh yes I can't resist Mary's tea and her cake is lovely too.' Mary went into the kitchen.

'Look can I call you Bill?' said Eric.

'Of course you can Eric, because you're my new, but old best pal' he laughed, 'so how can we help you today, take your time as both of us are now retired.'

'We have just pulled a body of a middle aged woman from the river about thirty five yards away on the opposite bank Bill.'

'Oh that's terrible Eric, how sad. Was it a suicide, if not who did it? Or did she fall in.'

'That's what we are trying to find out Bill. We estimate she was put in the water about maybe eight days ago now and we wonder if you can go back and try to remember if you saw anything unusual around about that time? It would have been we think very late at night, and look Bill I understand it's a difficult ask. I'm sorry to bother you but can you please try? I know it was a long time ago, I have a job to remember what I did yesterday,' he laughed. 'It must be old age creeping in or maybe it's the job I do.'

'Really how very sad, you should take a test for that Eric, there are tests you can take' shouted out Mary, 'I can still hear you and don't you two whisper about me, I know everything.'

Bill thought for a while then he said, 'funny enough there was a large dark coloured car parked over there at about 3.30 or 4am about eight or nine days ago. I saw this big man go round to the back of the car. I reckoned he took something heavy out the back of the car. He went down the embankment and was gone for about twenty minutes, maybe a bit more or even less. Say twenty five minutes, that should do it I reckon. But I know people use it as a toilet, let's face it where the hell do you go for a piss at night if you're driving after being out? There is nowhere for a piss is there, absolutely nowhere, they've shut all the public toilets and you can't take a slash anywhere now, bloody useless council.'

'BILLY, shut up, there's no need to be crude is there talking about piss this and piss that! You're so disgusting at times, you really are.'

'Ah I'm sorry my love, just trying to explain things that's all.'

'You had better listen to me right now because this gentleman is a serving police officer, or so he says. Even though he's gay, so have some respect if you don't mind, he may be gay but he's still a detective, he's in his rights to have you arrested. I'm so sorry officer, err detective, Billy sometimes forgets his manners, he's not usually as rude as this, are you Billy?' But then she scornfully stared at Eric's shoes again, she didn't like the look of them at all. If looks could kill he would be wearing a dead pair of shoes.

'Bill, can I ask you how come you saw someone at that time of the morning, what were you doing at that time, were you up?'

'I was in the toilet I got up for a pee, she was fast asleep as usual, snoring like a sailor.'

'Hey, what do you mean snoring like a sailor? I'm not a sailor. I'm your wife of 55 years.'

'Well it was sounding like a sailor to me,' laughed Bill.

'Billy,' asked DCI Fletcher 'what did you actually see? It's really important that you tell me please and take your time. I can't emphasize how important this is to our enquiries. Sometimes it's the little things that can help us to bring down a suspect. No matter how insignificant it may seem to you, it could be the clue that we are looking for. It's like a jigsaw puzzle, things can fit together and then we have the culprit. So as I said before Billy, please take your time.'

'Like I said Eric, I was using the loo. I always do about that time in the morning. I don't know why, but I always take a look out of the landing window as that's where the sun comes up. It's a habit I suppose, but it's so beautiful at that time, you can just see the sky line as the day starts. It can look lovely and you can just pick out the wildlife. You know the ducks and sometimes the swans, the colours are fantastic, I have even seen a few badgers and lots of rabbits too. Take the other day for instance an otter, well a pair of otters were running about without a care in the world, but she...' as he pointed to his wife 'is always snoring her bloody head off and never sees the early morning sights. She misses so much, I have seen a pair of foxes playing together and you do see the swans landing on the river too.'

'Shut up will you Billy, will you please just shut up. Look for god sake, the detective, err you are a detective aren't you?'

'Yes Mrs Bellman, as I explained to you before I am a Detective Chief Inspector.'

'Did you tell me that, if so when, three minutes ago you say? Well I wish you would speak up and say who you are. Billy, this gentleman doesn't want a geography or a nature lesson does he, and the BBC are not looking for another David Attenborough, so will you please just get on with it and will you stop interrupting for Christ sake. Good God we aren't going to get anywhere with your constant interruptions, on and on. What's the matter with you, it's me, me, me with you all the time!'

DCI Fletcher was now looking quite depressed he said to Bill 'what sort of a car was it.'

'Oh it was a big car, not a normal type but a large one, a 4x4 sort of car if that's how you say it? Jesus it's all changed since I was working, I can't keep up with all these changing cars.'

'What did the man look like? You said he was a big man, can you tell me anything else about him? Was he small, tall, slim, fat, skinny, long hair, short hair or no hair? Anything will help. Can you remember Billy?'

'Well he....look can you repeat the question again please, I'm a bit deaf.'

'Billy, you never told me about this man did you' said Mary, 'so why didn't you tell me about him, was it a secret? I'm your wife, that's of course if you can still remember that, so why didn't you tell me? Let's face it you soon forget don't you? He never tells me anything and we have been married for 55 years. He very conveniently forgets that I could have married into money, oh yes but I chose him! What a mistake that was let me tell you, because it really was over a big cock up.'

'Well, that's why you married me Mary, or have you forgotten last night?'

'Oh my God, isn't he so crude, why not tell the whole bloody road?' But she was giggling and she looked far away, but smiling!

Bill Bellman and DCI Fletcher were now sat on the dining room chairs holding their heads in their hands looking bewildered and confused. DCI Fletcher wished he was somewhere else. The light had faded from his eyes and his shoulders had slumped forward as he desperately stared at the floor and wondering how the hell he had got involved in all this. Bill put his hand on DCI Fletcher's shoulder and gave it a gentle squeeze.

'Mary my lovely darling, could you please make us that nice cup of tea you promised us, you know you make the best tea in the world, doesn't she Detective Chief Inspector?'

'Oh yes I can't wait. That's why I came to see you, your tea is wonderful and you're a legend down at the police station.'

'Look here then,' said Mary, 'if you two promise to behave yourselves I will do, but remember there are to be no secrets, and no whispering. Do you both understand what I'm telling you, well do you?'

They both said 'of course Mary, you're the boss.'

'The chap Eric was about.....hmm I would say 6ft tall and big. He looked strong and fit and was also well dressed. Sorry about Mary, but she's on the verge of dementia as you can tell.'

'I'm so sorry to hear that but I did guess as much Billy, sorry I mean Bill.' Then the door bell rang 'oh that will be my partner DC Buckley, shall I get it?'

Quicker than a king cobra, Mary was already at the door. She opened the door and said without first looking, 'no thank you not today we already have religion thank you dear,' and then she quickly shut the door in DC Buckland's face. She had taken him completely by surprise being so quick off the mark.

DC Buckland rang the door bell again and Mary now annoyed opened the door for a second time, but now she was really angry. She said to DC Buckland 'she was so fed up being interrupted by religious lunatics, also gay policemen who were now becoming an epidemic in this area.' Then she spotted his brown shoes. She stood there looking at them with a look of utter distaste on her face and looked as though she was going to be sick. She said out loud 'good God almighty!'

'Err can I please talk with.....? ?'

'Shut right up, are you stupid as well as gay? I just told you not today. Are you deaf, or just rude? If you don't go I will call the policeman from next door and have you arrested.'

'I am a policeman madam. I need to talk with you please.'

'Don't be so ridiculous and stupid, we already have a gay policeman in the house he is about to take my tea which I may add is considered to be the best in the world, and if you don't already know I have been told by the police I am a legend. You also have brown gay shoes on, well that's disgraceful. What the hell is going on at your police station? It all sounds far too debauched for my way of thinking, in fact I'll have a word with my MP about the state of your police station.'

She was now standing in her doorway with her freshly cleaned apron on, her hands formed into two fists now placed firmly on her hips. Her head was tilted to one side, her eyes glaring at him, 'gay policemen indeed!'

DC Buckland was now utterly bewildered and confused. He looked at his shoes muttering gay shoes? 'What....yes but....'

'Yes but, yes but... What is the matter with you, look bugger off now! I won't tell you again, go on move!' She slammed the door in his red face. 'Is that how you say it Billy, was that correct?'

Bill shouted out 'oh yes that's how you say it darling, very well done. I don't think he will be back to annoy us again, not today anyway, he can take his religion somewhere else and peddle it there. Well done Mary.'

'Do you know Billy he was also wearing brown gay shoes? What's the matter with everyone these days, policemen with gay shoes indeed, oh and keep your mouth shut, the neighbours don't need to know about our cock ups. I'm sure Mrs Prichard next door has lots of cock ups.'

Bill and DCI Fletcher were nearly rolling on the floor in hysterics.

DCI Fletcher rang DC Buckland's mobile and said 'wait for me in the road Ron. I will fill you in later. I won't be long now. No I can't talk at this moment. Yes I'm okay thanks for asking but it's complicated. So for goodness sake don't ring the bloody door bell again. Christ sake at this bloody rate I'm going to end up in a rubber room with you for company and who the hell needs that?'

DC Buckland had no intentions of ringing the door bell again as he thought twice was enough. Then again he looked at his shoes, what the hell was wrong with them? The forensic people had arrived across from the house, there were four of them. There was one he knew very well, a woman called Jenny Taylor who was one of his exes. She was about 5ft 4in tall and had a lovely figure. She had dark hair with a few red highlights; she had an attractive face with large bright smiling eyes and a very sexy walk. He called her over, 'Jenny do you mind if I ask you something?'

'No and no again.... I don't want to go out with you again Ron, not now, not ever, you got that?' You're just a two timing copper shit rat you must have gone through all the WPCs at your station by now!'

'Don't talk so bloody silly, there's two left to go. I was saving them for later. Anyway I wasn't going to ask you anything of the sort Jenny, and what's a copper shit rat when he's about?'

'Ha ha, here's a mirror' as she looked in her bag, 'so what do you want to ask me Ron? Did you know all the WPCs call you Ron the copper shit rat?'

'Yes I've heard that and I bet you love that too. Seriously Jenny, do my shoes look gay?'

'What? Did you say okay, grey or gay?'

'Gay. I said bloody gay!'

'Look Ron grow up will you, what do you mean by gay?'

'I don't know for God sake. You know gay, bloody gay, what do you think I mean?'

'Oh don't talk so bloody stupid! Have you been drinking again, for Christ sake Ron, look, go and get yourself a life and try to remember you're a serving police officer? You're so bloody dramatic these days.'

'Jesus wept Jenny, I only asked! It seems you can't ask anything simple these days about anything, bloody hell it was just a question. So do my shoes look gay?'

'Ron you're beginning to lose it, why don't you ask for some time off? Dear oh dear, you must be overdoing it. How the hell can you have gay shoes on? You have no heels on them have you, and they're not four inch sling backs are they?'

'No of course I haven't got bloody heels on, anyone can see that, and what's a sling back?'

'Why are you asking me if you have gay shoes on for?'

'Because the silly old bat across the road said I had gay shoes on, she's about eighty years old, and odd.'

'You're a stupid dummy. She's probably a little confused, you do that to people, it sounds to me you're heading that way too Ron.'

'Oh bollocks to you Jenny' he said as she laughingly walked off, giving him the finger.

'You're a dickhead Ron' she shouted, 'dear me what a state to get in.' She was laughing at the stupidity of it.

'Anyway, I haven't been through all the WPCs so don't get all jealous Jenny.'

He just caught the word 'twat' coming back at him and laughed. But he still fancied her though and as he recalled she did have a great arse. Anyway given time he would work on her again, but it would have to be later now. There was a fling with her but she caught him in a naked embrace with a new WPC and not having a sense of humour at all she had the nerve to dump him.

After what seemed to be hours DCI Fletcher came out of the house full of tea, carrot cake and biscuits. If he didn't have some biscuits, Mrs Bellman was ready to pounce on him she was watching him intently saying he had better like her tea and biscuits because she was now a legend. Someone had told her that and she thought it was probably the police and she didn't want to waste them on a gay policeman! The best though was her amazing carrot cake. She watched him like a hawk until he ate a very large chunk of it the size of a house brick!! But anyway, he was not going to disappoint her. 'This is lovely Mary the tea is superb, but the carrot cake is divine. I bet the queen would like to taste this tea and especially the cake.'

Standing with her fists clenched on her hips she said. 'Divine? What the hell does that mean, divine?'

'Mary darling, that's police talk for the best in the world, the very best.' Billy assured her.

When he finally came out an hour later DC Buckley was looking at his watch while glaring at him.

DCI Fletcher came running across the road to the pull in. 'For Christ sake Ron, will you get out of the bloody way? OMG do I need a slash, stand guard Ron.' He quickly rushed down the grassy bank, but in his haste he slipped on his arse as he hurried to go behind the thick bracken. Now swearing profusely he managed to get his zip undone just in time. Suddenly there was a loud sigh of relief and a cloud of steam emitting from behind the bush. Eric was peeing for about ten minutes, or so it seemed.

'That was the most bizarre interview I have ever had Ron. The lady is one shoe short of a pair, but the poor old girl has on setting dementia. Her husband is brilliant the way he looks after her, and they still get on. You could see they love each other to bits and her tea is very good, but the carrot cake was just about the best in the world. It was more than wonderful, what's the word for it Ron?'

'Nice sir, it was very nice indeed.'

DCI Fletcher could hear the disgruntled tone in his DC's voice. 'Nice, oh no Ron, superb is the word we're looking for here, absolutely superb.'

'Well that's fine for you sir, but I never even had a cup of tea. She didn't like me at all, and of course I got no cake or biscuits because piggy you ate the lot by the sound and the look of it. All I got was a bollocking about my shoes she accused me of being a gay policeman who's wickedly debauched.'

'Now, now Ron, I'm sorry but I think you're right, it was your shoes. She seems to have a thing about brown shoes and anyone that doesn't wear big black highly polished boots; well she thinks they've gone gay. Christ knows why, but that's why I told you not to knock on the door again, after all I was thinking about your welfare. Her father used to be a police sergeant for many years with big black boots which she used to polish every day. She has it in her head all policemen have to wear these big black polished boots, if not they're gay, it's as simple as that Ron.'

'What's the matter with her sir, is she homophobic or what?'

'No Ronald she has dementia, not full on yet but she's rapidly heading in that horrible direction. She makes a great cup of tea though and homemade carrot cake, let me tell you it was to die for.' He cracked up laughing at DC Buckley.

'How very nice for you sir and it serves you right if you get as fat as a bloody pig. I can see you're already heading in that direction now. Then he looked at his boss's shoes and laughed, 'oh by the way sir you've just pissed all over your gay brown shoes and down your left leg, you also have a very large green skid mark all the way from your fat arse to the back of your knees. You look like the jolly green giant who's gone and crapped himself.'

DCI Fletcher cracked up laughing then he stuck his stomach out and waddled back to the car in a first rate pantomime performance worthy of a round of applause, which he didn't get. It just pissed off DC Buckley even more. Who thought to himself, the greedy fat pig will have a job to get into the police car.

CHAPTER FIVE

When the small surgery found out that their district nurse Helen was dead, they were all in bits. Everyone including the three doctors and a lot of patients were terribly upset for days after. It was a very sad day, deep inside they had all known Helen was dead. Because it had been too long now, but sadly life has to go on and reality is reality, then it sinks in.

DC Buckley asked Katie Parish again if she could remember anything at all about what Helen had said about her date. All they had was a name, the name Dr Geoffrey Walker, but he knew that was a false name. He had also been on to the dating site, PLS - Professional Lonely Singles. That was mission impossible because his so called profile, whoever he was, had been taken down the same as hundreds who leave every day. There were also hundreds more new ones every day. They gave nothing away even under threat of a search warrant, it was a very closed shop and very difficult to police. The very last thing the dating site needed was bad publicity, so they remained extremely uncooperative. Yet all these dating sites seemed to be interwoven in some way.

This Doctor was apparently only on the site for a week, after that he came off. There was no information on him now as it was all an alias. Even the mobile phone he used was just a throwaway pay-as-you-go phone in a completely different name and completely untraceable.

However, Katie had said that Helen's date had a Mercedes 4x4 with cream leather seats, a dark blue one and that he was a Psychiatrist. He was 6ft tall with a devastating smile and apparently worked in Harley Street in a private practice.

One important call was made to Helen's nosey neighbour Mrs Ruth Wilkins who was to say the least, a little bonkers. She told him the same as Katie; she had a good look at Helen's date and the car. Her husband had said to her 'the car was a Chelsea Tractor, and that was it really. Anyway what's a Chelsea tractor doing around here though? There are no fields around here' she said. 'But it's such a shame, Helen was a good friend to her and she would miss her terribly,' and then she started to cry, but real tears. Her husband Derrick who was in the garden took her upstairs to lie down for a while.

When DC Buckland arrived back at the police station, DCI Fletcher was waiting to hear from him, 'so Ron what have you found out?'

DC Ronald Buckley repeated what he had been told. 'Apparently he has vanished off the face of the earth sir, we had better see if Helen had any enemies to talk about.' Then he repeated what he found out again, 'and that sir is that and what about you sir, any more news?'

'Well Ron, it seems the protagonist was 6ft tall and had a large 4x4 car. I was told he looked strong and was a nice looking professional sort of man. Apparently he said to Helen Burk he was a psychiatrist in Harley Street in the private sector. We checked Harley Street and no one has heard about him, he doesn't exist by all accounts. Well he does but he's a guy aged 77 years old, so that name was stolen by the murderer. Another thing he mentioned he'd purchased a house in Blenheim Crescent Notting Hill, number sixty seven but no one knew what we were talking about because it was definitely not for sale and never had been. It belongs to some Russian billionaire back in Russia who keeps a small staff on to look after the whole place when he's not around. We have also been round to the Italian restaurant Marco's and the Golden Bird Chinese restaurant to see if they had any CCTVs installed. They have but they don't keep the videos for this long so that's turned into a dead end too.'

'Have you searched Helen's house thoroughly Ron?'

'Yes sir and nothing untoward has turned up. We can't find out if she had any arguments with anyone. I can't find anyone who doesn't like her sir; she was a well liked lady. What a waste of an attractive lovely woman. Her two boys are devastated. At the moment their grandparents are looking after them. Both boys have taken time out of university. My god it's shocking sir.'

'You know what Ron, these women on these dating sites just seem to meet up with any bloke or so it seems, but without knowing anything about the person they're meeting. They like the picture of the man, then they like the sound of their voice and what they seem to have. I mean you could say anything and they would believe you. It defies belief, so all they're doing is telling a bloke what they have and what they like, then off they go to meet complete strangers. I have a feeling Ron this will not be the only killing we're going to find.'

'Why do you say that sir, have I missed something?'

'No Ron, it's just my own thirty two years experience. The facts tell me having studied this case this man seems to be a woman hater. Yet he never touched her sexually or even physically and apparently he drugged her with the date rape drug Rohypnol. We have just had the medical report back and it seemed she had a large amount administered to her, probably in a glass of wine or maybe something else because it's tasteless. She was then taped and tied up with garden ties and then her face was taped over except her nostrils where she drowned through them what a horrible absolutely horrible thing to do and then he dumped her into the river Brent where she very slowly drowned. She had no chance. It was a cruel way to kill a person.'

'Sir, this is one evil sod, but as you say it has the hallmarks of someone who hates women.'

'Well I can't imagine how she suffered, what a bastard he must be. No Ron this guy is going to strike again you can bet on it, and I'm willing to bet the guy is sick in the head. This was a terrible nasty way to kill anyone. This man just wants to kill women for the sake of it.'

After Helen's funeral, things gradually got back to normal, or as normal as they could be and life went on at the surgery. They had recruited another district nurse because needs must. Life was slow for some people who had been close to her. The police were no nearer catching the murderer and things seemed to be winding down, although behind the scenes the police were working hard to find Helen's killer, but no-one knew who or what the man was. It seemed there was nothing to go on, because he left no clues, or so it seemed.

In the meantime Alan Reed, alias Geoffrey Walker was going through the dating site hopefuls. There were still seventeen women to ring then he saw a woman called Lisa Davey. The urge in him to kill was rising to the surface once again and he had to satisfy his lust it was almost tearing him apart. He almost likened it to a pain in his stomach he wanted to kill a bitch as soon as he could.

This Lisa Davey was aged, or so she claimed, forty six years old. She was divorced with no children and lived alone with her Labrador dog called Donald who was three years old. She had her own hairdressers. Her height was 5ft 4in tall, slim with a nice shape. The hairstyle she sported was short, a sort of pixie style two tone blond colour and she wore large hoop earrings. She always dressed well even when walking her dog Donald, who even came to work with her in the salon. He loved ladies and was very popular with her clients. Every day he would sit by his favourite ladies, usually the ones who slipped him a biscuit which they had with their coffee as they sat in the salon chairs. Donald would sit next to the ladies with one paw on their laps and a pleading look in his eye, he was irresistible.

In his profile Alan said he was a Doctor but didn't mention what sort of Doctor he was. He was looking for an uncomplicated lady with a GSOH who must not have any baggage to speak of.

Lisa had posted a nice picture of herself. She looked fit and healthy and liked the outdoor life. She was looking for a long term relationship.

'Hello who's calling please?'

'Lisa? Is that Lisa Davey?'

'Yes, who's calling please? Do you wish to make an appointment?'

'Hi Lisa, well yes sort of' he laughed 'this is Stephen Bruce, Doctor Stephen Bruce from the dating site PLS. I've been away. Is it convenient to talk, if not I can call you again if you would like me to.'

'Doctor what doctor. Oh hi yes, yes of course I'm so sorry to sound so rude but that was a while ago now that we spoke. So have you been away somewhere nice.'

'I know it's been a while. I'm sorry about that is it still okay to chat Lisa? I'm so sorry to catch you unaware.'

'Yes that's fine I'm not going out for about two hours, so yes how nice to talk with you at long last, so you've been away have you Stephen, hope it was somewhere nice and warm,' she laughed.

'Yes actually it was and still is. I've just come back from the south west of France, in fact Carcassonne. I have a cottage over there, well actually a small farm house with some land and I have just been over to oversee a renovation building project and now it's finally finished, not on time, but at least it's been finished at long last. It also has its own vineyard, three acres all told. I have about three thousand bottles of wine in store at the moment and I could do with someone to help me get through them, the grape is a Merlot,' he laughed.

'That sounds like heaven to me,' she laughed.

'I have just had a large swimming pool put in and a gym plus another bedroom extension. I also had to check out the vines, as I said I have a three acre plot with good old grape vines and it's all going so well. I have someone who wants to buy most of them which as I said there are a couple of thousand bottles of wine now. However, I will keep a few hundred back for home consumption.'

'Love it Stephen, love it. Your profile if I remember, because you went off the site, said you were a Doctor. What sort of Doctor are you, and you said your name was Geoffrey.'

'Yes, I know but I have to be very careful as you can understand. My real name is Stephen Bruce.'

'Oh no that's okay Steven, lots of people use different names to start with.'

'I'm in Cardiology and I'm a heart surgeon, but in the private sector Harley Street, where I share my practise with other Doctors. Anyway Lisa, your profile if I remember correctly said that you're a Hairdresser and you have your own salon in

Primrose Hill, you are divorced with no children and a dog called Donald, and that you have no baggage.' he laughed.

'Yes that's correct that's about it, you seem to know all about me though. We didn't get a chance to speak for long before Stephen, as you had to shoot off quickly due to some building work being done.'

'OMG, yes don't remind me about all of that, but as I said it's all ok now.'

'Anyway, so you're back and it's good to hear from you again.'

Lisa told him all about her salon, her friends and especially her dog Donald and his adventures. She had been divorced now for four years. Her husband told her he wanted his life back so she said have it back then get on with it, but that was a stupid thing to say because he had formed a relationship with her one time best friend Laura. That was four years ago and it was all finalised and done with. She also explained she was brought up in a home and had no living relatives at all. There were plenty of friends around but no family and hairdressing was all she had known. She then asked him about his life.

'Oh as my profile says I'm a widower, but I'm not on the site anymore. I had such a large response but then I had to go to France so I couldn't cope with it. I only kept your phone number so here we are Lisa we are talking at long last.'

'That was nice of you to keep my number Stephen, shall we meet up for a drink or something, what do you think?'

'Yes, of course that's why I rang you, so when is it good for you Lisa? It has to be of an evening as I have my practise to run. How about tomorrow night as I have that free if you can make it?'

'Err... I was going out with some of my friends.'

'Ok Lisa, look I'll call you in a couple of weeks then, maybe three weeks. I can't be sure when as my life moves around my appointments etc, and I wanted to find someone to see if they would like to come to France with me. I also keep a boat over there and I have an interest in a large harbour side fish restaurant which has a lovely terraced flat overlooking the Mediterranean Sea in Nice which I own. Still never mind, enjoy your friends and maybe I'll give you a ring in about three or four weeks if that's okay with you.'

'Well I can put it off for another time Stephen. Seven of us were just going out for a pub meal, but it's not important and they aren't going to miss me, so anytime will do if it's still okay with you.' He detected the panic in her voice.

'Ok then, but I don't want to spoil your evening. We can leave it for another month or two.'

Lisa was now panicking, another month or two! She thought shit; I've blown it, Christ this is too good to miss. 'No, that's ok so where shall we meet, you say where, it will be fine for me.'

'I could pick you up Lisa, or we can meet up somewhere, it's up to you. If you do have anywhere in mind, I have a sat nav.'

'I live over my business called Lisa's Hair in Primrose Hill Road. It's a large shop and I have five girls working for me now. If we say eight pm, is that okay for you Stephen?'

'Yes that's fine by me eight pm it is then. We can go for a nice meal at an Italian place I know, do you like Italian?'

'Do I like Italian, god who doesn't? Yes I love Italian. What car are you going to be driving?'

'It's a dark blue Jaguar the latest one. I will be smart casual and I will ring you ten minutes before I arrive. Oh and Lisa write down my registration number and my phone number please then leave it with a friend or in your apartment. That way it makes me feel good to know you feel secure about our date. The Italian Restaurant is called Marco's, that's the one in Knightsbridge and it's on me so I don't want to hear any of this I'll pay half nonsense, is that okay with you?'

Lisa laughed 'yes that's fine by me and I'll see you tomorrow at eight pm.'

'He sounds brilliant' said Diane, Lisa's manageress. 'Have you left anything out I should know about? He sounds much too good to be true, you lucky bitch, so go get some girl!'

Lisa laughed. 'And he has this boat thing yacht or whatever you call it which is moored in Nice in the south of France. He has a skipper and everything but I haven't a clue about boats and things, or if you sail it, drive it or just sit on the thing.'

'Look love, just so long as you have a large, and it must be a large G&T in your hand darling and a large you know what in the other hand, you'll have cracked it, so don't worry about it.' They both laughed out loud, 'too right Diane, too bloody right.'

'This guy must be loaded Di, he's got all this property and his boat, he has a new Jaguar and he's got his own private practice. OMG I wonder what his house looks like.'

'He didn't say where he lives although it must be a lovely place. He's a widower with three children and they have all left home. God I don't need kids at my age as you know, I don't have any and never wanted any either. Donald is like a big kid. Hey Di, if we do go away will you look after Donald for me, you know he loves you.'

'Ha, ha you're jumping the gun lady' she laughed 'he could be a strangler or something or even worse, you never know.'

'Don't talk so daft, anyway he's going to leave me his phone number and his car registration number and his address. Hang on I have a text, oh look it's from Stephen and all his details Di.'

'Where does he live then, go on let's see. Christ almighty Lisa, Notting Hill, he lives in Notting Hill quick, get the street map. Bloody hell Lisa, Blenheim Crescent, you can't get much better than that girl. Hey I hope you don't blow this girl, blow him babe, but don't blow this.' They both cracked up laughing. 'And so you met this guy on a dating site.'

'Yes I told you, but it's not a cheap one, PLS it stands for Professional Lonely Singles. It costs us £2,000 a year payable in advance with guaranteed results or your money back. Let's face it Di I don't want to end up with a lorry driver or a window cleaner, so you reap as the saying goes, what you've sown. My ex was a mechanic, he scrounged off me for years and eventually he cleared off with the receptionist at the GP surgery, and he still owes me thousands which I won't get back. They now have two kids, twin girls so I will have to kiss the money goodbye. I reckon I could do with a break don't you Di?'

'Of course you do Lisa you owe it to yourself so go and enjoy it.'

'Di, let me forward all his details to your mobile if anything happens so you have the details for the cops' she laughed.

'Listen Di, I have a friend called Julia who sort of lives in Notting Hill in Chepstow Road about twice a year when she's not living in Moraira in Spain on the Costa Blanca. She's got a partner who's a brilliant Private Investigator. He's an ex flying squad officer called George Penny. OMG she struck lucky there, he's so gorgeous and a really lovely bloke. She has a nice hairdressing business in Spain and I get a free holiday whenever I want one so it's great you can look after Donald for me. If anything goes wrong, get in touch with Julia and George. So let me get their card for you.'
'Hey no problem Lisa, but nothing is going to go wrong is it.'

'Julia and George are due next week they are coming over for a month so we have a lot of catching up to do, and I may go over for a few days Di. I need a break so if this date turns into rat shit then I'm off to Spain for a while' she laughed.
'Too true Lisa, so you go for it, and don't you worry about Donald because Jim and I will look after him and the kids love him too. You only have six hours to go and you're away. Seriously play it cool honey and have a great time. Anyway I thought you dislike Italian food?'
'I do, I can't bloody stand it, but hey I'm not going to look a gift horse in the mouth am I,' they both fell about laughing.
'Lisa, you're so mercenary hey, but you're so right. But what if it makes you sick.'
'Then I'll swallow it in my own mouth.'
'Ha ha, it's the right answer' said Diane.
'Look I'm not getting any younger Di, so I have to grab my chance and if this is the one for me then I will try my best, what else can I do? Anyway I have no family and I want someone in my life, it hurts not to have anyone. I see everyone else with a partner so what about me? I'm going for it.'
'Yes let's hope it works out for you Lisa, I'll keep my fingers crossed for you, but don't keep your legs crossed!'
'DIANE........I don't know what you mean.' she laughed.

CHAPTER SIX

Alan Reed had been concerned that his rental car had stuck out like a sore thumb. It was easily recognisable. After a lot of thought he decided to take it back, but just before he did he decided to go to the car auctions because sometimes you could buy an old but luxury car at a really cheap price. While he was there he saw a fleet of London black cabs and then he had an idea. After half an hour he made a bid on a really clean looking London black cab. In the back of the cab there was an almost new wheelchair. He was going to take it back but then he had another idea. Maybe he could use it to transfer the women down to whatever canal, river or reservoir he was going to put them in. Now he became excited at this find he could put it to good use.

Two days later a woman called Mrs Belinda Mann from the London Car Auctions rang him. 'Hi Mr Reed, this is Belinda from the London Auction house. You have recently bought a second hand taxi from us. I wonder if you have found a wheelchair in the taxi, it was something you could hardly miss' she said.

'As a matter of fact, yes I certainly did, but I didn't want a wheelchair at this moment in time' he laughed. 'Anyway after I purchased the taxi I drove it into the compound outside where I checked it over also finding the wheelchair. I took it back into the receptionist area. I left it against the wall at the car auctions almost next to the office with a note with the taxi number plate number and my phone number. I did mention I had found it and didn't want it, but the office was so busy with clients paying for cars and getting the paper work sorted out I couldn't talk to anyone. You were so busy and I didn't have the time to hang about, anyway the note clearly said you should have it back and that was that, why haven't you got it? I did leave it there.'

'That's odd' said the office woman. 'Oh never mind I reckon someone stole it, there were so many people at that auction what with vans, taxis and all sorts of vehicles, anyone could have taken it. Well sorry to bother you Mr Reed.'

'I'm sorry to hear that, but honestly I did leave it there I promise you.'

In the meantime he had rented a lock up garage under the arches of the railway to keep a spare car. The rent was cheap and so was the area, but he still had his VW estate at home. Now he could keep the cab in the garage, it was in great condition and so was the wheelchair which was actually brand new. Even though the mileage was high on the taxi, it had all the hire lights on it and for all intent and purposes he could drive it around and illegally act like a taxi driver. This made him think he didn't need the women from the dating site anymore because now he could just offer them a taxi then take them off the streets. Then he could easily immobilise them and use the wheelchair to transport them into the water. Yes this was a great development, an exciting development for him as he was really almost untraceable. He would be when he put some cloned number plates on his cab from another one. There were about 21,000 black cabs in and around the London area. The thing was he was now on a mission to rid the world of greedy grabbing lying women and he couldn't wait to get started. Never worrying about getting caught because kill one or kill a dozen, the sentence is about the same and he didn't mind if he was caught. Time spent in prison he could also write about what he had done. There would be fan mail, so what was so bad about that he thought, yet he knew he would be caught someday. So in the meantime he still had a mission, he was dedicated 100%, but he knew he would take some stopping. For the first time in years he felt truly happy, yes he felt good, he was starting to feel clean, almost as though a layer of skin was being slowly peeled off and a fresh layer was exposed underneath.

The time was now 7.15pm on Tuesday 22nd of March when Lisa's phone rang. She thought oh shit he's going to call the date off. 'Hello?'

'Hi Lisa, listen I have a problem, you wouldn't believe this, but my Jaguar has been stolen and I've been down the police station, so I'm sending a cab to pick you up for 8pm or as near as he can make. It's a black cab and then he will pick me up outside my house if that is okay with you. I've had a rough day, but I am so looking forward to meeting up with you, do you still want to meet me? I should have a car tomorrow, but now it's too short notice to hire another one for tonight.

'Stephen, that's so horrible that's really not a problem. I'm sorry to hear about your car. Okay I will wait for the cab to arrive, see you soon and bye for now.'

Then Lisa's mobile received a text from Diane, saying good luck, hope it goes well and keep your feet off the glove box in his Jag...lol.

Lisa texted back some hopes, he's had his Jag nicked but he's sending a black cab for me Di.

Stephen arrived at 8.04 pm, then he sounded the horn three times then she appeared at her window, waved, then gave Donald her dog a doggy treat patted him on the head saying be a good boy I will see you soon. Look after the flat for me, she bent down kissed him on his head then she opened her door to leave her apartment. She locked the door and walked the ten yards to the cab and got into the back.

She asked the driver where he was going now. He replied 'Notting Hill, Blenheim Crescent.' She was pleased as punch and felt safe, snug and very happy. She closed her eyes to think, so far this was going well and what a nice area he lived in.

Stephen was sitting in the driving seat, he was wearing a flat cap and heavy rimmed glasses.

The cab made a sudden stop. He said 'in a false London accent, damn, I'm sorry Miss but I have a light come on my dashboard indicating your seat belt has snagged or something so I will have to adjust it.' He slowly turned round, got out of his cab, opened her door and said 'look the seat belt is twisted' then he shot her with a stun gun hitting her in the chest. Two seconds later she passed out. Very quickly he tied her hands and ankles with garden ties, and then he taped her mouth with gaffer tape and placed a dark hood over her head as a good measure. Quickly he drove to his garage and once inside he removed her earrings and a nice diamond bracelet too which he took along with her perfume. Excitedly he decided he would put her earrings with the other earrings from Helen in an old cup in his kitchen cupboard, but he thought he would have to get a small jewellery box to hold them in, because there would be more in the coming future. Now he checked the gaffer tape round her mouth making sure it was secure, but crucially he left a space so she could breathe through her nostrils. It was so important to him that they were still alive when they went into the water, because he wanted them to know they were going to suffer. Then he replaced the hood back over her head again. Now he was satisfied she wasn't a threat, although she was awake and making strange noises. Looking at the time it was 11.33pm. Without a care he took her back to the same spot where he put Helen in the River Brent. Needing her to be alive, he wanted her to know what drowning was like that was very important to him. It was important for her to know it was him who was going to end her life.

It was now approximately four or five weeks since he put Helen into the River Brent, and now he had weighed her body down with some heavy lead bolts wrapped in a supermarket bag, around Lisa's neck. She was now fully awake but couldn't communicate with him at all; he used the stun gun again to keep her still and to keep her quiet.

Making sure it was all clear there was no sound at all. Then he removed her from the back of his London cab and carried her to the water's edge wrapped in a large mat. After laying her down as quietly as he could, he was very alert listening and watching.

Hearing just the sounds of the still night he carefully slipped her into the water and then he pushed her out towards the middle of the river. The river had a greyish white ghostly mist floating over the surface of the water, but suddenly the cold water seemed to revive her. He'd noticed that before with his other victims. It must have been the cold of the river because she was now very much alive. She started to wriggle, but there was nothing she could do, she knew what was happening to her and was now in great pain. She didn't want to die, she wanted to see her dog, she wanted to live, this should not be happening to her. She felt like the light had gone and felt her lungs were bursting. Please she thought; I don't want to die. The water felt so cold and she had never liked to feel cold. Her feet touched the bottom of the river as it was only about five feet in depth at that point. She tried to kick off which made her head briefly come to the surface which horrified Alan. She was making a loud disturbing noise as river water poured out of her nostrils and her eyes were filled with terror with a pleading terrible look of pain and horror.

Quietly as he could he waded in for about three yards, he held her head then whispered in her ear 'please be still Lisa. Listen to me it will soon be over I promise you, so go back to sleep,' and then he held her under the water for about five minutes until she sank once more. Alan watched her but she quickly sank head first. He was pleased as he waited for about another forty seconds and then he saw some air bubbles come to the surface. Suddenly it all went quite and very still, the night turned back to normal and the ghostly mist returned once more on the surface. All the bubbles had now stopped.

Satisfied she was gone he casually looked around making sure no-one else was about, but then he heard voices coming from above. It was two men who had stopped for a toilet break so he kept very still. After what seemed like hours he heard the sound of two car doors closing and then a car drive off. Still keeping very still and listening for a couple more minutes, now satisfied no-one was there, he went back up the embankment very slowly to his car. If anyone asked what he was doing he would pretend to do up his trouser zip, but there was no one about. Suddenly he saw a movement to his left. Now he stopped in a frozen position, but it was just a rabbit sitting there giving him a curious look? Carrying on, he scared the rabbit which bolted off into the thick bracken. When he got back to the taxi, he realised his cap had gone. Quickly looking around but in the dark he couldn't find it and he couldn't afford to hang around any longer by using a torch. He just had to leave it there, but then realized he had also left the mat by the river bank. He pondered whether to look for his cap and his mat, but then a light appeared opposite in one of the houses which drew his attention away from looking for the items he had left. Hurriedly he got to the taxi, but he drove off slowly hoping he hadn't been seen. Looking at his watch as he slowly drove off the time said 12.47am.

His taxi was fitted with false number plates. As the moon was just starting to come out from its hiding place from behind a heavy layer of cloud, it started to light up the river with moonlight which held its grisly secret.

After he'd gone, Lisa's body had drifted into some reeds startling some moorhens. It became stuck with her feet protruding out of the reeds, her head now weighted down by the lead weights in the bag around her neck. There were no more bubbles because her head was wedged amongst the roots of the reeds on the bottom of the River Brent. She had earlier stopped wriggling and also stopped breathing. But she was dead, very dead.

Driving further down by the river he stopped and placed half a house brick in her bag and dropped it in the river, they would never find it there. Her money and her mobile phone and of course her earrings and perfume were in his man bag on the passenger seat.

Carrying on to his garage under the damp leaking railway arches, he drove his Taxi into the garage where he locked up. Having now secured it by a very strong lock which he had painted black so as not to show it was a new lock which could arouse suspicion. Getting into his VW estate he drove home with his prize, Lisa's hoop earrings, in fact she wore two pairs, there was also her diamond bracelet. There was still the smell of her perfume on the hoops, he was really pleased with the work he had done, but he could never use the river sight again he would have to find another place to drown them. However there were lots of places to take his victims.

Diane opened the salon door at 8.30am. The other four girls were already waiting to come in and the first thing she heard was Donald barking and making a terrible row. She shouted up the internal stairs 'Lisa, hey Lisa, are you okay?' At the sound of her voice Donald started to bark like crazy. Now concerned, she went up the stairs and opened the door as Donald came running out straight down the stairs and sat under the coat hooks in the hallway where his lead was kept. He kept looking at Diane then back to his lead and back to her again, while wagging his tail and whining.

Diane could tell he hadn't been out since last night so she took him round the back where he immediately went to the toilet and then bounced back in and up the stairs followed by Diane, but there was no Lisa. She looked everywhere but she was not in. The TV was still on because she always left the TV on when she went out for Donald; it was a comfort to him. Diane knew something had happened to her because Lisa would never leave Donald that long, not ever, he was her substitute child. The post was still on the mat which always arrived between 7 and 7.30am by the same postman. However, what she did find was her notepad and on the pad there was the mobile phone number of her date. She called it but it went straight to answer phone. A woman's voice said please leave a message.

At 10.30am Diane called the police who arrived at 2.47 pm. She was furious at the police for taking so long, but as they explained she could be having a great time with her new date. It was best to leave it for 48 hours and then the police would be concerned. After all she could be drunk or maybe in a hospital having had an accident, there could be a thousand reasons why she'd not come home.

'Yes and one reason is that she could have been abducted and murdered' shouted Diane, 'so you're not going to do anything for another two days then? What's the matter with you lot; she has a business to run and she also has a dog to look after. She employs five of us why would she not bother to come home unless something horrible has happened to her WAKE UP and start to look for her!'

WPC Abbey Little asked Diane 'have you checked the hospitals yet?'

'No I haven't.'

'Do you not think it's a good idea to find out then, so shall we try and see if she's been in an accident first, after all how would we know?'

After ringing around the local hospitals and having no luck they came to the beginning again.

'Look I'm certain something terrible had happened to Lisa,' she said to the WPC. 'I can feel it rather than explain it.'

WPC Anne little said 'we have to leave it for 48 hours because we can't go on people's feelings can we? Its evidence we go on, so if she hasn't been in touch and you're still concerned then give us a ring and we can take it from there. Honestly this sort of thing happens every day so we can't just drop everything on a hunch can we Diane?'

'No I guess not, but something has gone wrong I know it, she wouldn't leave the dog alone.'

'Yes, but she knows you will look after the dog if anything happens doesn't she Diane?'

'Of course she does, I always do and I have him when she goes on holiday, always have done.'

'Well then don't worry about the dog. If she turns up let me know down at the station, you have told me about the date she's gone on, and as I say she may be having a wild time.'

'Okay let's see what happens in the next forty eight hours.'

'Don't forget to call me. Look she'll turn up, people mostly do Diane. I'm sure she will.'

'Well I hope she doesn't turn up dead.' Diane had an idea, Lisa told her about a good friend called Julia who was also a hairdresser and had gone to Spain to live some fifteen years ago where she had opened a hairdressers. She was now living a nice life with a good business. Apparently Julia had trained with Lisa years before and Julia now had a partner called George Penny who was a PI and had an office in Notting Hill somewhere. Diane knew he was over here with Julia because Lisa was going to meet up with them for a night out sometime next week. She said he had a client who needed help and should have now wrapped it up. She would have a look for his details upstairs; it must be there in her apartment somewhere. Diane looked through Lisa's apartment being followed around by Donald the dog and found what she was looking for in Lisa's address book. There was also a phone number for George and Julia's apartment over his business address.

CHAPTER SEVEN

She found the address it was 87 Chepstow Road, Notting Hill. It said Julia and George Penny, Private Investigator. The apartment had two large bedrooms with a spacious kitchen and very large living room. It had a garage round the back for three cars and a beautiful large roof terrace on the top.

George Penny had been a policeman for twenty five years; he was a street copper for five years and then he was head hunted by the flying squad where he had to retire early after twenty years as a Detective Chief Inspector. He had been informed that his boss Detective Chief Superintendant Gerry Stanford had been having an affair with his wife. George confronted his boss with the evidence but his boss was making lame silly excuses at first he denied it ever happened. George said take a look at the photographs sir, it's all there and you still deny it. His boss just stood there with a grin on his large face seemingly not to care a fig about it. He said 'look George' which annoyed George so much he hit his boss who went right over his desk. It was a great punch considering his boss weighed almost sixteen stone. However it was folly to hit him in front of other police officers, so therefore ending a great career with a reduced pension rate of only 70% of his police retirement pension.

George started DCI Investigations which was now well established after seven hard but enjoyable years. There was no longer any need to advertise, because he was sought after and he also did some covert work from time to time for MI5.

At one time he was a brilliant amateur boxer with a devastating body punch. If you were hit by him you felt hurt and you stayed hurt, he had these heavy knuckled fists.

George was 6ft tall with light blue eyes and had receding grey silver hair, in fact he wore it shaven which suited him. He had a nice even row of strong white teeth and worked out daily, weighing in at 14 stone he was solid. There was always a smile on his face, his jaw was square and strong and he had a slightly broken nose, but it suited him and the ladies found him very attractive. He made them feel special and appreciated. He loved ladies and could pull a woman from across a crowded street, and had done many times. Above all, apart from being good looking in a rugged manly way, he was good at his job. George never stopped until he obtained a result, no matter how quick or how long or how far it took him to finish a job. He was simply the best.

George was a great friend to have by your side, but he made a terrible enemy. He was honest and told you as it was, like it or leave it. But he got results.

Diane thought she would leave getting in touch with him until the 48 hours was up as you never know Lisa may just turn up and say 'what's all the fuss about?' But in her heart of hearts, she knew that was not going to happen. She had an intuition she was already dead.

Twenty four hours later a couple walking with their dog saw some feet sticking out of some reeds. In fact they were looking at two Moorhens squabbling, probably over a female when Gerald Davidson saw the feet. 'Hey' he said to his wife Pamela, 'hey Pam look, some idiot has chucked a manikin in the river.' He laughed but he was not wearing his distance glasses, however his wife Pam didn't need any.

'Gerald those are real feet OMG they are. Gerald we have to call the police now!'

'What? Don't talk so daft' then a cyclist rode by, they stopped him and asked 'what does that look like to you mate,'

The cyclist, a man called Alan Kimberly said 'Jesus that's someone's feet and it's a woman's' He rang the police on his mobile, and within twenty three minutes the police arrived.

DCI Eric Fletcher said to his partner DC Ronald Buckley 'what I told you Ron has now come true, the madman has killed again, I told you he would. Christ we have a serial killer on the loose now. Let's fish her out and get this area cordoned off, and get the forensic people down as soon as they can.'

The forensic team gently took her out of the river. They said she was put in the river no more than thirty six hours ago and she had not been sexually assaulted, her clothes had not been removed or even moved as far as they were aware. She looked all but perfect except she was dead. The gaffer tape was still tightly wrapped around her face and head apart from the nostrils and her eyes. The team confirmed it was the same killer/s as before and he made her suffer by leaving the nostrils free so she drowned very slowly. She must have suffered the same as the last woman they had found, and that was just four or five weeks ago. The killer was now on a roll, or so it seemed.

Dr John Bishop who was the Chief Forensic Officer said to DCI Fletcher, or rather he growled in his deep voice, 'the poor woman, she had the same tape, gaffer tape wrapped around her head and we know she was alive when she went into the water. Her nose and nostrils and eyes were visible and not taped up which was exactly the same as Helen's were.

She must have known what was happening to her, he made sure of that. This is a madman who is a woman hater, he wanted them to suffer, and take it from me they certainly did, and so terribly.'

'Can you imagine being in the water and you couldn't do anything about it, but drowning through your nostrils? What a cruel bastard this guy is and I would say that going by the first one he killed she was picked up and drowned within about four hours. He does them quickly Inspector and this will not be the last one either!!

Dr John Bishop had one of those voices that commanded attention and when he spoke you listened. As an actor he would make a fine orator, as his voice carried a long way, but he always got respect which he deserved. Being a tall man 6ft 3in with a big frame, he still looked fit, yet at times such as this even though he was a hardened veteran of many murders, sometimes crimes such as these made him cry, that's just the way he was. Unlike the killer, he was a man who loved women.

DC Buckley asked Dr Bishop 'why did he kill them so quickly, what was the point in that because they were not molested in any way at all. What the hell was the point in killing them?'

'Because Detective Buckley, it seems to me he would be able to concentrate on his next victim and then the next one after that and so on, because this guy is going to keep on killing. He just hates women, but god only knows why though. They say there is a reason for everything so find the reason and you find the killer, but I'm sure it won't be as simple as that, however at the end of the day, it all boils down to the same thing.'

DC Ron Buckley said out loud 'what a sad depressing world some people live in.'

'Ron I reckon she went in the same place as Helen, this guy thinks he's clever, so let's go and take a look over the road' said DCI Fletcher. 'I'll tell you one thing Ron I'm going to nail this bastard. Sooner or later he'll slip up. They all slip up sooner or later.'

They once again knocked on all the doors in the road, there were again only a couple of people in until finally they came to Bill and Mary's house again. Eric thought he may get some more carrot cake, but anyway why not? Mary could cook a lovely cake.

'Look Ron, I'll deal with this one again, after all you caused problems the last time didn't you.'

'What! Why do you say that sir? I didn't do anything to her or even say anything to her.'

'Because Ron, I don't think she liked you at all, it must have been the shoes or your hair but you somehow seemed to upset her. It was probably your shoes or the way you stand, who knows? So I will deal with it. Anyway I don't want you to be forced to eat a lot of carrot cake now do I let's face it, you'll only pork out?'

'Hey that's okay sir never mind about me, you just go ahead and do it. I'll weep over it sir but I'll come out the other side a better person for it, and you know what, as you can plainly see I'm all broke up about it. But let's all be grown up about this because sometimes from time to time, shit happens to all of us, it just happens to be my turn today....again. Anyway I'm very disappointed to have drawn the short straw sir. I'll shed a few tears about the carrot cake I never had in the first place' he laughed.

'That's very poetic Ron, very poetic indeed. You should take up the pen.'

DC Buckley laughed as he walked back across the road ready to stand guard when DCI Fletcher would come rushing out again for a world record pee into the bracken once again. 'Oh and this time sir try not to piss all over your shoes.'

DCI Fletcher looked down at his black shoes and laughed as he knocked on the door once again.

CHAPTER EIGHT

Alan Reed was ecstatic because he had killed another one, that's three down and thousands more to go he thought, he was delighted. But now it was the turn of another hapless woman but first he had to find one. He hated the big headed ones, all glossy hair and lots of makeup, he would pick another one out, in fact he had seen one, having the telephone numbers of several more slappers.

Sitting down at his desk he read through the women who were stupid enough to have given him their phone numbers, but all of them were hoping to get into bed with a Doctor and live the high life and not do any more work, and to just take as they all did. He was going to enjoy his life for a change. He hated to have been discharged early from the 16th Med Regiment but there really was no other choice for him, he had to go. Late one night his CO tried to seduce him while he was worse the wear due to drink. The CO was a latent homosexual.

But Alan badly battered him and he was arrested then thrown into a military jail, but when the army's Psychiatrist, a woman, interviewed him his past came tumbling out and she recommended he was discharged at once on mental issues. Sadly he never wanted to leave so at this point yet another bitch to him seemed to have screwed him. They had to discharge him for being mentally unfit, but he had been in the army for over twenty years and he received a good enough pensions to get by on plus he had his gratuity payment enabling him to pay of the remaining mortgage on his house. As it worked out he now worked as a part time male model and as a film extra from time to time which brought in a few grand so he did okay money wise. Then again he was always being propositioned by both sexes but he always said he had a partner in France which was just a sham. So he also took to wearing a wedding ring but that never seemed to make a difference to any of them. No one doubted him as he was a great looking guy, he had plenty of chances to get women in the industry, but he kept well away from them. He wasn't unfriendly, but believed in the old adage don't soil your own doorstep. But he never spoke to anyone when he was working only to be sociable, and of course to his agent, and to speak when he was requested to do so, but did not want to leave any trail, or to get to close to anyone. Some in fact thought him a cold strange fish. They weren't wrong on that one he thought to himself.

Other people thought he was up himself and some thought he was a little weird, because he never mixed with any of them. While waiting for the shoots he was always reading books on the meaning of life and the making of great men such as books on Ideology. Women had tried to get to know him, he was polite, but was not interested he said his wife was a French lady who lived in Paris she was an artist.

DCI Eric Fletcher again knocked on the Bellman's door, but then once again and before he could take his hand away the door was wrenched open. Angrily standing there was Mrs Mary Bellman. 'I have told you before not to come here again not ever, how many more bloody times must you be told. I am very, very busy surely you can see that.'

'Mary can I please speak with Billy please it's rather urgent, is he in?'

'No I'm afraid he's not here anymore, he's gone.'

'Gone, you mean gone out? I don't understand. When will he be back Mary?'

'I'm afraid he won't be able to come back Detective Chief Inspector, not ever.'

'Oh I'm sorry, is he in hospital or is he ill, what do you mean by that?'

'Look Inspector, I'm sorry to have to tell you this as he was your friend, but my husband Billy is dead. He died three weeks ago after he was interviewed by the police so please go away or I shall get the policeman who lives next door to arrest you for indecent exposure, I hope you understand.'

'Mary listen, it's me Eric, DCI Eric Fletcher. I was here three weeks ago we had tea and some of your wonderful carrot cake together. You do make the best tea in the world Mary, you're a legend you should know that. Is Billy really dead? How did he die it must have been very sudden?'

'Yes it was; I now have to sell the house to go and live with my daughter in Cambridge.'

'What happened to him Mary? How did he die, oh that's so very sad I liked Billy I really did, as I like you too, oh what a shame?'

'Well he had another heart attack, his third one just after you had gone, it was the excitement you see it was after another one of his cock up's. After your visit he was always looking out of the dammed window looking for a man in a car. Look, I have to go so goodbye Inspector Fletcher. I have to pay the undertaker he needs his money, but I haven't got any. I think he was a gay undertaker because he wore these silly brown slip on shoes, that's a disgraceful thing to do for an undertaker can you believe that? So what on earth is the world coming to Inspector I ask you, undertakers wearing brown slip on shoes, and some police officers, they may as well wear slippers. Good god that can't be right can it, look here you're a policeman do something about it or this will get completely out of hand.'

'I will look into it Mary I promise you. No your right we can't have that can we.'

'Billy had his funeral last week. It was a quiet affair as we didn't want any fuss.' As she turned to go in the house she stopped and asked him 'oh yes by the way, why did he want to see Billy.'

'Oh yes I do beg your pardon, sorry Mary. It was just to ask if Billy had seen any other cars stopping over the road as we have found another lady dead in the water almost opposite you that's all. Anyway I will have to be going, so once again I am so sorry to hear about Bill.'

'Why don't you ask me if I saw anything? I have eyes too you know and I have ears, and I'm not entirely bloody stupid and I did see a car the other night outside. The man was not taking a piss as Billy would say, but he had an old carpet or rug with him which he took down to the water. He was a big man about your size and a nice looking one too, and a lot better than you I may add. You know you're face looks very debauched, terribly debauched, yours looks like melted cheese, you can do something about that you know as I don't think you're too old.'

'What?' DCI Fletcher was now feeling his face with the tips of his fingers with both hands. 'Mary, what was the car he was driving, can you remember what car it was?'

'It was not a car Inspector.'

'You said you saw a car the other night.'

'It was not a car; it was a London black cab.'

'A London black cab?'

'Yes, yes are you deaf or are you winding me up because you're repeating yourself like an echo, you sound as though you have dementia. I'm glad to see this time you have proper black shoes on too.'

'Yes well I did take your advice last time Mary. I'm glad you noticed them.'

'I'd like to say that's a very big improvement, but your colleague over the road still has silly brown shoes on, I do think he's a gay policeman, you know he is don't you Inspector?'

'Mary please, how long was the Taxi there for, can you remember?'

'I think it was for about ten minutes, the carpet or the rug he had was moving, yes it was wriggling I did see that, but when he came back it wasn't there, yes about ten minutes that's all he was there for, give or take a couple of minutes.'

'Did you see anything else at all? Anything about the man and can you tell me what time this was?'

'Yes it was about twelve thirty, he had a flat cap on when he went with the carpet or rug but when he came back he wasn't wearing a cap or carrying the rug. Maybe he must have taken his cap off, but I think he went looking for it. As I recall he seemed to be in a hurry, but there were two other men who turned up at about the same time, they wanted a pee, I saw them peeing behind a bush. Anyway they were there for about three to four minutes then they drove off. I was going to tell the policeman who lives next door about it exposing themselves like that. And then he drove off in his taxi just afterwards without his cap or his rug. Anyway he wasn't wearing his cap and that was that, perhaps he had a piss or maybe a dump, but he wasn't there long enough for a dump so that's all I saw Inspector.'

'Mary you have been brilliant and you know what.'

'What's that Inspector tell me?' She smiled.

'You are a legend, you really are.'

'Do you know what I miss about Billy Inspector, what I really miss about him.'

'No Mary, what do you miss about Billy, I would imagine everything.'

'I do miss everything but mostly I miss his cock ups, he did great cock ups.'

DCI Fletcher laughed out loud 'Mary you're not that bloody daft are you my love.'

'No Inspector, and when you're passing again pop in to see me I may still be here.'

'I will Mary, I will see to it. I promise you that I will,'

'You do that, but wait hang on a minute Inspector I have something for you, please sit down will you, she quickly disappeared into the kitchen he heard some paper crackling, she came back out minutes later with a full size carrot cake for him, this is for you Inspector, I know you like it.' The cake was in a large biscuit tin. 'I want my tin back Inspector off course when you have eaten it all, so you will have to pop in to see me now wont you.'

DCI Fletcher didn't know what to say, 'oh thank you Mary so much, this is lovely thanks, and I promise I will bring the tin back.'

She went to the door and opened it for him, she had put the tin in a supermarket bag for ease of carrying, but she had a tear in her eye, she turned away quickly to go indoors.

'Ron, Ron come with me, we need to look for a carpet roll or a rug and a flat cap.'

'What have you got there sir, is it evidence?'

'No it's a carrot cake Ron, a carrot cake. Mary gave me one which was so kind of her.'

'The colour sir, what colour are we looking for, you know cap and carpet.'

'Any bloody colour, it's not as though we have a choice do we, for Christ sake Ron, it's not a bloody carpet shop is it, just keep looking down the embankment and in the grass, keep looking and I'm joining you. Hey look Ron there is the carpet or the rug and hey, that's a flat cap! Get it Ron and let's see what we can get from it.'

The cap was a grey one and the rug was the large sort you get by the fireside. They called the forensic boys out to handle the evidence; there must surely be some sort of DNA on the items found.

DCI Fletcher was over the moon at the find, thank god he thought at last maybe the bastard has got a bit complacent, he told Ron they all cock up sooner or later, and then he howled with laughter.

'Sir, are you alright, why are you laughing so much?'

'Ah Ron if only I could explain, but I can't, it's a secret Mary told me and I can't repeat it, I'm sorry.'

They did get some DNA from the cap later and the carpet, but the only recognizable DNA was from Lisa, the other DNA from the cap was from a few other people which was very puzzling.

Alan Reed had stolen the cap from his barbers which had been hanging on the coat stand so it was anyone's guess who had owned it. There were several different types of hair to choose from and none were on the database, they were almost back at the beginning. They did have several DNA samples which baffled the forensic guys, but they did have evidence and if the killer was caught it would put him in the area. However, it could be classed as unsubstantial evidence and a good brief would throw it out of court with a resounding laugh, but perhaps they had the proof he wore it, only time would tell. Time as DCI Fletcher knew they hadn't got because he was certain he was now on a killing spree and the only way to stop him was to kill him or to catch him.

Alan Reed was busy on a photo shoot for cardigans and trousers for the magazine, Clothes First. He'd been working all day, and now he was eager to finish the last shoot, if it was good he could go. He was keen to get another woman now as he was on a roll and the feeling made him feel high.

Arriving home by 8.45pm he decided to ring a lady Estate Agent called Debra Carter. She was aged 42 so she said, she looked an attractive lady and very smart. You could see she had her photographs professionally done as they were enhanced with the soft focus look which to him was ridiculous to say the least and to him it was cheating so he had taken a dislike to her for her false impression she also looked like a bighead. He really didn't like big headed women and those bossy sorts. It would be a sort of bonus to make her suffer. He looked forward to that.

'Hi is this Debra Carter, it is? Brilliant! Hi again Debra this is Geoffrey Watkins the Doctor from PLS. I'm so sorry I had to go away to France, but I had some important work to do on some property over there, anyway Debra can we talk?'

'Hello Geoff, yes of course and I take it you sorted out the problem? The French workers can get, shall we say a little absurd with their estimates and working practises, and that's if they bother to even turn up.'

'Yes I know but I have now paid for a team of British builders to go over and sort things out for me. They send a report back every other day by email with pictures etc. Already they have done brilliantly, and twice the amount of work the French have. Anyway look Debra can we meet for a drink and a meal? I know a place in Mayfair, it's in Davies Street called Mr Williams and it is brilliant. It's only by invitation only at the moment and it's been open for less than a month. I took the chance and booked us a table for tomorrow evening, in fact they were the only seats left and it's a lovely table. Don't stare when you get there as there are a lot of show business types already who have been invited, and to be honest I do know one or two which is down to my work as a surgeon. Oh I'm a Cardiologist by the way, but I only work out of Harley Street.'

'Well Geoff that sounds wonderful, but I'm a vegetarian would that be a problem do you think?'

'No, I have seen the menu and the chef is Spanish. Apparently he's brilliant and world famous, they know how to cook vegetarian, so it's certainly not a problem Debra. Are you okay for that?'

'Yes I am and it sounds wonderful.'

'Debra I can send a Taxi for you at 8pm, he will then pick me up after you, so what's your address?'

'It's 49 Carlton Hill St John's Wood. So where do you live Geoff?'

'Blenheim Crescent in Notting Hill, so I will have the driver pick you up say about 7.45pm and then he will come to me. We can go straight to the restaurant and we can eat say from 8.30 to 9pm. It means going by taxi. I can at least have some wine without the worry of losing my driving licence. Let's face it you need a glass or two of wine, it's brilliant for the heart,' he laughed.

'Oh of course and that sounds good, how lucky am I.'

'I hope we get on Debra and you do look and sound nice. So are you selling plenty of houses at the moment?'

'Not really it's a little slow which is due to the economic climate at this time of the year but things could be a lot worse. Anyway I'm not complaining, my flat is paid for and I have a decent pension which is paid to me from my husband's estate after he died in a helicopter crash. He was a test pilot so he was well insured. He'd been a chief instructor in the RAF and a helicopter pilot. Anyway I own the business and all the property I bought ten years ago. So Geoff I am not looking for someone to carry me along life's pathway. I can do so very nicely by myself and I don't need anyone else's money, so don't you be thinking that I need a man for his money.'

'I wouldn't think that Debra, let's just see how this turns out, my god this is almost like a job interview isn't it. Oh in case you ask I haven't met anyone else and I have also deleted my account with the agency. You're the only one I wanted to take out to be honest, all the others were just not my cup of tea, or didn't seem to be. So anyway I will send a London black cab to pick you up first, is this acceptable to you?'

'Ha, ha Geoff that's fine I will see you tomorrow evening. Look forward to it and at least we can both have a drink.'

'That's brilliant Debra, just brilliant.'

Debra rang her friend Liz. 'Guess what, you know that Doctor we looked at some weeks ago on the site? You know you picked him out, well he's just rang me and he's taking me out tomorrow evening to a new restaurant and it's by invitation only, but at the moment all the show business people are using it and he has a special table booked. Jesus Liz this guy is loaded and he's a cardiologist who works out of Harley Street. He lives in Notting Hill in Blenheim Crescent, that's class Liz.'

'What does he look like Debra? If he looks the same as on his photo then he's considered gorgeous, so best of luck with the date and I'll keep my fingers crossed for you, he does sound nice Debs.'

'Listen Liz I have to get ready. I only have about 22 hours to go. I have to get it right this time, all the others have been losers, and I need to work on myself.'

Liz laughed, 'OMG you're not that bad Debra! You don't look 49 and he has to take you for 42, how would he know? Don't worry once you get him hooked he's yours, let's hope the lighting is not too bright,' she laughed. 'Debs can you do something for me.'

'Yes, mind you it all depends on what it is,' she laughed.

'Look I know this sounds a bit alarming Debs but will you please, please have your mobile pre-dialled to 999, so all you have to do is press send. If you get into trouble at least they will get a bearing to where you are. So will you do that in case you get into trouble, because you never know?'

'Hey Liz, don't you worry, but yes I will do that, why, do you feel it's not good or something?'

'Oh sorry Debs you know I can get strange vibes and feelings about things, just please do it for me.'

'Ok Liz, anyway it's a good idea. Yes I will do that but I'm certain he's okay and anyway a taxi is picking me up so what's to go wrong about that?'

Alan knew she had told him lies about her age because they all do. He could tell by the veins in her hands and her neck, so she was a liar and that made it all the more acceptable to him. This time though he had to change the drop off point. It was far too risky going to the same place again, so he checked out his map of the whole area. Having read the newspapers it seemed that so far there was a news blackout going on, there was nothing reported about a double killer on the loose. He was so disappointed in this. So he would ring the papers himself and tell them about the murders, but not reveal who he was. Apparently most daily papers had very good journalists who investigated crime, he had to be careful. At the moment he didn't want to be caught he was enjoying himself too much.

After studying the local area he found a good spot by the side of the Regent Canal, it was a place called Salmon Lane Lock. He took a drive round to the area and found a perfect spot, it was an area where the barges used to turn around some years ago and now there were reeds and algae in the water, this would be a good place to get rid of her. Pleased at his find he drove home and prepared for the following evening.

Debra was getting all excited and had been trying on all sorts of different outfits all day and still was unable to make her mind up what to wear. In the end she started at the beginning again and decided to wear a simple black skirt. The length was just below the knee and she found a cherry red top with a nice white scarf with black spots, and Julia Mays four inch stilettos. She knew she looked good. It was simple, but elegant and she accessorised it with some gold twirl earrings and a simple matching gold rope chain.

The time was now 7.38pm she was trying to keep a cool head. Then she had to use the loo again and then at 7.59pm she heard the taxi. It sounded its horn three times as she was told he would. Locking up her flat she met the taxi outside, the driver said 'Hi, I have to take you to Blenheim Crescent Notting Hill to meet Geoff, is that correct?'

'Yes that's the place,' but she suddenly had a strange feeling, she thought the drivers voice sounded familiar, but couldn't think from where, she sat back and tried to relax.

She asked the driver 'do you know this man Geoff?'

'No sorry I just had a message to pick you up and deliver you. Then he asked me to take you two out into town to a restaurant called Mr Williams in Davies Street Mayfair.'

'Do you know anything about this place driver?'

'All I know is it's beyond my reach and it's London's best kept secret and you can't get in because apparently it's by invitation only. It's supposed to be brilliant, and everyone who's anybody is fighting to get in the place. I have to say I can't see the point in all of that, give me a fish-n-chip supper any day' he laughed.

Debra felt a little more relaxed now, but there was still something not right, she looked at him again. He was wearing a black beanie hat, heavy rimmed glasses with a dark bomber jacket a sort of standard taxi driver wear.

'I have to say if you don't mind me saying Miss, you look brilliant, this guy is one lucky man.'

It was the word brilliant that shook her into reality it's not a word you hear every day and she had heard it before. Then she realised he was the guy she spoke to on the phone, it was Geoff!

She suddenly shouted out 'stop the taxi, I want to get out. Stop now please!'

'I can't stop here miss can I? It's in the middle of the street, I'll get a ticket.'

'Stop the cab now.' She shouted out.

'No I can't' he shouted back, and then increased his speed.

She took out her phone and pressed the send button to 999. She screamed 'London Taxi!'

A woman's voice said 'which service do you require?'

'Police, help me. Kidnap in progress, help me!'

Now Alan had stopped the cab. She was trying to get out with one hand on her phone and the other on the door handle. She felt a terrible jolt as he shot her in the neck with the stun gun. He watched her slump to the floor of the taxi cab but he had to get her phone which was still live and being recorded at the 999 centre. He was being tooted at by other cars as he was not parked in a good position so he had to drive off and was looking for a better place to park. Meanwhile the operator carried on asking if anyone was there because she could clearly hear other cars and the sound of his swearing, shouting out 'bastards, bloody bastards'. He was cursing all women, the bitches' he shouted then he found a slot to park in. As he got into the back of the cab she had started to come round and with one almighty shove she managed to kick the door open which was half open from her last attempt to get out. She managed to roll out of the wide door and fell into the gutter as a group of lady runners were jogging by. They stopped to look, but then realised what had happened and ran to her aid as Alan got back into his cab he drove off. She still had her phone with her and the operator was still listening and had already informed the police and a unit was sent to the spot by triangulating the last signal. She managed to speak to the operator, but the taxi had long gone. However the lady runners from the Primrose Harriers running club had taken the cab's number plate. One of the runners was a Doctor called Jean Lincroft; she sat Debra up and made her comfortable until the police arrived.

Stopping in a lay-by he very quickly managed to change his number plates back. They were simply held on by Velcro straps he also altered his appearance by getting rid of the beanie hat and thick glasses. However, he nervously managed to get back to his lock up garage without any mishap.

Locking up the taxi inside the garage he started up his VW estate then he drove off home. It was difficult to figure out what had spooked her, because the only thing she had seen of him was the picture on the dating site, but that couldn't have been it as he was wearing a beanie hat and thick glasses. No it was something he had said....but what was it? Then he thought 'brilliant'. The word brilliant which he did use from time to time when he became a little excited, he had always liked that word and he was sure he said that when he rang her to arrange a date and then in the taxi saying she looked brilliant, and then she recognised some part of what he said earlier it had to be the word brilliant, he was sure of that. That was the last time he would use that word. Devious bitch, she was a devious bitch now he wanted to kill her. Somehow he would make sure he would. There would come a day, and soon!

The police had interviewed Debra about what had happened to her. They asked if she was harmed in any way and why did she dial 999 in the first place.

All she would say was she felt somehow threatened by the driver and told them about the dating site and the man called Geoffrey, she was certain he was the same man as the taxi driver. She told them of her fears. She told them about the stun gun he used on her, but they had little to report when they returned to the police station. After all what could they say, as it was all speculative? She did say she wanted to speak to a detective if one was available, but there were none, not until the morning so they would report the findings to the CID and one would be in touch with her later tomorrow, if not she was to try again as they were the best ones to deal with a suspect kidnapping.

John Hutton was sound asleep with his wife when there came a loud banging on his front door. Now he was fully awake, he looked out of the bedroom window and there were three police cars and a couple of armed policemen standing outside his door.

'Hey you lot, what's all the noise about its 3.17am?'

'Open the door now or we will break it in. Do it now sir, please do it now,' shouted a burly six foot sergeant.

'If not' said another policeman 'we'll use the big red key,' which he had over his shoulder. It was a large heavy battering ram device painted a bright red which they use to get into the doors with.

The police sergeant decided John Hutton was a bit too slow to open his door so they did it for him anyway using the big red key.

John Hutton couldn't open his door as it was now in three different pieces lying in his hallway then the police charged in, 'where were you this evening sir?'

'Here, right here with my wife, we never went out, we had some friends round it's my wife's birthday, isn't that right Sheila?'

'Yes well it was my birthday yesterday so we had two friends round for a meal and a drink. Why what's the problem officers, are you going to arrest us for that, is it against the law?'

'Your taxi sir, has it been in your driveway all evening or has it been out? Have you let anyone else drive it, or at any other time sir?' said a sergeant Bellows.

'No not ever, what's happened sergeant? It must be very serious for you to come bashing in my front door, the neighbours will be delighted to see all of this bollocks going on. You will be hearing from our solicitor, you can be sure of that, and he takes no prisoners!'

'Look sir we are sorry, it looks like there has been some mistake because we think that your number plates must have been cloned by someone with a London black cab the same as yours, and he attempted to rape a lady this evening sir, and he may well have done so before tonight.'

'I'm sorry to hear that sergeant, very sorry, but as I said I never used my cab, and the last time was yesterday morning. I worked up to 11.30 am and then we walked to the supermarket, then the butchers and came home to prepare for the meal. Look let me write down the name and addresses of our friends, oh and the phone number. You can ring them now I'm sure they will be delighted to hear from you at this time of the morning sergeant.'

'Look as I said sir, we are just doing our job, and I'm sorry about the time. So we will leave you alone now and thank you for your time.'

'Thank you for my time! Are you having a laugh? So that's it is it, you break in my door at this time of the morning then realise you've come to the wrong house, then just as quickly you want to bugger off leaving my front door in pieces. You don't seem to care at all, so now I can't go back to bed before we get our old door replaced with a new one. I have to go to work at 8am, I have regular clients to pick up and my wife who is a midwife has to be in work by 6am if not sooner.'

'Look sir, again we are very sorry, but rest assured I will make certain one of our trusted joiners will be along at about 7am and here's my station number, name, rank and phone number. As I said at the moment we are chasing a serial offender, so again rest assured I will sort it out sir. I am very sorry but I really do have to go.'

'I can tell you now I will be putting in a complaint about you, because you're just a bit too hasty with that big red key thing and if I lose my clients because of you I will sue the arse of you. You can put your house on it and I mean every word sergeant and it may just come to that, because it's you I will sue, and then the police themselves. Now get out of my house and thanks for clearing up this mess....not!'

The sergeant left the house with his tail between his legs, but he was not amused. He got on to the joiner Duncan who was fast asleep at the time, he woke up to hear the sergeant asking him could he go round like now this minute to fix the door, it would be a favour to him and it was very urgent.

'Oh I see you've screwed up again have you Tony? Well this is going to cost you mate and its double or nothing, plus the favour still stands you got that? You have, good... then give me the address.'

DCI Eric Fletcher had a note on his desk saying could he pop round and speak with a woman called Debra Carter about a possible kidnapping and something about being kept against her will in a London black cab. It was something to do with a dating site, she had jumped out of the taxi after being hit with a stun gun or some other apparatus and could he please ring the lady ASAP.

DCI Fletcher looked at the note then it hit him a LONDON BLACK CAB. That's exactly what Mary had said she saw parked up in the same space as where Helen and Lisa were dumped. 'Ron, get in here now we have a lead on this bastard so move your arse. We have to go and you had better get here pronto.' He put the internal phone down when DC Ronald Buckley came running through the door.

CHAPTER NINE

'Ring this woman now Ron and tell her not to go anywhere, because we need to speak with her immediately so get on to it. Why are you still standing there just do it?'

'Mrs Carter, Mrs Debra Carter? Oh good morning this is DC Ronald Buckley. We understand you had an altercation with a taxi driver who used some sort of stun gun on you and something to do with a dating site. We need to talk with you as soon as possible, could we see you right now? We can, that's good Mrs Carter. We will be along in about twenty five minutes give or take a couple of minutes.' They quickly walked to the police car park and drove off with their siren wailing and the blues and two's flashing. Within the given time they arrived at the address where Mrs Carter was waiting for them.

She endeavoured to explain about the dating site and then gave a good description of the man and his taxi cab. She told them she was hit with some sort of electrical device and it hurt. It temporarily knocked her out, and then she woke up, but managed thank god to roll out of the taxi door where she fell into the gutter. She was rescued by a ladies running club who were going by at the time.

DCI Fletcher said to her 'what made her think it was the one and the same man that she was about to meet.'

She said 'it was the word just brilliant. He said that when I agreed to meet him at the end of the phone call and then when the driver said to me the same word brilliant again, I knew I was in big trouble. Why else would the same man disguise himself as a taxi driver and the word which made me suspicious was the use of brilliant, it's not a word you hear every day. It was the way it was said with a sort of excited tone about it. I can't explain Inspector, but thankfully, I was right after all.'

After the interview they looked at each other, both were horrified at what she had told them. DCI Fletcher knew now they were in big trouble because the man had a perfect disguise, a London black cab. He wouldn't need to use a dating site now, because he could virtually pick any women up at will late at night. This was now a very bad situation. They couldn't stop all black cab drivers from working and the guy could clone any number of black cab number plates, so now they had to somehow try and stop him. This was the third attack within six weeks, but they knew he was going to try again. After checking the stats they found out there were over twenty one thousand black cab drivers in London alone. So the future was looking a little darker.

But it was going to get darker for some, and very dark indeed. Alan Reed was now going to attempt to get another woman. Being so disgusted with himself at how he nearly got caught and now he wanted to get even with this Debra Carter.

Eleven days later Alan drove to the Estate agents. Standing outside the agent's window he looked inside the time was 9.30pm on Sunday. There was a house for sale in Rochester Road Bayswater. It was a four bedroom house in the region of £363,000. He took the reference number and on the Monday morning at 8.30am he saw Debra Carter unlock her shop which was just down the road from her flat. Suddenly he was having a job to control himself he wanted to kill her so badly. Now he wanted her to suffer.

At 8.45am he rang her asking about the property in her window. Using an educated accent, he was plausible and good at accents. Now he used the name Bruce Green. He asked her if it was possible to view the property at 5pm and could he bring some carpet with him.

She asked him 'carpet?'

'Yes, well you see my brother has a carpet business and this one particular colour is in plentiful supply as my brother has a warehouse full of it bought from a German company that went bust. Its good quality I could carpet the whole place out with good quality carpet but very cheaply.'

'Yes that's fine,' she laughed 'as long as it's not too large.'

'No it's just a small roll. I want to see how the colour scheme would look as the carpet had the colours I liked. The advert also said the decor is in excellent condition and that you understand would save me a lot of time and money.'

'No that's okay Mr Green.'

'My wife would be able to come the next week, as at the moment she is in Spain at our villa with her mother and sister, but if I like it I would be able to give the okay. After all it is me, who has the money,' he laughed. 'To be serious I'm looking for another investment and I see you act as rental agents. This could work out and I won't be requiring a mortgage, it's a total cash buy. I want to see if it's worth converting into four apartments. To me it certainly looks as though it could be.'

Debra Carter said 'yes that's a great idea. You would have no problems in renting them out as there is a desperate shortage of good quality flats to rent in this area, I could fill them now this same day. I don't think for a moment you will have any objection from the local council to turning it into apartments, because as I said at the moment there is a great shortage of apartments. I know for a fact the council will welcome more apartments in this area, as long as the plans confer to their wishes. I have a number of contacts who can put you right on the planning aspect, and of course we have a few architects that we can recommend. We also have as you say a rental department where we can check out all the references we also collect the rent. All this is in a brochure. I will see you later Mr Green. You had better have my mobile number so please ring me if you can't make it later or if you're running late.'

Checking out the house he noticed there was no driveway, none of them had, but he had an idea in mind. At 5.23pm he rang her to say he was sorry, but he was on the way and would be five minutes late, the traffic had been extremely bad. He had driven from his house in Walworth which he was renovating, there had apparently been an accident with a cyclist, but he had now arrived.

She had been looking at her watch wondering where the hell he was and getting more and more wound up because she and her friend were going out for a meal to celebrate Liz's birthday.

He knocked on the door but she had seen him cross the road a little further down. Well she presumed it was him although somehow he seemed familiar, he was blowing his nose as he crossed the road which helped to cover his face. She was irritated now because he was a little late, yet she badly needed a sale. She told herself to stop moaning, not to look desperate and to calm down, look confident and not too eager.

Knocking twice on the front door Debra answered it and stepped back inside to let him step in, but suddenly she had the horrible thought it was the man in the taxi who had attacked her.

Having now stepped inside he hit her straight away in the neck again with the stun gun, then he tied her wrists behind her back with garden ties her ankles were also tied with garden ties, but her face was taped all the way round with gaffer tape, except for her nostrils and her eyes, all done in four minutes.

Finding a bathroom on the first floor with a large bath, he soon filled it up with water. Now satisfied, he went down the stairs, picked her up then carried her back up the stairs and into the bathroom. Being very gentle with her as he always was with his victims, he didn't want to mark them.

'Now look Debra,' he said slowly. 'I know you let me down the first time by ringing the police about me and as you know they always manage to get the wrong end of the stick. But that was a silly thing to do. Still in the end there's no harm done and I bear you no malice. I do have to say though this water is a little cold, but please don't worry it will soon be over. I've had a lifetime of hurt so think yourself fortunate it will soon be over, but for me I'm afraid it will just go on and on.'

She couldn't hear him she was still unconscious, but there was a distant voice coming from somewhere.

Carefully placing her in the bath, he turned her over so her face was in the water he held her there for a while. She was fully clothed, but he took out her twisty gold earrings and put them into a small pill box in his pocket. He looked at them and smiled, oh yes he liked them very much. 'Thank you for these lovely earrings my love, they're gorgeous, they really are.'

Debra slowly started to struggle a little as the cold water revived her. She was now beginning a sloshing splashing desperate kicking, but her legs were not working properly her arms seemed to be paralysed and wouldn't work. But she was a very strong woman. It was then she saw her previous life flashing by and most seem to be from a distant past she was not familiar with. Then she saw the old bath and the broken wall tiles and the smell of an old unkempt building and then suddenly her granddad was holding her on his lap where she was eating an ice cream at some seaside town, but a dog a small tan and white dog was trying to snatch a lick and her granddad was laughing. There were several seagulls flying around and some were by her granddads feet all waiting for a small morsel of food for her to drop and she laughed too. Suddenly she was back in the living.

'Oh dear, please don't struggle Debs darling,' but she carried on struggling as hard as she could. She knew she was going to die, she just knew. But she wanted so hard to live and not to die in some uncared for old porcelain bath tub of years gone by now full of cold water. Now she felt her strength slipping away, she wanted it to stop but then out of breath and now out of strength she gave in.

Holding her feet up in the air while she was still in the bath and saying 'I'm so sorry, I wanted to use warm water Debra, but there was only cold water. Keep still and it will soon be over. It's harder if you struggle Debra, so let the water take you on your journey. Please don't struggle anymore. Listen to me it will be a lot easier if you let the water do its work on you, trust me it will. I'm a Doctor and I know about these things, but of course you already know that don't you darling Debs.'

She was fully aware what was happening to her and knew she could do nothing to stop him, but she tried so hard. She kicked and strained, shook her head from side to side, but to no avail.

She felt her lungs bursting, there was no breath left and she was in pain all over, but then she saw her past flashing before her again in a mad merry go round of light and dark as she finally passed out to die in a strange old bath tub of a long forgotten owner.

Alan was holding her feet in the air as she slipped all the way under the water until she stopped thrashing about. He noticed she had lovely legs. Suddenly he became annoyed she had to be punished because she had recognised him, so for that reason alone she had to go. Twenty minutes later after letting her feet go into the bath he checked to see if she was still breathing. He had kept a pair of surgical gloves on all the while he was there he did so with all of them, but she was dead. The time was now nine minutes past seven pm.

They had to be killed quickly because he left no clues and mostly had no time to talk with them, he just wanted it over and to take their earrings. The problem was he didn't like to hurt them physically but wanted to feel better for cleansing himself and the world of these wretched women.

Looking around he went through her handbag where he took all her money, there was only £96 but it would come in handy. Dropping her bag in the bath next to her was the best place for it. Checking the street, he was about to go when her mobile rang, it said Liz. This threw him, he thought should he answer it or not and what could he say? Getting into his Mr nice guy mode to find out what she wanted, as she may be outside or something and he didn't want to be seen by anyone, so he reluctantly answered it.

'Hi Debs are you still okay, and you took your time to answer. Are you still okay for later, I've managed to book a table are you still up for it?'

'Oh dear, I'm afraid she won't be coming to see you this evening Liz.'

'Pardon me, who is this please? Is Debra there, can I speak with her?'

'I'm afraid not, because at the moment Debs has gone swimming, I told her not to. And now I have to say the silly girl has got into difficulties it's not looking very good. I did try and tell her the water was extremely cold, but you know her she wouldn't listen to me or anyone else' he laughed.

'Hey, who are you? I want to speak with Debra now please if you don't mind.'

'Sorry Liz, that's no longer possible I'm afraid, she's wasn't very good at swimming was she?'

'What? What are you talking about, she hates swimming and I do know her. Who are you, please tell me!'

'I was her new swimming instructor for this evening. I'm afraid she's had some breathing difficulties it doesn't look good. So sorry she can't even swim the silly girl, and now she's not even moving.' he laughed out loud.

'What, now listen to me, you tell me who you are, where you are and where is Debra? What have you done with her you BASTARD, tell me where you are!' She heard laughing as Deb's phone went dead.

She rang Notting Hill Police station and asked for DCI Fletcher.

'Oh yes, in what connection may I ask madam?'

'Murder, I believe my friend has just been murdered, please can I speak with him, it's very urgent.'

'Where are you, and who are you?' asked the custody sergeant.

'Mrs Elizabeth Downing, I'm a friend of Debra Carter and she's just been abducted by a taxi driver a few days ago. Please put me through to him, because he's on the case with DC Ron Buckley.'

'They're both off duty now madam, but I will make sure he gets this message as soon as possible.'

'Idiot' she shouted, 'you're all bloody useless! Tell him I told you that my friend has disappeared and I'm reporting you for being an obstruction.'

The custody sergeant Terry Mosley thought about it then rang DC Buckley and told him what this Elizabeth Downing had said.

'For Christ sake give me her phone number Terry. What's wrong with you?'

'Hello Mrs Downey, I'm DC Ronald Buckley. Can you tell me the reason why you rang the police station?'

'Yes, my friend Debra Carter who you interviewed last week in connection with a dating site and a taxi driver who abducted her, well she's now gone missing. I have just spoken to her abductor or killer and that idiot Desk Sergeant you employ was not much help.'

'Stay where you are, I'm on the way so give me your address Liz. I will be about thirty five minutes, if not sooner.'

He rang DCI Fletcher who was fast asleep in his recliner with his Jack Russell dog Herbert on his lap. His wife was annoyed because it was his work mobile. 'Not again' she said out loud, 'I'm getting bloody fed up with all this, never any peace.' Her early night promise had now gone out the window.

She had to answer it, 'hello Ron yes he's here I'll get him.' She woke him up and the dog looked really annoyed at being disturbed and showed his teeth at her.

'Don't you show me those teeth you little shit or I will pull the lot out with pliers,' she said to the dog.

'Eric, Eric.' She gently shook him. 'It's Ron and it does sound really urgent.'

'Thanks love.' Ron told him what Liz had said. 'I'll be about thirty minutes, you're already on the way, ok see you in five then.'

'Look I'm really sorry honey this madman has struck again so I have to go. I'll try and catch you later.' His wife Jenny looked very fed up, 'still you have Herbert for company, and I just want to catch this lunatic. We all do.' He bent over to her where he kissed her, 'I'm sorry my love.'

Ron had driven off towards DCI Fletcher's home and was now just three minutes away. Eric was waiting for him. Slipping into the passenger seat they were now off to see Liz who was at the estate agency, she had a spare set of keys to the office. They had tried Debra's flat but no answer so they met at the agency. They found the day diary and saw the entry to the address. They also saw there was a spare key in the cupboard behind her desk where she kept all the keys together with the spare keys to all the houses and apartments she had for sale. They saw the time of the last appointment and raced to the address, leaving Liz behind just in case Debs turned up, more in hope than anything.

When they arrived at the address it was a three story old town house which had seen better days. The paint was peeling off the front door and step, while the railings guarding the small front garden had began to turn rusty and the windows needed a good window cleaner.

You could see the old sash cord windows had not been opened in years and odds on, you wouldn't be able to open them now, and someone had painted several layers of thick white paint over all the frames. The cobwebs were thick and full of dead fly carcasses.

They went to try the key, but the door was unlocked so they went into the house. It was a very gloomy place with bare floor boards and the hallway was thick with leaflets and free offers of this and that, plus free newspapers. The house had been empty for some time. Ron found the junction box and turned on the lights. DCI Fletcher said 'check the bathroom first Ron, while I'll check out the kitchen and the ground floor area.'

DC Buckley searched the five bedrooms, and then checked the bathroom. As he walked in he saw water all over the floor, but he saw Debra's feet, then he saw the rest of her. It was obvious she had died in terrible pain as her eyes were closed very tightly, but she had somehow managed to bite through the gaffer tape surrounding her mouth showing her bloodied mouth and her top teeth had bitten through her bottom lip. He wanted to cry, it was a horrible and a nasty way to die like that.

'SIR, sir up here, she's up here, but dead, very dead. Christ how did we miss this sir? What did we do wrong? I feel so guilty now, the poor woman's dead in the same manner too. I'll ring forensics sir.'

When DC Buckley saw poor Debra she was floating in the water with her face on the side. She had been drowned in the large old cast iron bath with heavy solid floral feet. The equally large bathroom felt cold even though it was a warm evening.

There was a tiled wall, which extended from floor to ceiling, also a very old shower unit over the bath. It had a huge shower head and some of the old small white tiles surrounding it were now cracked with some missing. The floor was tiled in real old fashioned black and white tiles. Some of these were also cracked and made from a material called lino. And some tiles were curled up at the corners and there was also a few missing. A couple of spiders were hanging from their webs above the bath in the corner. He could see the bath was stained a light brown colour under the two old grizzled taps from years of the taps dripping. He could see the taps were inlaid with white porcelain with the words Hot and Cold written on top of the old worn taps in black. It had a terrible surreal look about it, maybe because she was wearing a bright red scarf. The bathroom look was what you see in an old folk's home about to close, or one of the bathrooms you see in HM Prisons. The radiator was an old cast iron job. God knows how many years old. He doubted they even worked because there were so many layers of old paint they would probably not throw out any heat anymore. It was the same murder scene as the other two women. All had been tied up with garden ties and they all had their faces bound with gaffer tape except for the eyes and their nostrils. Her hands were tied by the wrists behind her back and her ankles were tied the same, but there were signs of a frantic struggle as she had obviously wanted to live. There were blood stains on the edge of the old bath as she had smacked her face on the rim of the bath while trying desperately to live. You could see the large cut on the bridge of her nose and one of her ears was very swollen and her left eye was almost closed with another cut on her eyebrow. You could see she desperately tried so very hard. This sight of Debra upset him. He felt empty, lost and sad, and then he became angry.

DCI Eric Fletcher could see how upset his understudy was he said 'Ron, now you listen to me, you have to let go and keep your anger inside because believe me that anger will destroy you. When you're upset you miss things, you have to keep a cool head. Believe me I want to catch this mad sod, all of us do, so don't let him win. We all have to try and keep calm, take in the details and look for clues.'

'Sir I'm sorry, but sometimes it gets to me. Anyway I reckon he held her feet up in the air as she struggled to get out, but being tied like that and her head being heavy she wouldn't be able to breathe. Even you or I would perish in the bath sir if even your wife was to hold your feet in the air. There was a murderer who did that a long time ago now. I've forgotten his name, but they hung him.'

'George Joseph Smith, said DCI Fletcher. He was involved in the Brides in the bath murders in the 1900's, about 1913 I think but don't quote me on this. He married these women three in all. He had taken out large life insurances and they all managed to die by having fits in the bath. They reckon by lifting up their feet well over the head whilst still in the bath they passed out and then they drowned. The crucial thing is by having the feet held above their heads they can't struggle as they are trying to breathe and then that lets the water in, but it was never conclusively proved that's the way they died. However die they did, and it seems to me you are right Ron as this once tough little lady did struggle and if she did he held her feet out of the water we think, but the thing is she's dead, murdered by the same madman and woman hater. She hasn't been assaulted either, but her mouth is a mess, you can tell she suffered a lot.'

The forensic team arrived and Doctor John said 'bloody hell Fletcher, another one is it? You guys are getting to be a habit around these women. It's un-nerving and yes, it's definitely the same method, meaning the same man or the same woman.'

'I know, I know' said DCI Fletcher, 'but we can't find a bloody motive except he must hate women.'

'Well that's a motive, so work on that then. He's a man who hates women' said Dr John Bishop who was the head of the forensic team in his usual booming theatrical voice. 'But this guy must have a very good reason sad as it is to hate women, but find out why and you have your killer. It seems simple to me Inspector, very simple.'

'Does it really? Well how many nut cases are there on our files, and how many not on our files Mr Bishop. It's not that bloody simple; we only wish that it was.'

'I know Inspector Fletcher, but we all want this madman caught, it gets to us too you know.'

Alan Reed was now excited, he was on a roll. He wanted to do another one so he looked at his dating book. So far he had now crossed out three women, but there were another 13 or 14 on the list. There was bound to be some who had already met men. He rang another one, this one was called Annie Martin and she was a primary school teacher and lived in Camden Town. She had told him she lived in Camden Street as she trusted him on the phone. After all he was a Doctor and she was keen to form a relationship with another man after her divorce from her husband Peter who had walked away with the woman from the corner shop. They were now living in Australia and he was also a teacher, a maths teacher. The trouble was the kids she taught were not the only ones with homework. She had plenty to do most evenings which didn't leave a lot of time to socialise with anyone. So this online dating seemed the way forward for her. She had spoken to some right idiots and the odd nice man, but even this was not an easy option. Her life was in disarray but loneliness is a horrible thing, especially when you're still so young. People always associate it with the elderly but that was not the true picture. She didn't like living on her own not at all, but it was so hard to find someone suitable.

Annie was 45 years old and had been a teacher since leaving Teacher's Training College some twenty two years ago. Alan Reed had all this written down as best he could. Happily she seemed to be a suitable candidate so he was going to ring her now.

'Annie, it is you, good. Hi Annie this is Doctor Geoffrey Walker. I rang you about six weeks ago. Listen are you seeing anyone, if not would you like to meet for a coffee or a meal or a drink, sometime soon like now' he laughed. 'Sorry to be so direct, but I have just come back from France, I have a small vineyard over there in South West France. I had to have some building work done, but now it's all sorted out thank goodness. By the way do you like France? I could live there with ease and I intend to do so in the not too distant future.'

'Hi Geoffrey, it is really nice to hear from you, so that's what happened to you then. Yes that was six or seven weeks ago now, but who's counting?' She stood there with her fingers crossed.

'Yes as I said, I had to go to France to oversee a project on my farmhouse and vineyard it took a lot longer than expected. Anyway it's sorted out now, so I'm free at last. To be perfectly honest Annie, your phone number was the only one I kept as I'm off that site now. I had so many emails I had to delete them but I did like yours. You don't seem to be pretentious like most of them, so would you like to meet up?'

'Yes, yes that would be nice, you've talked me into it' she laughed. 'If you can think of a place to meet, that would be lovely.'

'Annie I know a nice little Italian place in Notting Hill, do you like Italian? You do, that's great. If I can send a taxi for you then he also picks me up after you, we can share a bottle of wine. That way I haven't got to drive so I can enjoy the evening without worrying about the breathalyser' he laughed. 'I do like a nice bottle of red to share, don't you?

'Yes that would be lovely Geoff, what time are we talking about?'

'Shall we say 8pm? If the taxi picks you up at 7.45 I'll book the table for 8.30pm, let's say tomorrow evening. Is this good for you?'

'That would be perfect and I love Italian. I speak a little as well as my mother was from a small place in Tuscany, but no-one has even heard of it, such a small place with about ten houses. I think everyone left and it's not there anymore. Anyway I'm looking forward to it and thank you for ringing me, I didn't think I would hear from you again Geoff.'

CHAPTER TEN

That night Annie had a job to sleep so she took a sleeping pill, the trouble with that is they make you feel so dozy, but she didn't want to go looking haggard so better dozy looking than haggard.

Alan Reed was well pleased with himself. He wanted to kill as many as he could before he was caught. It was obvious sooner or later he would be caught at some stage, but he didn't really care. He wouldn't even mind, because after all he had been a prisoner all his life trapped in his own head thanks to his mother and women in general. He was worse than a misogynist, he could charm the birds out of the trees, but that's as far as he would go. He still had to rid the world of these greedy gross women. This was now his mission in life.

DCI Fletcher was stumped, this killer had left no clues, only that he may be driving around in a London black cab. The guy, who had tried to abduct Debra, must be the same man who'd drowned her in the bath.

At 7.55pm the taxi arrived outside Annie's house with cloned number plates tooting his horn three times. After two minutes she opened her door and waved, she locked her door and walked the few yards to the taxi. She got in the back and as soon as she did, he stepped out of his door and opened her door. He said a light has come on again. It's the seat belt, I'm afraid it's twisted. Let me untwist it for you. She looked on then he hit her with a stun gun and she immediately passed out. Quickly gagging her he drove off for about a mile then went to the back of the cab and secured her with garden ties. With her hands behind her back and her ankles tied, he gaffer taped her mouth and laid her on the floor. The taxi sign said NO SERVICE. He drove off to a prearranged place, the Lime House Basin in the Regents Canal.

Annie couldn't move, she was tied up securely and the only way she could breathe was through her nostrils. She was terrified, she was in a panic, but there was nothing she could do.

She just lay there praying she would be alright, yet she knew she was going to die. She started to kick out, but he just used the stun gun again on her and then she was still. The time was now 10.37 pm. Getting the wheelchair out he secured her with Velcro straps then covered her with a blanket and pushed her along. Making absolutely sure no-one else was about, he undid the straps and carried her to the side of the canal. Tied around her neck there were two large bolts in a supermarket bag. Carefully lifting her from the wheelchair he slipped her into the cold dark water of the canal. Very carefully pushing her out into the middle, where she sank head first into the gloomy depths of the Lime House Basin. The bubbles from her nostrils soon stopped as she slowly drowned. He dropped her bag in the Basin further down after having weighted it with half a house brick where it quickly sank, but not before taking her mobile phone and some perfume and money from her bag she also had a nice small bracelet which he also took from her bag, he never bothered taking any watches from his victims, just small items of jewellery and their mobile phones.

Satisfied she was dead; he walked back to his taxi cab pushing the wheelchair and drove off back to his lock up garage. Pleased with her earrings he was feeling them and smelling them. They were small gold studs, and when he was home he would put them in his kitchen cupboard with the other mementos. Now he counted the money she had with her which was only fifty five pounds. Feeling utter elation that another had gone he smiled; this was easy, but in all seriousness it had been too easy. It would be a good idea to take a couple of weeks off and let things settle down for a while, maybe he would go away for a few days. Everyone from time to time and he was no exception could do with a break. Suddenly he had three days hard modelling jobs to do. This time it was men's hats and jeans he had to get to Fulham to the studio for the day. It was just a morning shoot then he was free for a while. He told his agent he would maybe go over to France and take a look around Paris again for a week. So he checked the airlines; Ryan Air did flights all the time to Paris, so it was a no brainer. Being in two minds whether to go or not as he still had this urge to kill, it felt like a hunger pain. Booking a flight he spent the entire week in Paris. Booking into his favourite place the Hotel Albe St Michel which was in the centre of Paris, he looked forward to eating at his favourite Restaurant Le Stella which was in the Avenue Victor Hugo. The average meal was about £65, but excellent. It had real character he was so looking forward to just eating, drinking and seeing the sights. It was about time he enjoyed a break where he did nothing but eat, walk, take photos and sample the restaurants. He could speak French really well as he was taught in the Para's, yet he could also speak fluent Spanish.

At ten thirty in the morning after the drowning, there was an art class from the local school on a field trip to do some sketching of the Lime House Basin. There were reeds and moorhens, swans, ducks and a couple of old barges no longer in use. There was plenty to see and paint for the kids. They all set up their fold away chairs and sat down to sketch. Some of the kids were caught messing about but the teacher Jackie Swanson soon sorted them out they were told to get back to school which was only about a hundred yards away.

'Oh Miss we won't do it again, honest we won't' said two cheeky twelve year old lads. She warned them 'any more nonsense and you will be barred from coming out again.'

After an hour Jack Reading who was twelve years old, the same as the rest of his class mates, was enjoying his sketching because that's what he did the best, he was a natural artist. When Miss Jackie Swanson saw his sketch, it stopped her in her tracks.

Jack was a very good young aspiring artist and his work was hung in the school's hallway, and two more in the Headmaster's office. He was not the sharpest knife in the box, but he could draw and paint. She saw a body upside down and asked him crossly 'JACK! Why have you drawn a horrible picture of a body, why?'

'Miss it's in the water, you said we could draw anything we wanted. Look over there, it's there look, it's a tailor's dummy.'

When she looked she could see nothing but an old sack, but then the sack turned over and a pair of feet bobbed up to the surface again, it kept moving with the water movement from the swans. There were now about eleven curious swans in the area where the body was.

'OMG!' she shouted when she went over to take a closer look at the dummy. When she was really close she realised it was a middle age woman who was trussed up. 'Children listen to me. All of you get back to school now. Terry you take charge take them back please, and don't mess about.' It was only a short walk back to their school of a hundred yards or less.

'Oh Miss.' came the cry. 'Do we have to?'

'Yes, DO IT NOW.' she shouted out, and then she rang the police. She could clearly see it was a woman by her feet. Her head was still under the water but popped up now and again. The police came within ten minutes where they soon secured the area with police tape and a couple of burley police officers.

DCI Eric Fletcher was in the police canteen with DC Ron Buckley when a young WPC came hurrying up to the pair and said 'Sir, I'm sorry to bother you but they have found a middle age woman in the Lime House Basin, she's been drowned and it's apparently the same scene as the others sir. The area has been sealed off and Forensics I'm told are on their way.'

Both officers now had to abandon their full English breakfast with much annoyance they had only just started, but that had happened before.

Both the detectives managed to cram their bacon into a sandwich; they both took a mouthful of baked beans which made them unable to talk very well. DCI Eric Fletcher was particularly annoyed because he was driving and he had to give his sandwich to DC Ron Buckley, who greedily scoffed both sandwiches while smiling in-between mouthfuls.

DCI Eric Fletcher looked at DC Ron Buckley and said 'my god you're eating that bacon sandwich as though it was going out of fashion.'

'Well it is' said DC Buckley as he spitted bacon bits everywhere, 'what about you and the carrot cake, you pigged all of it, I had nothing so you owe me' he laughed 'oh my god that was delicious.'

'It was nice Ron, nice will do!' When they arrived within the next few minutes, there was a large crowd which had now gathered all of them were rubber necking trying to get the best position to see what was going on. Ten minutes earlier there was no-one about only the school kids, now the area was filling up with all sorts of nosey people.

'Clear this bloody lot out of the Basin Sergeant Stocker. Get rid! They could be trampling all over the bloody evidence for Christ sake. Wake up; what's the matter with you. Get it done now, any moans you can have then arrested,' said DCI Fletcher.

'Arrested sir, on what charge?'

'For being bloody stupid Sergeant, now that also includes you. Interfering in police business and for acting like a bunch of time wasters and being dick heads. I don't know Sergeant, for Christ sake use your loaf, but just get them out of here,' shouted DCI Fletcher.

'Ron this is number four now,' said DCI Fletcher, how the hell do we stop this madman?' Then the forensic team pulled up and Dr John Bishop who headed the team ambled over. 'This is now number four Eric. What's the matter with Buckley, has his teeth been giving him problems?' asked Bishop.

DCI Fletcher looked at Ron who was picking bacon bits out of his even teeth and then he was trying to wipe baked bean juice from the corner of his mouth, and for some inexplicable reason he had some bean juice on his left ear lobe. 'What?' asked Ron, 'what's the problem now? Jesus, I can't seem to do anything right these days.' Both men were looking with amusement at DC Buckley's antics.

'Well you're right on that one Ron,' said DCI Fletcher. 'You should see yourself, what a fine example of a detective you are. For God sake Ron, get a grip will you? I don't know, look at you, there's bacon in your teeth, you wear gay shoes, plus you have baked beans in your ear. What's the bloody world coming to?' He said to John Bishop.

'Yes, and anyway I can count John,' said DCI Fletcher to Bishop's sarcastic comment. 'How the hell is he getting all these women? It must be the dating site. I reckon he has a list, who the hell knows? This guy is not going to stop not until we catch him, because sooner or later we will.'

Suddenly DCI Fletchers head swivelled round. All heads were now turned to look at the direction he was looking. 'Shit, there's that bloody conniving reporter Lovett, who the hell told him about this? Whoever opened their big mouth I'll have his balls on a bloody skewer for this. You see if I don't.'

DC Buckley looked at DCI Fletcher and thought, you see if I don't, what the hell does that mean. He was about to ask, but then he thought better of it. He'd had enough bollicking's for the one day.

CHAPTER ELEVEN

'Oh no sir,' said Ron 'he's on his way over to see us, how the hell did he know? What's going on and who told him, Jesus this will be all over the news anytime now?'

'I know I can't stand the man he's a scene stealer' said DCI Fletcher, 'and a shit stirrer if ever there was one. The guy is poison, but once he's discovered a story he doesn't let go. The bastard always get's in the way we could do without this at the moment.'

'Cant we just get rid of him sir' said DC Buckley.'

'Ha, if only we could Ron. I'd better go and ask him what he wants. Hey where do you think you're going Lovett,' shouted DCI Fletcher angrily 'and who told you about this?'

'This one, what about the other three women,' asked Lovett a local reporter 'this now makes four Inspector, so how far exactly have you got on this one, because our readers will want to know?'

'How did you know about this Lovett, who told you? Come on who told you, there is a news blackout on the other investigations.'

'Other investigations, don't you mean killings Inspector?'

'Don't talk bloody rubbish Lovett?'

'Oh rubbish is it Inspector, really? Look I had a phone call from a posh sounding bloke who called himself The Primrose Hill killer. Does that make sense to you? He told me number four has just been found and they all drowned, but very slowly, and he told me the directions of the other bodies which is now four counting this latest one. He said there were going to be a lot more and Notting Hill is a den of filth with marauding bitches everywhere and his job is to clean up the whole area. Apparently he's been told to by his Angel's voice in his twisted head. This guy is obviously round the bend and very dangerous.'

'How long ago was this Lovett? I hope you're not going to write this up yet, we need a break on this one. He's one clever bastard so what did he sound like?'

'He rang me about thirty five minutes ago. This mad-man was laughing and then saying there was going to be a lot more bitches to be put down because he has the tools to do it in his little black bag. The voice of his sounded a little posh, but I had the distinct impression he was putting on the voice as it didn't sound quite right to me. Listen I have it on my phone; it was a message he left. It said get down to the Lime House Basin and see the school kids painting and they would find number four, and that the police were pathetic, rubbish and a total waste of time.'

'Oh he did, did he? The bastard' said Ron.

'Yes he did' said Lovett 'he also mentioned not to try and triangulate the mobile phone because it's a throw away phone and now it's destroyed. He would use the phones he had taken from the dead women's bags.'

'Let's have a listen Lovett, come-on give me your phone.'

Lovett handed his Samsung over saying, 'hey Fletcher I want this back.'

DCI Fletcher put the phone to his ear. After listening to the message he said 'I'm confiscating this phone Lovett, as we need it for evidence.'

'Hey you can't do that I need my phone, you can have a copy Inspector, but I do need my phone.'

'Don't get your knickers in a twist we will be as quick as we can, but as you can appreciate Lovett we need the recorded message and I know you have another phone. Look I'll deal with you, on one condition no one else will be told, and it's you who will have the full story.'

Simon Lovett had been an Investigative journalist for 29 years. Now he worked as a free lance, but mostly all the time now with the Daily Echo he was very good at his job. Once a week there was a column in the Echo called 'Lovett's Column.' He knew this was a story that had to be run, because if he didn't then other newspapers would run the story. It's not every day you meet or hear from a serial killer, and this would earn him a nice bonus too. Simon Lovett had a way of winkling out the truth. Being a journalist he had a lot of informants that he paid well. Also being a gay man he was well known in the gay community of London and also in show business circles. Yet he was still a very popular man amongst his peers, but the police had no love for him because sometimes he managed to obtain vital information before them. But he was very good at what he did and he didn't much care how he got to the truth. He was always a loose cannon. However, he was a very good investigative journalist. His paper paid him a lot to keep him.

It was well known he had bent the truth at times, but you also had to remember for all his faults, he was very good. So when he put his mind to something he would not let go of a story, especially a good story as this would turn out to be.

DCI Fletcher told him 'he wanted a news blackout on this killer'

Lovett's reply was 'you must be joking! Our readers are in great danger and they need to know Inspector, so therefore the duty of the newspaper was to tell all its readers to take special care when walking in the area.'

They named the killer The Primrose killer. The police loved that.....not!

CHAPTER TWELVE

SERIAL KILLER ON THE LOOSE IN NOTTING HILL.

Screamed the Daily Echo's head line and all the details that Lovett had were as usual exaggerated. They sold out their papers within the hour and had to do reprints. The whole area around Notting Hill was now gripped with fear. People openly panicked and now the police were inundated with stupid people trying to report on rapes which never happened and suspicious looking men who had been seen lurking in shop doorways and car parks, and strange men doing odd things on the top of Double- Decker busses. One man was stopped and searched for innocently scratching his balls inside his trousers at a bus stop, his wife was furious. She was next to him at the time, but the woman police officer ignored her. She had asked for assistance as it started to get out of hand with the wife threatening to slap her for being so fucking stupid!!

Lovett had turned the whole thing into a circus. Now the paper was openly condemning any dating site it could get any information on. It was encouraging anyone with a story to tell about dating sites to contact them without delay with a guarantee that no one would have their details exposed. After all they may very well be helping in apprehending the killer/s.

The police had to bring in more staff to sift through the rubbish that this newspaper was producing, but what a lot of papers they were selling. That's why they paid guys like Lovett so well. Lovett was even on the local TV station giving out interviews on how the police were progressing and according to him they were not doing very well. So he said if anyone has information please do get in touch with him through his newspaper the Daily Echo. Any information they gave would be treated in the strictest of confidence.

DCI Eric Fletcher disliked Lovett and all his kind with a reverence. They caused such trouble and they delayed the case with all the stupid disruption, but sometimes they did get information on the perpetrators and passed it on to the police, often when it was far too late. After all the papers come first and let's be honest, it was the papers which paid Lovett his wages.

DCI Fletcher could do with a break on this case. The killer had left no clues, only that he told them he was going to do it again and again until he was caught. But at the moment he had no intention of being caught as he was enjoying the attention and off course getting rid of all the oversexed bitches.

The guy was a complete madman, but a clever one at that. He was now openly called the Primrose Hill killer in the newspaper the name was penned by Lovett. Also, the killer so it seemed was a very cunning individual, but what alarmed DCI Fletcher was his confidence. He told them there were more bitches to be put down because he loved his new work and the police jolly well knew he was good at it and he certainly wasn't going to stop now. It was a case of catch me if you can.

He contacted Lovett again and mentioned he would like to give him a photograph, but at this moment in time he loved his work, yes he was on a mission.

DCI Fletcher said 'he's teasing the police but he knew they had no clues. That was the most frustrating thing nobody had any idea who he was and why he was killing these women,' he said.

The police had worked out Alan Reed was a loner who was not married and had no children, that was just about all they had on him.

CHAPTER THIRTEEN

George Penny, private detective had landed with his partner Julia late the day before. Now they were back in his flat over his office in No 87 Chepstow Road, Notting Hill while Julia did a little bit of shopping for things such as milk, bread and all the other bits and bobs you needed. She said she would do a big shop later, but in the meantime George had phone messages to answer. Looking at his watch the time said 9.38 am.

Diane walked along Chepstow Road with Donald who was Lisa's dog. Diane had now given him a permanent home following Lisa's death. Donald knew Diane and her family, but he missed Lisa, especially in the salon. He'd been staying with them for about three years now on and off when his owner Lisa Davey was away on weekends or holidays.

She had been looking for number 87. When she finally arrived she saw the name on the door which read (DCI) Discrete Confidential Investigations (Private and Business confidential enquiries) with a phone number. She tried the door and it was open so she walked in to see George sat behind his large desk going through a pile of paperwork. Looking up he said 'oh please come in and how can I help you, excuse me haven't we met before? '

'Yes George we have, I'm Diane Court. I sort of feel as though I already know you well. My boss Lisa Davey as you probably know was found murdered by this mad sod, The Primrose killer.'

'I'm sorry Diane can you repeat that again, but slowly, Lisa is dead? What, when, how? You mean my Julia's friend from Primrose Hill, Lisa's Hair? I can't believe this. You say she was murdered by The Primrose killer? Who the bloody hell is he when he's about, because I've never heard of him.'

'Yes it's true, it's been in all the papers George, and probably in Spain too I shouldn't wonder.'

'Julia and I have been on holiday coupled with an assignment to China for nine weeks. We have only just got back into circulation so old news is new news to us. Look hang on let me get Julia, she's upstairs cleaning the flat as there's dust everywhere, well according to her there is, I couldn't see any myself' he laughed. 'Hey babe can you get down here now please honey....., babe are you deaf?'

'What's all the shouting about George' asked Julia as she came into his office it was then she saw Diane. 'Diane how are you babe, are you ok? Hey listen, has Lisa told you next week she's coming round for drinks and you're very welcome too, we'll have a right laugh. No men though' she laughed. 'We can have plenty of wine and a takeaway, and George here will pick you guys up and take you back home won't you George?'

Suddenly Diane burst into tears and she started to sob. Julia stared at her.

'What's the matter Diane, why are you crying, tell me!' asked Julia who tenderly put her arm around her.

'Look babe, please sit down. Diane has some awful terrible news to give to you' said George.

Diane sobbed out the story whilst Donald the dog sat with his head gently lying on her knee looking at her with his tail slowly brushing the floor. Diane struggled to tell them what had happened to Lisa.

Julia couldn't speak, she was in shock. She was a good friend of Lisa's and had been for many years. She had gone to school with her, and then both had enrolled in the same hairdressing college. That was about seventeen odd years ago now, or was it twenty...

When Diane had finished telling them what happened to Lisa, George asked her if she knew who the police officers were who were handling this case.

She told them a 'DCI Eric Fletcher and a young man DC Ronald Buckley.'

'Really, I know Eric pretty well, but I have never heard of the young DC. Eric's a good cop though and he doesn't suffer fools easy, but sometimes he misses the point by reacting too quickly. Does he still work out of Paddington Green Diane?'

'No, he works out of Notting Hill Police station in Ladbroke Grove.'

'Ah he's been moved then,' he thought it must be due to his age.

'Look George I have his card, it's got his details on it and you can have it. There have been four women murdered by drowning, they were all tied up from behind and their faces were gaffer taped, except for their nostrils and eyes. They drowned slowly and must have been in a terrible panic.'

'OMG that's a disgusting thing to do to someone, that's not human. Which number was Lisa Diane?' asked Julia.

'She was I believe the second one to be drowned. The first one was a district nurse called Helen Burk and then Lisa. He quickly moved on to an estate agent called Debra Carter who was drowned in the bath in a house she was selling. Yet she actually got away the first time he grabbed her or met her, I'm not sure of the true story; She jumped out of a taxi which the would-be killer was driving and then he drove off, but the bastard went back a week later and this time he killed her drowning her in an old bath in one of her client's old houses which was up for sale. Last week no 4 was a primary school teacher called Annie Martin who was murdered in the same way as all the others by drowning. They were all about the same age around 44 to 50 years old and all from a dating site, and all from the same area. That's why he's called the Primrose killer George.'

'What did these women have in common Diane?'

'It seems they were all looking for love George. Apparently they were all on the same dating site. He's now killed four women in the last seven or eight weeks.'

'Look let's take a break Diane,' he looked at Julia who took her upstairs 'I'm going to have a word with Eric I worked with him some years ago and we got on very well,' said George.

Julia took Diane upstairs; they both had a stiff brandy and a good cry. They told a few stories about college and about customers, about life and why Lisa needed to find love on a dating site in the first place. 'She was after all a very attractive woman, but she always wanted more though' said Diane 'always more, the trouble was she seemed to be so fussy, she was a hard lady to please. I know she was no pushover, but she always wanted the best. The thing that started her off was a couple of her clients who had been on the site for months and one for only a few weeks, but both managed to find really nice men and both men were wealthy. They are both living the high life you know the dream. One has gone to the South of France somewhere and the other now lives in Cornwall in a cottage by the sea. They both managed to persuade Lisa to have a go on the site.'

'What was the site called Diane' asked George. 'Mind you there must be hundreds of these sites on the internet none are really that safe.'

'I have no idea what it was called, I mean I'm so happily married I never took any notice of what it was called, but I do know it was well over a thousand pounds to join. It was essentially for well off people, and by all accounts it did seem to work. I wish to god she never went on it, but you knew what she was like Julia. She was so independent and would always have the last word on anything once she had it in her head. She was well away, and now she's dead.' Diane burst into tears again.

Julia put her arms round Diane and said as she hugged her. 'I knew Lisa from about eighteen or twenty years ago and she never had a family of her own, that's all she ever wanted. But now this shit head has murdered her. George will sort this out trust me. Because once he has his nose in front of a case he won't stop until he catches them, he is so tenacious, oh and ruthless too.'

'OMG I hope so Julia. I hope he gets the gutless bastard, what a coward he must be. This man is a total shit who needs to be stamped on, rubbed out, eliminated and then melted down. Everything a human can suffer. Yet he can't be human the way he kills these women can he?'

'I do agree with you Diane, but George has that look in his eye now and that means only one thing. He won't stop until he nails this scum bastard of a man, believe me he won't. George knew Lisa very well. You know she often stayed with us in Spain, we had some great times together, and he is gutted trust me he won't stop until he gets this evil man.'

'Could I please speak with DCI Eric Fletcher?' asked George.

'Yes who's speaking please, I seem to know this voice' replied DCI Fletcher.

'Ha ha, Eric it's George Penny. Haven't you been retired yet? I see they moved you down the line, that's a demotion for sure mate, anyway that was always on the cards.'

'Bloody hell its old George Penny. Hey I heard you had hit the good life posing in the Spanish sun and just ambling along like an old fart, have they handed you a stick yet mate, or a mobility scooter.'

'I've just been measured up for one Eric. Also a gold topped cane with sequins.'

'Christ, you used to work out for hours years ago, I bet you're too knackered now' he laughed. What do you mean moved down the line you cheeky sod? No George I'm here in a sort of training capacity for new DCs and DSs we get good results too as these youngsters are keen. They all seem to be so educated, however one thing seems to be missing with a lot of them and that's good old plain common sense.'

'I have to agree mate. Hey less of the old Eric! I still do a few hours a day here and there, you know go a few rounds. You have to keep trim as you never know what's round the corner do you, like this mad man such as this Primrose killer bloke. What the hell is this all about Eric? I've been away in China for nine weeks on a paid working holiday. Some client paid me to find his wife and daughter so I had to go with my partner Julia to look like a couple on holiday. Anyway it all got sorted out in the end, but all these killings Eric. Can we meet up, we need to talk this through if you don't mind and I can be useful. The problem is I know nothing about these murders. It's the first time Julia and I have heard about them so I would like to get in on the act. Remember Eric, I do have good connections and a good reason for asking you.'

'Hey come on mate it's me you're talking to not some bloody wannabe. So what's your angle on all this George because there's always an angle, you taught me that, remember?'

'Yes I can still remember telling you. Lisa Davey, the number 2 who was murdered, well she was my partner's best friend. We want to help find this bastard Eric and I knew Lisa pretty well too. She used to stay with us in Spain from time to time, such a lovely woman and Julia has known her for over twenty years now, so that's my angle.'

'Ok then, look George I'll see you in the Red Bull at 12.30. I can tell you then about what's been happening so far. You have to promise me you are going to keep quiet about what I tell you, because some facts are not known to the public. I'll help you if you help me too, I don't care if you kill this bastard of a man, and he needs to be put down, but quickly or better still slowly.'

'That sounds good Eric and you know even under pain of death my lips are sealed, but as I said Lisa was a good friend of my partner. I find it hard to comprehend Lisa's been murdered. I'll see you later in the Red Bull. I find this still very upsetting for Julia and myself.'

Eric thought George could be an asset or a pain in the arse, but he knew that once he had something between his teeth he would never ever let go until he solved the problem. It wouldn't matter now because if he was on the case and being an independent operator he could get to places where Eric wasn't allowed to go. Sometimes loose cannon's can be a problem, but they can also be a great asset. Nevertheless, he thought George would be a great help. He was and is still a great detective and the way he was booted out of the flying squad was nothing short of scandalous, it was also a great loss to Scotland Yard.

'Hey George you haven't aged a bit you silly old tart, how the hell do you do it?'

'Clean living and a bloody good woman Eric, and the occasional drink. You also have to keep busy and of course the odd rub of wrinkle cream to keep the wrinkles away. I see the one you're using hasn't worked' he laughed.

'Yes very good George, very funny I see you haven't lost your sense of humour. So what's your interest? I know you told me, but tell me again.'

'She was my partners best friend has been for twenty years more or less. Can you tell me more about Lisa Davey Eric? I was asked to help on this as my partner Julia would very much like me to have a go at finding out who killed her, and the others. So take it from me I will do my best to find this evil bastard. Who kills in this fashion Eric? The guy can't be normal can he?'

'I knew you were going to get involved George, as you are a private investigator I can't stop you, but don't get in my way. I have a job to do and I do know your reputation for finding out the truth. I will help you if you help me, but there has to be a line drawn because it's my job to keep some things, shall we say discreet between us and I know you can get into places we can't because we have certain standards where you are a loose cannon so to speak. I don't have any objection if we could help each other just so long as we work for the same end, to catch this bastard before he kills more women, believe me he will do. He's an out and out serial killer and now he's going to be hard to catch. Now he wants the world to know, that's what the headlines were all about. He phoned that toe rag Lovett and left him a message which I have transferred to my phone, it's creepy mate, have a listen.'

'Mr Lovett, it's such a lovely day. If you go down NOW to the Lime House Basin, you will see school kids on some sketching and painting exercise, but just over from them you will see my latest bitch creation floating in the water. She's number four and there will be many more, because it's my duty, it's my orders. I have to follow my Angel's orders you must understand this. Do you know of the other three I've drowned because there is nothing in the papers to say so. Anyway I'll get to the point. This is now four missions I have been on, and as I say it's my duty to carry on regardless. We don't ask questions we obey because I have my orders. Yet I can't understand why the police have not informed the public, which after all surely it's their duty to do so. They seem to want to keep things to themselves and maybe they don't want to alarm the public, but listen to me, my mission is to get these harlots off the streets. So I'm telling you now I have more missions to carry out, and I will do so as quickly as I can, so you can print this in your paper Mr Lovett. I salute you for printing this and I know you

will do just that, because after all you have orders to follow too, and your duty is to your readers.'

'We wanted to keep it low key as long as possible George, but now the headlines read as follows and Lovett is responsible for this.

SERIAL KILLER ON THE LOOSE, PRIMROSE KILLER HAS FREE REIGN.

Police haven't a clue. When will the murderer strike next and where? Who is next on his murder list? Why have the police kept quiet? Our duty is to our readers we will keep you all informed.

'Then the paper wrote as much as they knew about the victims George. But they were all linked to a dating site and all were in their early forties and single women. They dare not mention the name of the dating site or they would be sued to the last penny.'

'Eric, surely you must have a clue as to who or what he is, so what do you have on him? He must have left some DNA or prints?'

'No we have nothing he leaves no clues. It seems now the latest is, he's got himself a taxi, a London black cab. Now all he has to do is go out late at night or anytime and he can take his pick. After all there are over 21,000 black cabs in London alone George and the streets are teeming with women in short skirts and practically nothing else on. It will be easy for him to take his pick of the drunken women waiting outside any club for a Taxi.'

'Well you better add mine to that Eric because I have a London black cab. I use it for the occasional covert work when needed, so who told you he has a cab?'

'A victim told us. She was kidnapped but managed to get out of his taxi. About a week later he went back and killed her in a bath. We also have a lady who saw him take the body of a woman down to the River Brent, or at least we think she did in a Black cab.'

'What does that mean Eric, think? Don't you know?'

'The witness has oncoming dementia, sometimes she's ok and sometimes she's not. Her husband saw the killer the first time, and we think it was with the District Nurse Helen Burk. It was early in the morning from his landing window. The guy had just taken a pee and on the way back to his bed he looked out of the landing window next to the bathroom where he saw the man. But unfortunately he's now dead. He died a week after that event with a coronary. According to him he did say the man was about 6ft tall and nice looking, fit and had a 4x4. A couple of weeks later he went back to the same spot with Lisa, but this time he was in a London black cab. This time the information came from his wife.'

'Yes, but in her condition she's not reliable is she Eric.'

'Well Diane Court, Lisa's friend said he was calling for her in a taxi because his car had been stolen. Then Debra the estate agent was attacked in a London black cab. She was hit with a stun gun and later on down the road he stopped. However, she managed to escape. She fell out of the cab into the gutter and was then rescued by the Primrose Lady Harriers, that's a running club for women. They were just going on a run and were going by when she fell out of the cab, but we think it was the same guy who managed to go back and kill her in one of her houses while showing this madman around. He was pretending to be a client, he drowned her in an old bath at the property and she suffered terribly you could tell.'

'In all my years Eric, this is probably the worst way to kill anyone.'

'I know so it seems easy to kill women? Let's face it George that's an easy kill. However none of them were sexually molested and none were touched as far as we can tell. No clothes were removed, they were just drowned in a cruel way and that's about it really, but he will strike again and that's guaranteed. So have you any idea from what you've just been told, does it ring any bells? Oh and we think the guy collects their earrings and other small items of jewellery.'

'Earrings, how do you mean earrings? So tell me what's that's all about Eric?'

'None of the women who were found were wearing any earrings, but you could see they had them in because what woman goes on a date without earrings? No he takes them, but god only knows why!'

'This doesn't sound too good to me Eric. Look these guys are hard to catch. They have total confidence. By what you have told me this one wants the whole world to know, especially the police that somehow he's been wronged, probably many years ago. By becoming a serial killer he will at long last get noticed, he craves the publicity to feed his ego, he seems to be very ill.'

'My fear George, he's now on the rampage, so how the hell do we stop him?'

'It seems to me Eric that this guy could be ex military it sounds to me he's a woman hater, that's for certain. We have to find out why if that's at all possible. However, he hates women and he is aged about I'd say in his late forties. He's picking women in their late forties and older too, so I would take a wild guess and say he probably hates his own mother for some reason. Sex also seems to repulse him because as you have stated, he hasn't touched any of them in a sexual way. His mother probably or a carer hurt him, or even both in some way, maybe in a sexual way. I think he is also ex army by the way he spoke on the phone to Lovett. But this Simon Lovett is a shit! I remember him from my days in the flying squad, he gets a sniff and there's no stopping him. He's a freelance which are the worst, but they do get good money and can at times be very useful to us, sorry I mean to you, but I am going to try and find this man Eric, and when I do you will be the first to get him. There's no glory in this for me and I'm also a freelance like Lovett, but I won't be billing anyone for my work and I won't be disrupting your enquires. I'll inform you all the way, so let's try and catch this madman because that's what he is, an out and out madman!'

'Okay George, so if we can pool all our information together we may have a chance and for a change no-one's ego is on the line. Let's do this together, but incognito.'

CHAPTER FIFTEEN

George's partner Julia was still in bits. She had known Lisa for many years and when she found out how she had died it upset her terribly. Lisa used to pop over to Spain often to see Julia and now she was gone. It also upset George to see Julia so upset. The whole thing was upsetting, but he was going to do his best to find this man, the Primrose killer, which is how Lovett described him.

George disliked Lovett for his underhand ways, but he could also be useful if he was handled in the right manner. 'Oh on second thoughts can you let us see Lisa's body Eric, because Julia wants to say goodbye and to be honest so do I.'

'Yeah sure George and I'm really sorry she ended up like that, same as all the others.'

George held Julia's hand as they stood next to the window in the morgue as they drew the curtains across to reveal Lisa lying on the table with a sheet over her body from the chin down. She looked peaceful and calm but that was not the way she died. She died in great pain and misery and must have been terrified. There was no way of knowing what happened,

Alan Reed was extremely pleased the papers had printed the story at long last. He didn't much like the Primrose killer handle but he could live with it, and now was a good time to tell the world he was coming after the evil women. Today he was looking at his list again to see who would be next, but something made him stop and have a rethink. No, he would use his taxi this time. The West End would be a good place to start and to see who was about. He may just take a run out to-night then he could see what women were about at around say 1am there were bound to be a few stragglers he could trap. He knew the police could not stop every taxi so the thought very much excited him. Anyway, now he had to calm down and keep it tight, and to always wear his surgical gloves. Looking in the kitchen cupboard he took the four sets of earrings out of the old cup and now put them in a nice little jewellery box he had bought he decided to keep it on the top of his bedside drawers. Also in the box he now included his mother's earrings. Every night he opened the box to look at the earrings because it thrilled him. It was the only time he could get a strong sexual feeling but he didn't want to get that feeling as it sickened him. Even the thought of him with a woman made him miserable and weepy and then the painful memories would come flooding back.

He looked at his watch the time read 1.17 am. Having driven around the West End several times he had not yet seen a suitable candidate there were plenty of slappers about but none stood out yet, but he felt lucky. Looking at his watch he thought about going home, but then suddenly he spotted a young girl, yes she would do nicely she was wobbling a bit and seemed to be a little confused.

Sheila Evans was in the club called Rascals. She had dressed for the occasion and had good news to tell her partner. She was dressed in a short black skirt and a nice light blue top. She had 4 inch sling back heels on and had a shoulder bag with her. It had the pregnancy testing kit inside she was so pleased it showed the device as positive. She was over the moon and hoped Adam would be too. She had treated herself to a pair of long 9ct gold twisty earrings to celebrate. The place was so busy due to a couple of Hen parties, it was a Thursday night. When she met him he said 'hey I love the earrings honey' he could see they were new 'what's the occasion for them?'

Adam could see she was very excited about something. However, when she told him he just went ballistic there and then. They had an almighty row over her trying to get pregnant again which he didn't want her to. He'd told her a few times he did not want to be tied down with young children. Telling her he was not ready for the family thing, it just wasn't him.

'Right, you can now consider yourself dumped' he said to her and stormed off with his mates. He didn't want to know because he told her over and over again, not to get pregnant.

Sheila would never listen to anyone and he didn't want to get trapped, but now he would be.

A couple of people she knew came over to calm her down and they all sat down and then talked. After talking for a couple of hours to her friends she realised the time was getting on. As she had to start work for 9 am she decided to go home so she said 'goodbye to her friends.'

She had to try and grab a taxi home because she lived in West Kilburn in Bravington Road with her parents. They had made a self contained two bedroom flat for her in the large house they owned. She had just turned 25 years old. She left the club at 1.33am and she'd had a few drinks, despite the fact that she was pregnant. She felt she needed a drink after the horrible row with Adam, and now she couldn't care less about anything. She wasn't drunk but tipsy is the term some people used. She said goodnight to the two doormen and told them she was looking for a taxi to get home. At 1.36am she had walked from the club in old Bond Street into Piccadilly when she saw a London Black cab, it belonged to Alan Reed. She saw the cab approaching and stood almost in the middle of the road to flag it down, but she was now wobbling a bit on her heels.

Alan saw her and noticed no-one else was trying to get a cab at that moment, so he stopped next to her and said, 'where to Miss?'

Looking into his cab she said 'Bravington Road, West Kilburn please.'

He indicated and slowly drove off with her, 'you had a good night miss' he said to her.

'No not really, it was a really shit night. I've just been dumped by my rat of a boyfriend. He's pissed off with his mates again and left me on my own as per bloody usual, but that's it now he can clear off in the future, because I've had it! I'm so pissed off with him.'

'Oh look love, he'll come round and realise he's made a mess of things and will soon be phoning you. Let's face it you're a very attractive lady and make no mistake about that.' said Alan.

'Do you think so' she asked him, 'because I feel a waste of bloody space at the moment?'

As he was now in Great Western Road he stopped and said 'hang on a minute miss, my seat belt light has come on and I think it's yours, so I'll just take a quick look if you don't mind. I don't want to get fined, I just need to readjust the belt, and it won't take a second. Opening her door into the back of the cab he rammed a needle in her upper arm. It was 15mg of the drug Rohypnol the date rape drug. He held his hand over her mouth with his left hand while holding the needle with his right hand. She struggled a bit but was no match for his strength. After a few seconds she was out to the world so he carried on. He had already taken her gold swizzle earrings and put them in his pocket, he also took her small fake diamond bracelet. He drove a little further and came to Elkstone Road and turned right into Kensal Road which ran alongside of the Grand Union Canal. At this time it was very quiet and the area was deserted. He was amazed at how warm it was the night was still and calm. Stopping his cab he made sure nobody was about. He tied her up with the garden ties with her hands behind her back. Then he also tied her ankles and used the gaffer tape to wrap around her head and her face, but leaving her eyes and nostrils free so she would drown through her nose. Satisfied no-one else was around he took her to the canal side over his shoulder then he carefully slipped her into the water with two heavy railway bolt weights that he always kept in a bowling bag. He put them in a supermarket bag tied tightly to her neck so her head was under the water. Yet he hardly made a sound as he was now getting used to this. After he checked the time it was now 2.18am. Quietly he watched her as she slowly began sinking in the murky Grand Union Canal. Within ten minutes she had gone, she had momentarily come to, but soon lost consciousness again, then a barge chugged on by and the water was disturbed then she bobbed back up to the surface for a minute. The wake had carried her along for a while, but she became stuck between the stern of a stationary barge and the canal bank where she remained stuck tight until the morning.

When he arrived back home and after parking up his taxi in his garage under the railway arches, he took a look into her small bag. He was horrified to find it belonged to WPC Sheila

Evans from Paddington Green Police station. Her police warrant card was in her bag with a couple of other personal things including a pregnancy test kit along with her mobile phone and a bottle of perfume. He looked at the pregnancy kit and saw it had been used then he saw it had a long thin blue line going through it, so what the hell did this mean? He thought bloody stupid things that women had in their daft bags, who could understand the mind of women? There was also along with the other stuff £167 and seven loose condoms with writing on the packets saying Ultimate love sex. Mutual climax Ribs & dots to speed her up and lubricant to slow him down for extra pleasure. That's what the writing said on the small individual packets. Ribbed for extreme pleasure Dots, what the hell did Dots mean he thought. This made him glad she had gone he thought serves her right, because now he felt disgusted and she was a WPC too. How could a WPC with a lust for sex like that be employed by the police? He wanted to complain about her, but now it wouldn't do anyone any good would it. He thought the bitch has gone and good riddance to her with an attitude like that. So now these bitch women were corrupting the local police force as well, how evil is that, he thought to himself I have much work to do. Now he felt completely justified in what he was doing. However, he did like to keep the perfume the women had in their bags, he had kept them for the lovely smells they made. So he put her gold earrings and her bracelet along with all the others he had collected in his jewellery box the top of his bedside drawers. There were now five sets of earrings and they were all so nice. When he smelt the inside of the jewellery box he could smell the women. That's all there was left of them but now he owned them, he owned all the women. He was the only one with any connection to them. Yes he was in charge; he was the one with the power. It was easy to spray the inside of the box with another perfume to keep the smells alive, this was most important to him now.

The idea of picking up lonely women was a great way to meet women. It would be good to do that again and maybe he could do two women at the same time. There were several drunken girls he'd seen earlier on staggering about the streets. He'd give this some thought.

However, in the morning he knew this latest bitch would be found and then the shit would hit the fan because she had been a WPC bitch.

The police would pull the stops out for this one because the cops looked after their own. He'd better keep his head down for a while and anyway he had a week of modelling coming up. Out of the blue he had been asked if he could go to Bristol for a modelling shoot and the money was good. When he came back he would do another one. Yes he would sleep well tonight feeling happy and peaceful. It did this to him and now he had found his true vocation. So far there were five slappers, but lots more to come so yes he would sleep well. In the morning he would drop her bag in a supermarket skip.

There had been a phone call from his agent Delia Swan. She asked him could he get to Bristol now as the shoot was brought forward due to a hotel cocking up the booking arrangements. Emailing her back he said he was on his way and mentioned because of the inconvenience he ought to be paid some more as his weekend was ruined.

Delia said that wasn't a problem, but just to get there today, like now if possible. He couldn't use his estate car because it needed a new ball joint and it was going into the garage, so he decided to use his taxi and besides he needed to give it a good run which would do it the world of good.

Dropping off his VW estate at the garage for repair he took his taxi on the drive to Bristol. When he arrived at the Premier Inn in the middle of Bristol the parking was in the three story car park almost next to the Inn. Now he had this strong urge to kill again and decided to leave the false number plates on his taxi and take a cruise around later to see what he could do. He had plenty of the date rape drug Rohypnol and a couple of his stun guns.

The modelling job was in the Bristol Marina, he had to do one job for men's hats and another job for men's jeans, and also some men's jumpers. It took them five days to finish the shoot then he was free until the next job came up. He was paid very good money and managed to earn up to £500 a day because he was a very popular model. There again he never argued like a lot did, thinking they were above everyone else, he just got on with the shoot and delivered. Alan was also very handsome and fit because he worked out on a daily basis which paid dividends in the end. He was 48 but only looked about 38. Some thought he was even younger, but it was all down to his healthy living because he didn't drink and had never smoked, also making certain he had plenty of sleep which he was doing now at long last thanks to collecting earrings from his victims. All his meals were healthy he was almost a vegetarian in his eating habits and it showed in his looks. In fact he was proud of the way he looked.

Leaving the Premier Inn to walk the short distance to his taxi, every night he toured around the night spots, especially Anchor road and the Bristol Marina. Deciding to see what he could do at the end of the week when he had finished working he'd come across an area with plenty of night life. Friday night would be good as there would be plenty of slappers around and he would get rid of another one then drive back to London the same night. The lust for killing was almost consuming him. Suddenly it was as though he was in fact starving hungry and had to kill the same as he had to eat, so when he had killed it was a wonderful release for him until the next time.

CHAPTER SIXTEEN

The same morning the Grand Union Canal was covered in a light hazy summery mist giving you a hint of a lovely day to come. You could see in the near distance the sun which was a soft dullish orange colour where it was slowly climbing out of the morning mist. There were still a couple of evening stars still clearly visible in the very pale light blue sky. As usual there were a few ducks and moorhens paddling around squawking and looking for food which was their normal behaviour. They certainly knew where to find some because it was the same routine most mornings. All of them were all waiting around the stern for the sound of the alarm clock from John and Grace Fullerton's narrow boat that reminded the wild life to be ready for the bits and pieces of bread thrown in amongst them.

They were all waiting in a large gang trying to anticipate when the food would be thrown to them, the experienced ones were usually the big ducks, the bully greedy ones who always got in first and then they muscled the others out of the way like prop forwards in a rugby match.

Suddenly there was the shrilling sound of an alarm clock and the gangs of ducks, moorhens and a couple of swans made themselves ready for the feed to come. They paddled around in circles getting anxious in case another one got in front of them. It was the same ritual every morning. The big ones got to the front of the queue first. The smaller moorhens were rushing about bobbing their heads backwards and forwards with their red beaks trying to get to the front of the screeching herd of ducks and swans while all the time losing their place at the front of the mad bread queue.

John Fullerton had been awake for about twenty minutes he'd been listening to the morning sounds, especially the sounds from the herd of ducks and moorhens. That would soon increase in intensity when he fed them. Looking at his sleeping wife Grace, despite being married 48 years he still loved her dearly and he still loved to look at her sleeping face.

She was woken up at the usual time of 5.30am by the screeching alarm clock. They hated the sound, but it did its job well. Watching her stir as she slowly sat up, she stretched her arms above her head holding her hands together. Bending down in front of her he kissed her heavy breasts the same as he did every morning. At her age she loved him to wake her like this. She was grateful he still found her sexy and closed her eyes and let him fondle her. Now she was getting that lovely strange feeling in her tummy, but it would have to wait until later because she badly needed to use the loo.

After kissing her sleepy face and saying 'good morning' he stood by the bed and stretched his arms out a few times. Grace was now sitting up rubbing her eyes and looking out of the port hole window she said 'hey it's looking like it's going to be another glorious day.' She noticed how hard he had become. She held it in her hands and laughed 'we'll have to leave it until later John. Anyway, you have to feed your family outside. Listen to them they know the sound of the alarm clock, they're not daft are they.'

'No they certainly are not. I reckon you're right love.' John slowly put his underpants on followed by his dressing gown, then his slippers. Slowly he walked to the stern of their narrow boat. On the way he had put the kettle on and then waited for Grace to bring him his usual mug of tea. They always sat at the stern of the barge to drink the tea and to drink in the atmosphere of the canal life they loved so much. They adored the first light in the mornings.

Most of his life John worked as an accountant for a large city corporation and Grace was a PA to an oil magnate, but they had become so sick of the hours they worked and the stress of modern life. Disenchanted, they moved onto their narrow boat which was bought with their savings seven years ago they renamed it The Grace & Favour. They had let their home out for an income and anyway they were both now getting their pensions so they had a pretty good relaxed life. The thing that began to worry them both was the canal, because it was beginning to become a little too popular and the waterways were now becoming congested. It now became very difficult to get a mooring and what they charged was astronomical, but they could get away with it because the demand was there. They wondered how long they had left to enjoy the canal before it became too expensive for them. They blamed it squarely on all these TV programmes which seemed to highlight the good bits, but not the bad bits. They had noticed a new phenomenon, something you only found on the roadways, road rage. They called it canal rage because inexperienced people heading to the canal locks found themselves having to wait in long queues and then moaning how long it took to get through the locks. Sadly there were people barging into one another. The nice atmosphere was fast disappearing.

After picking up some stale bread from the bread bin John was now doling it out into the midst of the wildlife in small pieces acting like a conductor waving his arms about. The noise they made sounded like a mad choir while he was throwing the small pieces of bread. It always made him laugh he recognised most of them because this was a daily ritual.

The strange thing was they never bothered with brown bread, you could clearly see brown bread pissed them off as they spat it out in disgust which made him laugh even more.

John always attracted the bully ducks first and threw their bread a lot further away from the gang knowing they would make a mad dash to grab it. He tried to evenly throw bread to the others so they would all get a fair share. The ducks and moorhens were going frantic and squabbling amongst themselves. But then majestically along came a pair of swans so graceful and beautiful to watch, which reminded him of why they gave the so called good life up for a life on the narrow boat, it was a no-brainer. They were now hissing at the other greedy ducks because they wanted their share too.

'Grace my darling that was a lovely cup of tea thanks' then as per usual he always emptied his mug by swirling a small amount of tea three times anti clockwise then carefully slinging it over the side into the canal because someone said they thought that was lucky. Standing up he swirled the tea around and was about to sling it in the canal when he suddenly saw Sheila's face staring at him from just under the water. At first he

thought she was a dummy and then he shouted 'Grace, will you come and take a look at this please.'
'What is it' she shouted back 'I need to use the loo badly.'
'No you don't, come and take a look at this.'
'What, look at what John, what are we looking for?'
The body of Sheila had sunk again. Then another large barge sailed by and the water was disturbed again. It was the wake from the large barge that did it. Sheila's body popped up out of the water and quickly sank again, 'Christ sake that was a woman's body John, a young girl's body. Call the police now, quickly go on call them hurry. Bloody hell where did she go, she's sank again.'
Then Sheila bobbed up again and Grace managed to hold on to her with the end of the gaff rod. When she saw that she was tied with her arms behind her back she wept. Oh Christ, look at her such a lovely young thing, she's been murdered. Oh why, why, who does these things, why does it happen, John why?'
'Honey I can't begin to answer that I wish I could.' John already had his mobile in his hands and dialled 999. He told them what they had found, there was a dead woman's body in the canal partially wedged between the stern of the barge and the bank but it was obvious she was dead. They were told not to touch anything and to give them directions. There would be a team down ASAP.
'Give her to me Grace, now go and make another cuppa please love. I'll look after her till the police arrive, go on make a big pot we're going to need lots of tea for these guys when they arrive. You can see she has only just been put in the water, yet we never heard a thing. I reckon she was put in the water further up and she's drifted down the poor young girl, and as you said Grace she's a lovely looking girl.'
DCI Eric Fletcher had just woken up when his phone beeped. Answering it he was out of the house within eleven minutes. The first thing he did was to call DC Ronald Buckley, he told him to be up and ready to go in five minutes. Putting on his blues and twos, he raced to pick up DC Buckley who was standing in his driveway still putting on his shoes and still

unshaven, but he had his electric razor in his pocket for just such emergences as it had happened before in the past. There was toothpaste round his chin and soap was stuck to in his ears. He looked as though he had just got home from a rough night out when he jumped into DCI Fletcher's car.

Fletcher looked at his brown shoes and asked him 'Oh Christ Ron, are you still gay? You have those bloody gay shoes on' he laughed hysterically.

'Don't you start all that again for heaven sake sir once was enough thank you? So what's the panic, where are we going?'

'Down to the canal Ron and this time it's a young girl.'

'Oh shit no, not another one sir, who is she?'

'Haven't a clue yet Ron, there will be no ID will there, if the others are anything to go by. Anyway let's go.'

By now the local plod had taken her out of the water where she was laying there on her back. They had put a sheet over her from the Grace & Favour narrow boat.

When the sheet was removed DC Buckley said 'OMG no! That's Sheila Evans.' The gaffer tape had become undone and some remained around her mouth. DC Buckley could see who she was.

'Sheila Evans, do you know her? Hang on a minute she looks familiar to me as well, wait on Ron doesn't she work at Notting Hill police station?'

'Sir, she's a WPC down at our nick. I went out with her about four years ago for about ten months or a year and look that tattoo on her right thigh. It's a spider I recognise it. I saw it enough times.'

'Are you sure are you certain it is her' said DCI Fletcher.

'Yes I'm more than certain sir. She had come down from Hendon, the police training college. Both of us were on an advanced driving course.'

You could see Ron was visibly shocked, she was a lovely looking young woman and he remembered her being so kind and she was great fun to be with.

'How long did you say you knew her for again Ron,' asked Fletcher 'was it for long?'

'As I said sir it was for about a year maybe a little less she was lovely.'

'Ron, are there still any WPCs you haven't been with, is there?'

'Yes sir, there are two others, but I'm working on it as we speak,' he laughed a little nervously.

Forensics quickly arrived they said she was put in the canal between 1 am and 3 am this morning. She was caught in the undercurrent probably by a passing barge. The canal isn't very wide in this section and that's why she became wedged between the side of the canal and this narrow boat. There was a supermarket bag tied around her neck which had just one weight in it, but the other weight had somehow come out leaving just the one weight in the bag. So now it was virtually the same scene as all the others.

John Bishop the forensic Doctor said in his lazy baritone booming voice 'Look Inspector Fletcher, this madman is really on a roll, and now a WPC is on the list too. You have to catch this crazy sod and make it bloody quick because there will be more of them to fish out.'

Then the most hated freelance journalist Lovett, suddenly appeared again. After taking a phone call from Alan Reed to say the WPC he had just been murdered, and she was now floating in the canal. It was an inclusive story and he should go and take a look. Being as he was a journalist could he tell all the clubbing and drink swilling bitches that he was on his way to see to another one and very soon? He signed off, the Primrose killer.'

DCI Fletcher asked him how he had heard about this murder and how did he get to come down so quickly and what did he know.

Lovett told him about the phone call he'd had.

'What phone call Lovett, so who was it that rang you and when was this?'

'It was about twenty five minutes ago now, it was the killer.' Lovett could see it was the same scene as the last one and he asked if she was a WPC.'

'Yes' how did you know that, she was dressed in a short black skirt and a blue top? She had been bound and taped around the face as before except for her eyes, leaving only her nostrils to breathe through.' Lovett told him the killer mentioned to him she was a WPC.

After talking with Lovett DCI Fletcher asked him politely to sod off as this was a murder scene and now he was obstructing the police from doing their job.

Lovett raced back to his office at the Daily Echo and shamelessly wrote for the second edition.

PRIMROSE KILLER STRIKES AGAIN, WPC SLAIN THEN DUMPED IN CANAL.

By the evening the whole area was now in a blind panic and the nationals had also got the story, but now it was running in all the red tops as well, it was insane. At Notting Hill Police station there were reporters everywhere and the BBC news teams along with the other TV networks. Lovett was in his element, but after all he was only doing his job and getting paid big money too.

George Penny heard about the latest murder from DCI Eric Fletcher with a phone call, they arranged to meet at his office in private for a chat.

George asked DCI Fletcher how old the young WPC was, he was told she was 25. It seemed to him she was picked up in his false taxi and he's now changed the rules on this, and that makes him far more dangerous.

'How do you work that out George?'

'Because the other four women were all aged about the same age so far, they were in their early to late forties and older who were all from a dating site. This new girl was picked up off the street, so don't you see she was not on a dating site was she, and not like the others. It seems he's trying a new tactic. Now he's using his taxi to grab women and he doesn't have to give any profile, age height photographs or anything else. All he has to do is stop when one looks vulnerable, this is now becoming much worse Eric, we have to catch him and be quick about it.'

'Sure George, let's go out and get him then shall we? He clicked his fingers just like that. Easy eh, but it isn't, is it! We have no idea who or what he is, because he leaves a smoke screen behind him and then starts all over again. Yeah lets go and get him, are you coming too?'

'I didn't mean it quite like that Eric, and I can see you're stressed, but we have to look harder because as sure as god makes it rain, this lunatic is going to kill again. I meant no offence Eric and you should know that.'

'I know George, and your right I can't even sleep for thinking about this maniac. My wife is frustrated as I have not been able to give her any of my time.'

George had been given Sheila's address and went round to speak with the parents. He asked them where she went on that fateful Thursday night. They gave him Adam Chives' address and phone number and said 'they were always falling out over any little thing, and they think she went out to see him that night. Apparently she had some very exciting news to tell him. She never told us, but we reckon she was pregnant, she never told us so, but what else was she going to tell him?'

'Yes we met outside the club Rascals' Adam told George. 'We did fall out because she got pregnant and never asked me if she could. I didn't want her to get pregnant as I don't want a family yet, I'm too young but she never listened to anyone. Anyway we had a quick row and then I walked off with my mates at about 11.30 I think or about that time. We all jumped into a taxi and I left her there with some of her friends she was a bit upset, then we went to Celia's club. Now I feel terrible, it's my entire fault she's dead. For Christ sake it feels as though I've killed her. I loved her to bits and I still do, what am I going to do without her now and it's all down to me. It's my entire bloody fault, I killed her.'

'No it's not your fault Adam, it's the person who killed her and he's the one I want. Look I will let you know what happens, but you have to tell the police the same as me if you can think of anything else here's my card so keep it, and thanks for your time. You did not kill her, everyone falls out now and again and you can't blame yourself for her death Adam.'

George thought to himself...well if he hadn't fallen out with her and stumped off with his mates she would still be alive so he had to live with that terrible thought for the rest of his life. Maybe next time he would think twice about leaving someone else alone at that time of the night.

George walked into the club Rascals and had a word with the two doormen. One was a guy called Tommy the Tool because he had a head that looked like a hammer and a flattened nose. At one time he used to be a useful pugilist, but as he got older he never liked to get hit, it just annoyed him so he retired. The other one was called Big Ben for obvious reasons. He was 6ft 6 in tall and weighed in at about 22 stone. He was solid but as nice as pie with a strange high pitched lisp which had apparently got him into more fights than Muhammad Ali.

Both doormen told him that Sheila had walked off about 1.30 pm and went to look for a taxi. They saw her turn left out of Bond Street then walk into Piccadilly. That was the last time they saw her, but taxis were going by all the time so it was impossible to say which taxi she flagged down. They said they didn't see her get into a taxi as she turned into Piccadilly and that was the last they saw her. Big Ben said 'she had a few drinks but nowhere near drunk. She wasn't staggering, well not too much and walked fairly straight. However she did seem to be a little upset.'

George asked Ben, 'was anyone else with her and was she on her phone to anyone and how upset did she seem.'

Ben said 'he could tell she had been crying, but that's nothing new these days, couples often come together and leave either on their own or with someone else. Most of the trouble is with couples, they fall out because the bloke gets flirty with some other girl and the same with the girls. It's a merry go round and they try to pick up the pieces. However, once they leave our premises they are on their own and we can't be responsible for them. We can't go chasing down the street after idiots because they would leave the door open for anyone to get inside, but neither of us saw her get into any vehicle we hope this mean hearted bastard would soon be caught.'

'Can you remember what she looked like Ben, and can you too Tommy?'

'Yes she was a really good looking girl for sure' said Ben. 'She had a tight, I think black skirt on with a blue top and high heels and she had these long sort of twisty earrings on and looked very sexy. The guy who dumped her must be stupid or blind, maybe even both or worse, gay.'

'Oh and she had a small shoulder bag' said Tommy.

'Is there anything else lads that you can remember about her? Can you let me know why you noticed her earrings' asked George?

'You could tell they were new' said Ben 'they were dangling about because she was shaking her head about. She was upset over something and it was hard not to notice with her short hair. They were long and sparkly and I must say very nice, and that's about it. I can't think of anything else to say about her, she was a lovely looking girl.'

'Well thanks lads. If you do think of anything else please get in touch, here's my card.'

'George, how are things going?' Julia asked him. 'Are you getting anywhere yet?'

'Well I have established he collects earrings. I reckon the guy is ex military, and Eric missed that one as well. This guy hates women. He's a good looking bloke, big and strong and also drives a black cab.'

'Careful babe he's beginning to sound a bit like you with that description.'

'Does it? You know Julia this guy has left no DNA or any clues at this moment in time, unless the police are not sharing any with me. But I know this much he's going to be difficult to catch. The way he kills them puzzles me. It's not a normal kill he has to drown them through their noses. Why does he do that, and look there has to be a solid reason because there's a formula for everything.'

'Perhaps it goes way back to his childhood George. Maybe his mother mistreated him and something to do with water? Perhaps she nearly drowned him or it's got something to do with a sexual thing, maybe he was abused by someone from years ago.'

'It's really odd there is no sexual contact with any of these women and they were all good looking ladies' said George. 'Then there is the earring issue why does he collect them, and what for? So why would you do that. I mean they must be trophies of some sort or something. As far as I know serial killers do normally keep something from their victims.'

'Well I wouldn't know about those things George.'

'So it's just the earrings he keeps Julia, or so it seems. He also we think keeps their perfume and other small jewellery objects like rings and bracelets. Oh and their mobile phones. He's used them to ring other women, it's so bizarre, but he's a clever one.

'Perhaps it gives him pleasure George; in some way maybe he gets his sex through the earrings.'

'Christ that must hurt babe.'

'Oh yes, trust you to think of that George and I wouldn't be the least bit surprised with the size of your handy tool you daft sod. Seriously though, perhaps he looks at the earrings and he gets a thrill from owning them like he still owns the women he kills, maybe it gives him power. But so far you say there are no bags found from the women. They must be hidden somewhere. You say he used a dating site but the last one was last seen heading to get a taxi. If that's his new method George then he's really out of bloody control and he can strike anywhere with impunity, or maybe it was an opportunistic moment he had. If not this has gone beyond serious, he's gone nuclear, you have to stop him George.' Julia went into the kitchen to make a coffee.

'Yes you're probably right babe, if only it was that simple. You would make a good profiler. Did you hear babe, babe did you hear what I said, honey are you okay?' As George came into the kitchen Julia was sat at the table quietly sobbing.

'Honey, hey babe come on we'll get him.' Sitting down besides her he put his strong arms around her to offer some comfort. He hugged her then kissed away her salty tears. Come on babe we'll get him.'

'I know George but it won't bring Lisa back will it, she's fucking gone. It's not fair it's simply not fair at all. She was my best friend and has been for the last twenty years. Lisa did have a terrible upbringing and now I won't see her anymore. She's gone before her time, what a total shit this bastard is. You have to catch him George and make him suffer too.

'I know Julia, we have to try and stop him, but he's left no clues so far, none at all.'

'George I really want to see him hurting. What the hell has gone wrong with this world we live in, it's full of pain and misery and bastards that kill. What do we do when we catch them? Some idiot writes a book about them and then a film is made and they end up inside making millions and living the bloody life of Riley? I want to see him dead George. I hope the bastard goes in great pain, he certainly deserves it.'

'I know honey, I know. We will nail him sooner or later.'

'George, I don't want to see him behind bars, I want to see his filthy dead body all screwed up in absolute agony the bastard, that's less than he really deserves.'

CHAPTER SEVENTEEN

Alan Reed was now in Bristol on a photo shoot modelling various men's wears. He was there for a week he was staying in a Premier Inn in the middle of Bristol near Caveat Circus. Bristol was not a place he liked he didn't really like the area, but it had lots of canal waterways which gave him an idea. While quickly thinking about it he promptly forgot the idea. If he was ever connected to Bristol he would be in trouble because if he did another woman, it may come out that he was on a shoot there so best he forgot about it. However he was restless now and he needed to kill another one as soon as he could.

There was only two more days to go. He would soon be back home, and then he would go back to his dating site to check it out again. Mind you he still had about 13 women left on the site to contact. The taxi pick up was a bit too soon to try that one again in London. Then again he thought that Bristol would be an easy touch if he drove down on the Friday night and came back the same night but late. After doing his homework he was shocked by the amount of women who were walking about half naked, pissed and falling about. He had to try and rid the world of these creatures. He just had to go back to Bristol because it needed a wakeup call, it needed cleaning up, it was debauched.

However he was home on Friday by 3.30pm and looked through his list. There was one he'd marked down, her name was Fiona Blackwood. He remembered her well. She said she was a solicitor, but wouldn't give out where she worked for obvious reasons, which he said was perfectly acceptable. After the conversation he did say he would ring her in a couple of weeks. She only gave him her mobile number and he thought she was a bit too stuck up and canny. She sounded like a snob, the very sort he despised, the very sort he would like to kill. Yes he would enjoy this kill. Looking at himself in his full length mirror in his bedroom he was pleased he would look the part for her she was obviously upper class and a total no-all.

She would have to pay for all her snobbishness was his thinking; yes he would enjoy this kill. Then he reached for his phone and dialled her number.

'Hello, is this Fiona? It is, oh hi Fiona this is Doctor Adam Moss. I know it was a few weeks ago now I do apologise, but I had to go to France. I stupidly left all your details behind in the house I had to oversee some building work. Sadly it was a total nightmare so thank god it's all sorted out at long last.'

'Well that's a long time ago now Adam. I have met someone else. Mind you I don't think it will go anywhere though, he's just gone to Australia as he's filming out there. He's an actor and won't be back for about three months, so yes okay, I guess I'm free at the moment.'

'Look Fiona, would you like to meet up for a meal or a coffee or drink?'

'We could do all three Adam, and why not? I'm pretty much free these days as I only work part time now and I'm pretty much sick of working I don't really need to these days. My husband died eighteen months ago, he was a bank manager and the stress got him first I'm afraid. I warned him he was doing too much, but it transpired he was screwing the manageress of the building society next door to the bank. They were having it away on her office desk during her lunch break; I think they call it a grub screw! Anyway she was underneath the fat idiot where he had a heart attack at the critical moment' she laughed. 'Serves him right for being unfaithful the fat sod, but I get by very nicely. Where do you recommend we meet up?'

'Oh my God you certainly get to the point' he laughed 'but that in a way is so sad and so bad but such is life as the French say. Do you like Chinese? I know a great place, the Golden Bird in Brompton Road, Knightsbridge, are you up for that? I can recommend it. All the show business people go there and I can get a table as I know the owner very well.'

'Yes Adam, I've heard about it, a colleague of mine went one evening. Her husband had to wait for three months to get a booking because it's so sought after. She said it was amazing. There were all these show business types in there. Apparently it's supposed to be almost impossible to get a table did you say you know the owners?'

'As a matter of fact I do, between you and I he is a client of mine; remember I'm a Doctor, a cardiologist and I practise out of Harley Street. I can't be more specific than that, it's like you Fiona, confidentiality is part of the job.'

'I have the day off tomorrow Adam so I can meet you say tomorrow evening if that's okay with you.'

'Yes that's fine Fiona. Is it okay if I send a taxi for you say at 7.45pm and then I will meet you inside as I work until about 8pm? I will be inside the restaurant at my table, I'll have my lap top but I will finish when I see you I promise. I will be at the table in the corner and I will see you when you enter the front door I can't miss you.'

'I hope so Adam as I've had years of working until *midnight* but no more. There's more to life than killing yourself just for money.'

'I reckon you do have a point there Fiona. Where do you live? I will need the address for the taxi driver. I use him all the time, his name is Jimmy. He picks up all my clients and takes them home etc; he's very good so what's your address?'

'Oh yes its 16, Priory Road, Sudbury and you say 7.45pm? Great I will see you inside the restaurant. See you tomorrow evening Adam.'

'Yes I'm really looking forward to that Fiona.'

'Same here Adam, same here, **Qui-Sait-Seulement** as they say.' (Who only knows?)

If there was one thing that Alan hated above all, it was the snobby irritating privately educated posh bitches with money because they always looked down on ordinary people. Oh dear god was he going to enjoy sending her on her journey, yes he thought yes this one I will enjoy. She was going to be put in the Serpentine in Hyde Park.

'Fiona Blackwood was 5ft 7in tall with a nice enough figure. Her best asset was her hair which was thick and curly and it suited her down to the ground. She was a bit mannish in her mannerisms but still an attractive lady aged 49. After she had put her phone down she thought for a while about the conversation she just had with Alan, alias Adam Moss. She was a trained criminal Lawyer. In fact she was a barrister of some repute and had been for many years, which Alan didn't know about because she told him she was a solicitor. She was that as well, although she no longer took part in the dealings concerning conveyances on houses any more. The more she thought about the conversation the more uncertain she was about this charming man. Hmm he was just that bit too charming, there was something in his voice it was a little too eager and too oily it was hard to put a name to it. Conman came into her head.

Her thoughts were he was just too good to be true. She also thought about the Notting Hill murders. There was some creep wandering around killing women from a dating site. This man was no longer on the site and she thought being picked up by a cabbie called Jimmy sounded a bit silly and a little Mickey Mouse. What could he do in a taxi she thought, well a lot actually?

After thinking about it for a while she remembered a PI called George Penny who had his office in Notting Hill. She also remembered he was a great looking bloke who she immediately fancied. She could certainly remember that about him. Her firm had used him to great effect more than once. The office girls drooled over him, she thought the silly cows at the time, but they were right she laughed, and he was very good at what he did. He was in Notting Hill somewhere so she decided to contact him merely as a precaution her woman's intuition had now strongly kicked in. That was something that had never let her down before and especially at crucial times in court.

She worked as a partner in a firm called Hogan, Blackwood & Ball. The office was in fact in Pembroke Road, West Kensington not far from the centre of London. At 7.48am the next day Fiona's phone rang waking her up. 'Shit, shit' she said out loud 'it's the bloody office emergency phone. Yes Fiona speaking. What all bloody day? You're joking Clive, can't you get anyone else for Christ sake? It's my fucking day off and I've made plans. So you can sod of this time.'

'Sorry darling no-can-do we need you, there's a flap on because Gilberts have screwed up the American connection big time and the amount is seriously enormous. If we can't fix this damn situation then we will be a laughing stock, so get your cute arse back in the office ASAP. Oh and be prepared to work late tonight.'

'Oh bloody shit Clive, I have a date lined up and he's so bloody hot.'

'I don't care if he's ultra hot shit, get down here now. Try to remember you're a partner. Sorry but it's more than urgent Fiona. Can you imagine how the share situation will pan out if this gets out? We're talking bloody millions in losses. Fiona, you know as well as I do that if that happens we may as well commit Hari Kari on the Town Hall steps with me on top of you with a massive hard on dressed as a bus conductor with a bad lisp due to a serious overbite.

'Oh bollocks, what a terrible over active sick imagination you have Clive. So you can stuff that. Let me tell you again you sick pervert, your imagination sucks. I certainly don't need that, and thanks for the gross picture you've installed in my head never to be forgotten. You're a bloody old weirdo. I'm awake now ok I won't be long, see you in a while and you'd better get the coffee on and not that insipid crap we give to the juniors either. I want the real Columbian that the best clients get and a bloody large whiskey to go with it otherwise you can forget it, oh and lunch thrown in as well from Peter's Brassiere. The last time you ordered sandwiches from that grotty local cafe they tasted like they were made from horseshit, you tight sod.' Clive laughed.

Fiona worked until 7.30pm, she phoned Alan Reed alias Adam Moss to say she was not going to be able to make it as she had worked all day and by the time she freshened up it would be far too late. Plus she was too tired to go out so could he ring her tomorrow to arrange another time. He was out so she left the message on his answer phone.

When he read her message Alan Reed was really pissed off to get her phone call. He wanted her badly he was so looking forward to ending her big headed greedy life.

'He rang her back. Ok thanks for letting me know Fiona, but that's a shame. When can you make it again?'

'Well it seems tomorrow is good for me Adam, or the next day will be fine just so long as nothing else interrupts us, so what do you think?'

'Can we make it the day after tomorrow which is Thursday if that's okay with you?' Alan asked her. Say at the same time, is that good for you Fiona.'

'Yes Adam, that would be perfect see you then. I look forward to it.'

'She detected the irritation in his voice. Now she could tell it wasn't disappointment but irritation which made her even more suspicious. She had worked all her adult life with crooks, cheats, murderers, rapists etc and she didn't like the tone, it was definitely irritation. Her instincts were now on high alert and there was something not right about all this. She would most defiantly ring George Penny first thing in the morning.

CHAPTER EIGHTEEN

'George Penny, please.'
'Speaking, how may I help you?'
Fiona said to him 'could she see him as soon as possible. It was about a man from a dating site who seemed to be not what he claimed to be, or maybe not who he said he was. My name is Fiona Blackwood and you have done work for me before, or rather my firm Hogan, Blackwood & Ball.'

'I have a window at the moment so could see you now Fiona. Yes I do remember you and your firm. I believe we had a good result didn't we? Twice in fact if my memory serves me correctly. So come round now the coffee is on.' He gave her his address and within twenty five minutes she was there sitting in front of him. Julia brought the coffee in 'how do you like your coffee Fiona?'

'Oh black please, its Julia isn't it?'

'Yes, George and I are partners.' She smiled at Fiona who Julia could see was dressed to the nines and was definitely out to impress George. Julia knew most men are thick when a woman dresses like that, they think it's normal. They are too stupid to take notice what a woman is up to, so she decided to hang around as a sort of minder. She hated other women to sniff round George especially attractive ones such as this Fiona, but that's the way Julia was because underneath that jolly exterior she was a very capable woman, but there lurked the jealous green monster within and she was not slow to show that side to George. Although like most women she would always earnestly deny it.

When Fiona started to explain about this man called Dr Adam Moss. George and Julia were on the edge of their seats listening intently to her story. 'It was just a hunch that the guy was not who he says he is' said Fiona.

George went over her story again 'and you say he was going to have you picked up in a taxi, what sort of taxi was going to pick you up Fiona?'

'Well he said a guy called Jimmy would come for me in a London black cab, he used him all the time for his clients. Look with all these murders the press are banging on about I thought I would check this out with you and to see if you have any idea about any of this. He may be perfectly legitimate I may be over-reacting George,'

Julia told her about her friend Lisa who had been one of the Primrose killer's victims. 'She was victim number two with what we know about all this, he uses a dating site to research his victims. He makes dates to see them but now we believe he uses a London black cab to pick up his victims, so we think he does something in the cab to incapacitate them and then he drives more or less straight away to either a canal or river to drown them. My advice is not to meet him on your own, or not ever.'

'So George' said Fiona, 'do I inform the police to be with me on this date or should I just walk away?'

'No, no don't do that. If you can trust me I will come on the date with you and make sure he doesn't kill you.'

'So how do you propose to do this, after all he's picking me up at my house at 7.45 pm tomorrow evening. You can't come out with me can you George? Where will you be and will my life be in danger? Christ sake it's the only life I have. However, I would like to help catch this man. If you can think up a way of apprehending him then I'm all for it.'

'Fiona, I can be parked up next to your house in the road in a van and Julia here my lovely assistant will be in a car the other side of the road. The guy will be parked outside and he'll become wedged in the gap in the middle. Trust me he won't get away and you will have a tracker on your body plus a wire and another tracker in your bag. I will arrange for you to have a powerful ladies stun gun in your bag, but you have to hold it against someone for 4 seconds. It's a pink one and looks like a torch but it will disable a big man, are you okay with this? Look it's up to you and if we tell the police about all this, trust me they will not sanction it. They will screw it up with court orders and god knows what other documents, you don't need me to tell you that do you.'

'Yes that's right George. Sometimes the police are their own worst enemy. Can you show me one of these stun guns please George?'

Julia opened her bag and produced one in her hand 'look it's very feminine but very powerful.' She leant over George's desk, opened the bottom drawer and took another one out and gave it to Fiona saying 'try this for size, it's not heavy and it's very easy to hide.'

Fiona gripped the torch like stun gun and aimed it at George she said 'stick your hands up, I want to search you' and laughed.

'Well done Fiona, but there will be no searches today I'm afraid' said Julia giving Fiona a hands off look. 'We have just charged this today and so it's ready to operate how does it feel in your hands?'

Fiona said, 'hmm I reckon it will feel great' she said looking straight at George.

He sat there looking completely clueless like most men would. Julia knew exactly what she meant and was not amused by it at all. She was livid, but also at George for being so stupidly dumb.

'Fiona we have to keep this between us' said George.

'If only we could though,' she knew she was winding up Julia who was trying her best to humour her.

Julia had a look on her face like she'd just eaten a slimy cockroach sandwich from a down and outs toilet seat.

'If you want to go to the police you're free to do so' said George. 'However, I can get into places others can't get into.'

Fiona smiled then she looked at Julia who was now rolling her eyes. 'Well okay you can organise it George, and if that's right what you said about the gap it will be easy for you to slip in and sort it out,' said Fiona.

'Right so let's get this show on the road,' said George. 'We will both come to your place tomorrow evening and wait until he turns up then I will arrest him.'

Julia was now getting visibly annoyed at this situation with Fiona who made it obvious to her she fancied George like mad, but he sat there doing his job and not realising what was going on between the two women.

'See you tomorrow George, and you Julia.'

When she left, Julia tore into George. 'You stupid daft sod, what are you playing at encouraging her like that? She obviously wants to shag the arse off you, you bloody idiot. You're not going round her place on your own either! Are you blind, daft and bloody stupid?'

George looked perplexed. 'What? What the hell are you talking about? I never said anything to indicate I fancied her babe, what's the anger for? I don't fancy her, I love you to bits; you should know that, hey come here.' He grabbed her and laid her across his desk, she had a job to hold on to the edge of the desk as he furiously made love to her. Just as Julia was screaming out in ecstasy, neither of them noticed the office door silently open to reveal Fiona standing there.

'Oh, oh I'm so sorry I left my mobile phone here, I'm so sorry.' She picked her phone up then backed out of the office as Julia was looking round the side of George. She had a great big smile on her face, Fiona hadn't.

'You come when you want Fiona,' laughed Julia.

'Next time lock the door babe' said George.

'Yes I will but that's taught her a lesson, now she knows what she's missing.'

'It seems that I'm missing something too babe,' he said with a puzzled look on his face. 'The show has to go on' he laughed as he carried on. In the back of his head he thought women... I'll never ever understand them?

CHAPTER NINETEEN

Alan Reed had a strange feeling about meeting Fiona; his sixth sense had kicked in. Something wasn't right, he couldn't explain it but somehow a voice told him not to go. After thinking about it for a while he ordered a London black cab to pick Fiona up at the pre-arranged time.

Yet he would be parked in the road a little way past Fiona's house, after all he still had her address. He would be reading the paper. At about 7.15 he was watching for anything unusual and then he saw a silver Ford Transit van parked up on one side and a dark blue BMW parked on the other side, leaving a gap outside Fiona's house. The van had a man sat in the driving seat and the BMW series 3 had a woman sat in the driving seat. No one had noticed his VW estate car but at 7.48pm a London black cab arrived outside and beeped the horn three times. Suddenly the van closed up to the front of the taxi and the dark blue BMW parked at the back moved forward blocking the taxi in tight. A big fit looking man rushed out of the driving seat of the van and grabbed the driver of the taxi, held him in an arm lock and pinned him down to the floor. He saw Fiona Blackwood standing there smiling. He also saw Julia as he drove by. Yet he also saw her looking at him for a second. But it was more like a casual stare.

Alan Reed had slowly driven past them with his window wound down. As he looked out he saw all of them now standing in the driveway. The taxi driver was being held in an arm lock by the big man. He saw the taxi driver asking what he had done and what was going on. Now there seemed to be the whole area getting involved and asking what the taxi driver had done wrong.

This was the time to slowly depart and leave them to it, so he drove home. Now incandescent with rage because the bitch had almost caught him but she would pay for this. But he had her address. There is nothing as satisfying as sweet revenge was his thinking.

George asked the taxi driver 'what's your name? Come on tell me your name.'

'My name is Gerald,' said the taxi driver 'Gerald Knowles. Hey I have no money honest, I've just started ten minutes ago so I have no fares yet, let me go.'

Fiona asked him to tell her where the Golden Bird restaurant is and how long he'd been a taxi driver for. She also asked if he had done the Knowledge which is the London taxi driver's gruelling driving course. Without having passed the test you could not be a London black cab taxi driver.

'I did my last Knowledge test six months ago which I passed. It took me five years and four attempts to do it. I have just got my own taxi, and the green card. Look what is this? Are you the police or what are you?'

'It's not him,' said Fiona,

'How can you tell' asked Julia.

'Because it's not his voice, the other guy had a plain accent and I'm rather good at remembering voices. It's not him but I want to know who sent him as if we couldn't guess.' She asked him 'who sent you to this address Gerald?'

'It was some guy, and I was to pick a lady up. I was to beep my horn three times and she would come out, but no-one told me I would be assaulted. Look I'm going to tell the police about this, I haven't done anything wrong, have I? You can't just go around jumping on people for no reason mate,'

'Look' said George, 'I'm afraid this is a delicate story. Here Gerald, take this money please. I'm sorry to have caused you alarm hopefully it wasn't a wasted trip for you and you're not harmed are you?'

'What's the money for,' asked the taxi driver.

'It's a hundred quid, so at least you've earned out of it, so it's not all bad Gerald. I'm really sorry about your arm. I'm a private detective and we thought this lady was going to be abducted, believe me we did have a good solid reason. The man who sent you should have come himself, but in a fake taxi and for some reason he got wind of me. I'm sorry about this Gerald it sounds to me as though the man we want has sent you as a decoy to check out if it was safe to come here. This guy is one smart man and a very cunning one.'

Gerald looked at the cash and said 'ok no harm done at least I got paid, anyway can I go now?'

'Yes sorry, you can go.'

'Haven't you forgot something' asked Gerald the taxi driver.

George scratched his head 'no I don't think so, what have I forgot?'

'A tip mate, where's my tip?'

George handed him another twenty pounds and said 'yes you can go now Gerald, but how the hell did he know we were going to be here I wonder.'

Gerald answered 'no idea mate it all sounds a bit weird to me.'

Gerald now pleased said 'no harm done mate' as he drove off.

'This is one clever man Fiona. Try and remember you're still very much in danger.'

'In danger, why am I?'

'Because he knows where you live and he's already gone back and killed one lady who had previously escaped. She gave him her address too and he went back to her work place, where he drowned her in a bath. Look he's well capable of coming back to get you out of spite or out of revenge, but I do believe he will come back for you.'

'You know George I did see a car leaving afterwards,' said Julia. 'It was a black estate car. There may not be anything in that but you never know. Anyway I've made a note of it, but I couldn't get the make of it or the number. And I didn't see the driver properly as it was too far away. But he was I'd say middle age dark hair and good looking for what I could see of him.'

Fiona was now worried about this man who was probably the Primrose killer because now he knew where she lived. She was due a holiday and her business owed her several weeks, so she decided to take off somewhere for a couple of weeks. The following morning she visited her travel agents to book a holiday to Rome but she couldn't get a seat for two weeks. She knew some people over there but they were themselves away for two weeks, it was bad timing. She had wanted to go that evening, but there was nothing available and that was the only available plane seat left.

George was pleased she was going to go away for he knew this Primrose killer man would try and get to Fiona and kill her. All he had to do was find him, he was ever hopeful.

Meanwhile, Alan Reed was desperate to get another victim, yet on second thoughts he thought he ought to leave it a while now because this could have spelt disaster and his work had only just begun. Someday he knew he was going to be caught he didn't care about being caught, but not yet. However, this woman was going to have to pay for the all the trouble she had caused. He would seek her out later when she thought all was well yet the urge to kill was now almost out of control. Alarmingly he wasn't sure he could contain his feelings for very much longer.

Deciding to take a sleeping tablet to calm himself down he went to bed and took a stiff drink of whiskey which he didn't much like then he popped a sleeping pill into his mouth. Within the hour he was fast asleep.

When he awoke at 8.23am the light was streaming through his bedroom window. Somehow he had to try and get another victim. Yesterday he felt annoyed about this Fiona and now he felt the strong urge to kill again. Walking through to the kitchen he made a coffee and then reached for the list, there were now 13 names left.

Abigail Westwood was a Pharmacist working for Miller & Drummond who had a large chain of chemist shops; this one was in Oxford Street, London. She had just arrived home when her phone rang. 'Hello, Abigail speaking.'

'Hi Abigail this is Doctor Peter Strong, we spoke a few weeks ago now from the dating site PLS. I had to go away urgently on business to France, is it still okay to talk?'

'Oh hi yes I remember you now, how are you? I haven't seen your profile on the site, have you come off Peter? That usually means you've met someone.'

'Yes I came off it. I decided I'd had enough as I had so many replies, and to be honest with you I only kept your phone number so this is why I am ringing you. Anyway you're a Pharmacist are you?'

'Yes I have been for many years and to be honest I could do with a change. I envy people that work outside and move around instead of being cooped up in a small room making up prescriptions all day long and seeing the same four walls. What sort of doctor are you Peter?'

'I'm a Psychiatrist and have been now for many years. I have a practise in Harley Street, but look let's forget work for now. Would you like to meet up for a meal or a drink sometime?'

'Yes that would be nice, when are you thinking of? I'm okay for most evenings and weekends, it's up to you.'

'Ok good, how about tomorrow evening. I know a great Steak House that also serves fresh fish too, and the wine they serve is wonderful. It's in Kensington.

'Oh that sounds lovely so where shall we meet up.'

'I think the best place to meet would be by taxi, because if I send a taxi for you then they can pick me up too, it means we can both have a drink without having to worry about driving.'

'Oh what a nice thought thank you. I better give you my address, have you a pen handy? It's 54 Pembroke Close Primrose Hill.'

'Okay thank you Abigail, shall we say 7.45pm? I really am looking forward to this. I will get the taxi driver to beep his horn three times then he will pick me up in Blenheim Crescent Notting Hill right after you. Until tomorrow evening Abigail.'

'Yes I'm looking forward to this as well Peter, so see you tomorrow at 7.45pm.'

Abigail had not been on a date for at least six months, the last date was an utter disaster as the man she had agreed to meet said he was 6ft tall which she liked as she was actually 5ft 8 in tall and if possible wanted a taller man. The man was in fact a little smaller than her and was also as thin as a jockey's whip. Plus he was also an ardent smoker and she could smell cigarettes on his breath and his clothes. There was also a strong smell of alcohol on his breath and his finger nails were filthy.

The worst date she had was with a so-called property millionaire who turned up with a large shaggy unkempt grey beard. He was also about 5ft 8in tall with a belly so large that the table seemed to be too far away for him to reach his knife and fork. His dress sense was appalling he turned up wearing a dark blue blazer covering a grubby once white T-shirt and some light coloured chinos. Removing his blazer he placed it on the back of his chair and sat down to reveal several stains, and under each arm there was a large sweaty patch. That was her first date since her husband cleared off with another woman eleven months ago. Unsurprisingly she was pleased to hear from Peter. Anyway he seemed to be a genuinely nice man and hoped this was true. Anyway, she decided she would give it another go.

Abigail was now forty seven years old. She'd been with her husband for twenty seven years and had not been with anyone else sexually or indeed with hardly any men before him. She was a little nervous about meeting up with Peter. There again she had to start somewhere. However, she was a very attractive looking lady, but her husband was a complete control freak and a bully. She couldn't even buy any clothes without him approving them and she was never allowed to go for a drink with her friends, not ever. Consequently she had no friends left at all to go out with. Being on her own was not what she had expected. It was hard and lonely it was a way to lose your confidence and such a shame to see this attractive lady going to waste sadly being so unhappy, yet she had a most amazing figure with lovely shoulder length thick light blond hair.

She wasn't too fat or too thin, just perfect. Considering she was aged forty seven she didn't look it, but her confidence had evaporated to a very low level.

At 7.45 pm the next evening there came three beeps from a taxi. She looked out of her window to see a London black cab waiting outside her small terraced house which she was now renting. Abigail quickly opened her door and told Jasper her small cross breed terrier to be a good boy, to look after the house while she was away and that she wouldn't be long. She made sure his bowls had food and water and gave him a couple of tit bits of dried liver; she patted his little head then closed the door and quickly walked to the taxi. Jasper ran to the sofa which backed onto the window, jumped up onto the head rest and looked out to see her disappear into the taxi. He was distraught at being left alone and jumped back down. Running to the door he cocked his leg up over the door frame and also the carpet. Looking depressed and lonely he started to wail as usual which pissed off the neighbours.

She had got into the taxi and the driver said 'good evening Madam.'

Abigail said 'good evening to you too.' They had driven about two miles when he pulled into a side street and said 'I'm sorry about this Madam, my seat belt light has come on indicating it's yours so I will have to check it out. I won't be a moment, I don't want to get a fine' he laughed and opening his door he got out. He opened her door to adjust the webbing of her seat belt, but hit her with a stun gun and five seconds later she collapsed and slid off the seat onto the large floor area. Quickly injecting her with Rohypnol and then he was securing her hands by the wrists behind her back using garden ties. To keep her ankles together he used more garden ties. Quickly he taped her mouth so she couldn't make a sound. Closing the taxi's doors he took her to the Regents Canal. After finding a parking place he pulled out the wheelchair where he sat her in it and wrapped a tartan blanket around her body which was held upright by Velcro straps. Placing a head scarf around her head she looked as though she was asleep. He was wearing a long dark Trench coat and a trilby hat pulled over his forehead and his usual surgical gloves.

The time was now 9.37pm, he started to trundle her along the pavement when all of a sudden she woke up but she shouldn't have done as he'd injected a lot of Rohypnol into her. Abigail not realising where she was tried to move but she couldn't so he stopped the wheelchair and saw what she was doing. He looked at her almost lovingly.

'Abigail please listen to me there is no need to struggle it only makes it much harder for you and for me too. Please just try to relax and when I put you in the water just let go and think of the good times you have had in your life. Try to remember this as a journey to a better place so you have to let go my dear,' but she had a look of absolute terror on her face and for some unexplained reason this upset him greatly.

'Good evening' a voice spoke to him as he walked along the towpath of the Regents Canal. The sound made him jump because he hadn't seen anyone coming and he was far away in his distant past. The voice came from an old lady while her husband said 'good evening' as well. They were walking their dog, a stumpy fat little Corgi. Alan said 'good evening' back and carried on pushing the wheelchair.

'Oh it's a nice evening' said the lady who was aged about seventy and her husband was about the same age.

'Yes it is and my wife has fallen asleep but she likes the canal at this time of the day when no-one else is around, she's very shy. I'm afraid she's been very ill.'

The old lady said 'oh look at her eyes, they are busy, she can hear us I'm sure' as she noticed her eyes darting about almost pleading with them to help her. 'Is she alright, she doesn't look too well' she said to Alan.

'Yes she always looks like that when anyone speaks to her. She can't speak I've clearly just said she isn't very well.'

'What's the matter with her' the old lady asked him in a sympathetic way.

Abigail was in a sort of semi comma, but she was half aware of what was being said and she could make out the old couple now earnestly looking at her. She could not speak but she felt as though her eyes were spinning in her sockets. Try as she might she could not get out of her paralysis.

'Look I don't mean to be rude' said Alan, 'but this is a boner (Army speak for pointless) we have to get a move on. She doesn't like to stop and talk, strangers make her panic. So if you will excuse us we have to go. You two have a nice evening.' he slowly trundled off with Abigail in the wheelchair.

'Well how rude was that' said the older lady to her husband, 'he was strange to say the least. Toby come here' she said to their dog who stood there looking at the wheelchair. 'What a strange man he is' she commented.

'Yes not very friendly was he' said her husband David. 'Still that's the way of the world today and hey my love we tried our best. He was a handsome man though and he obviously cared for his wife. He was taking her out for a walk my love, or rather a ride in her wheelchair. Anyway come on Toby lets go,' but Toby was still staring at the wheelchair as it slowly disappeared as the towpath turned left under a bridge.

'I think he was very odd, and what on earth was he wearing surgical gloves for? I can't help getting this feeling that there was something very wrong about them. She looked absolutely terrified to me, poor woman you could tell by her eyes. It's just a feeling I have David, a feeling that all was not as it seemed to be, look can we go back the same way home?'

'Margaret you and your feelings, but still most of the time you always seem to be right.'

Alan was now annoyed he had been seen, he didn't want to go back with an empty wheelchair the couple would be wondering where Abigail had gone to, that's if he bumped into them again. He found a nice quiet spot and said to Abigail 'oh look this is a nice place to go.'

He started to take the blanket off her, and also her scarf from around her head. 'Look please don't panic Abigail, it will soon be over. I promise you it won't take long. I just have to put this bag around your neck that's all and it has some lead weights in it to help you.' So he tied the bag around her neck and then lifted her out of the chair and into the canal. It was now 10.27pm as he gently put her into the canal. She was not going easy now and she wriggled and tried to kick out so he reached for the stun gun again when he heard 'HEY, WHAT THE HELL ARE YOU DOING, STOP!' David and Margaret seemed to suddenly come out of the gloom.

Abigail was now in the canal and had sunk to the bottom. Toby the small fat Corgi was running up to Alan snarling as he ran. Alan dropped the wheelchair into the canal and ran off leaving his hat behind.

David saw what had happened and jumped into the canal after Abigail while Margaret was already dialling 999 for the Police. Managing to grab Abigail by her thick mane of hair he pulled her to the surface. Thankfully the canal was not that deep in this area and he managed to get help from a group of lads who had been larking about on their way home after a couple of drinks at the local pub. They undid the tape from her mouth so she could breathe properly.

A passing police car was already in Clifton Gardens having dealt with a domestic call out which was very near the canal. After they took the call from HQ they were there in three minutes. They took over and gave her first aid until an ambulance arrived. The police officers spoke to the police station and asked them to get hold of DCI Eric Fletcher as they believed the woman had been abducted by the Primrose killer.

Alan Reed managed to get back to his taxi without being seen where he'd left it in Johns Wood Road. He drove the taxi back to his garage under the railway arches and thought about how he was almost caught. Still he'd managed to keep her earrings which were small gold hoops, but now he had to have a rethink. Yet he was amazed that no newspapers had mentioned the dating site and how he managed to pick them up. He was quite concerned now because Abigail would tell the police what he looked like, but on the other hand what could she say? In future he would get rid of the women during the early hours. The trouble is the old couple had also seen him and he'd lost his hat, again! That was the second hat he had lost and he knew they would get his DNA from it, but he had no record except from the Army records because of his assault charges. How would they know he was once in the Parachute Regiment so he dismissed that, he knew the police had no access to the army's DNA base?

DCI Eric Fletcher was informed almost immediately, also DC Buckley. They were on the scene with the forensic teams within the hour.

DCI Fletcher introduced himself to David and Margaret Salter, the couple who managed to save Abigail who was now in hospital. DC Buckley was at her bedside interviewing her about what had happened.

Margaret told Inspector Fletcher what they had seen and gave him a good description, well as best as she could do in the circumstances. 'What made you suspicious of this man Margaret?' asked DCI Fletcher.

'It was strange, he was acting a bit suspicious I also noticed he was wearing surgical gloves, but the worst part was his wife's eyes. She looked terrified, and Toby the dog also disliked him. My woman's intuition told me he was a wrong one. We can tell Inspector, we women can tell.'

DCI Fletcher thought well he'd managed to kill a few and none of the women could tell?

After gleaning all the information he could from Mrs Salter and inspecting the scene, DCI Fletcher had the wheelchair removed from the canal for the forensic gang as he called them. But now he also had the hat the killer had dropped, so as it was now dark he headed to the hospital to link up with DC Buckley. Abigail was not that well informed. She said to them 'she had spoken to the man called Dr Peter Strong on the phone then she'd been picked up by the man posing as a taxi driver. But she was out cold for most of the time;' although she did say 'he had this soft well spoken voice. There was not a lot more she could tell them.'

DCI Fletcher and DC Buckley were pleased about the hat Alan had dropped, but DNA was of no use if there was no name attached to it, nevertheless it was kept on the record and later it was found his DNA was also on the other hat he had dropped by the river Brent putting this man in the frame for the murders, whoever he was?

Apart from that, frustratingly, there were no clues except he took the earrings belonging to Abigail and the wheelchair they pulled from the canal had no fingerprints on it either. It was annoying the hell out of them, especially Eric as he was somewhat impulsive at times especially times such as this.

The next day DCI Fletcher called on George Penny at his office in Notting Hill. 'Hi Eric what have I done to deserve this? I bet it's not a social call.'

'Jesus! This place must have cost an arm and a leg mate, check you out! It's really posh, that's the biggest desk I've ever seen and get you, a real coffee percolator and a good one too. You're doing good George, and believe me I'm so pleased to see that. You were crapped on by your boss, but look on the bright side and look how well you're doing now and Julia is lovely, what a find she was for you.'

'Ok, ok Eric save the plaudits. I don't need medals, but nonetheless thanks all the same.'

'Right let's get down to business George.' He told George of the latest developments, and what had taken place by the side of the Regents Canal. 'There are no clues as such mate, all we have is the guy is about 6ft to 6ft 2inches tall. He has massive shoulders, and to him being slim, so on taking an average he is 6ft tall and broad shouldered. Oh and very good looking.'

'Eric was there anything in the way that he spoke to them, any phrases he used? What was his dialect like, was it loud, soft, broad, anything at all you can tell me?'

'Yes he had a softly spoken voice and apparently he sounded posh. Look, whilst the iron is still hot so to speak, pop round to see the Salter's and ask them what they saw. A fresh approach might bring dividends George. So here is their phone number and address.'

'Yes Eric I was going to ask you if that was OK, I don't want to piss on your parade though, but as you say a fresh set of ears can pick things up we all miss.'

George rang the door bell and almost immediately he heard a dog barking, 'Toby shut up, come here now this minute, get into your bed and keep quiet.'

The door opened to reveal a woman aged about seventy, but as bright as a button and very attractive. She was in prime condition for her age; being about 5ft 6in tall with blond greyish hair. She had her make up on and was wearing a nice dress. She also smelt very nice too.

'Come in Mr Penny' said Margaret, 'take a seat, thank you for phoning us. Would you like a coffee or tea, we are about to take tea so it's not a problem. David is upstairs and won't be long.'

'Tea will be nice thank you Mrs Salter.'

'Oh call me Margaret, please George. It's okay to call you George is it?'

'Yes of course it is'. Margaret went into the kitchen to prepare the tea.

George looked around the living room, it was neat and tidy with various photographs of their grandchildren and of their own children, a boy and a girl who were now in their fifties. The grandchildren must be in their early twenties or late teens. Toby the fat stumpy little Corgi was licking George's hand and letting him stroke him. The room was comfortable and you could see the sofa and the two chairs was some years old, but very comfortable. There was a sideboard where all the photographs were placed, and a fruit bowl with apples, oranges, and bananas. A dining table with four chairs and a vase of flowers in the middle stood in the corner. Toby had his own miniature sofa to lie on and to sleep behind the door next to the radiator. The dog was spoiled rotten and he knew it, he stumped around almost with his nose in the air, but he liked George. Margaret poked her head round the door and said 'one spoon or two in your tea, sorry I mean sugar. My, you must be a bit special because Toby doesn't take to everyone I can tell you, he's always been a bit fussy you know George.' Then he heard the toilet flushing and could hear Mr Salter coming down the stairs. 'Thanks Margaret, no sugar thanks, but I do like dogs. Oh, hi Mr Salter I'm just about to try your wife's tea.'

'You must be George Penny. DCI Fletcher told us you would be calling round, but I don't think we have anything more to add or say about it really, well I can't think of anything.'

Margaret brought the tea and placed it on the small coffee table in the middle of them, 'this one's for you George so now how can we help you?' She was looking at him thinking he's a bit of alright.

'Could you please just go through the events again and try to remember exactly what this man said to you, it's very important that you remember and I'll record it on my phone, if that's okay with you.'

'Yes okay George I'll try my best for you. Well let's see. I first saw the man coming towards us about 9.45pm maybe a bit sooner. Anyway he didn't seem to be all that confident in pushing a wheelchair. My curiosity got the better of me and when he drew near I said good evening to him and his wife, but he didn't seem to hear me because when he did see us he seemed to be a little jumpy. Then he said good evening back. Strangely he was also wearing surgical gloves and a funny trilby hat, but I think you have his hat. The thing which alarmed me was his wife's eyes. They were pleading with me to help, I'm positive about that. The thing is George, I did thirty three years as a psychiatric nurse at Broad Moor and patients often spoke with their eyes, she looked terrified and also so helpless. When I asked what the matter was, he just said oh nothing much it's a boner and quickly walked away.

'What happened then' asked George 'what did you see?'

CHAPTER TWENTY

David Salter said 'we decided to turn back because Margaret has this uncanny sixth sense whenever something is wrong. We hurried along and even Toby ran out in front of us, and as we came from under the bridge at Edgware Road we saw he was on his own and his wheelchair was now empty. It was obvious he had dumped his wife into the canal or she had got up and ran away, or maybe she had been taken by aliens but she wasn't with him. Then we saw the bubbles so I jumped in and brought her to the surface, she had these metal bolts around her head in a supermarket bag and she was almost dead. After removing the gaffer tape from around her mouth I gave her the kiss of life, she was lucky as she was almost gone. It was then we called the police but she couldn't speak properly. My wife said her eyes were dilated and she'd been drugged.'

'Did you hear him use the word boner David? Did Abigail say anything at all which made any sense to you two, any word, any remark, anything at all?' Said George.

'No she said nothing that made any sense to us. She was mumbling and trying to clear her throat but she said nothing intelligent at all, the poor woman.'

'So he never used the word boner. Think David it's very important.'

'Yes he did. When Margaret asked what was wrong with her, he did use the phrase it's a boner. Why, does this mean something George?'

'It could well do, but at the moment I'm not sure yet David, I have to check it out. It may mean something or nothing. Sometimes words are clues, and that's why I ask you to tell me every word he said to you. The Police and even I can miss things if we don't listen properly, and when you're tired sadly we all do.'

After two cups of tea and some assorted biscuits George thanked them for their help and returned to his office where

Julia was sitting behind his desk working out invoices and bills etc.

'Hi George, how did you get on with the Salter's, and you've got biscuit crumbs round your mouth you big kid, and on your jumper' she laughed.

'Julia, I reckon this guy is ex military.'

'How do you figure that out?'

'Because he often uses words the army use amongst themselves. For instance he used the phrase 'Oh it's a boner,' which means it's pointless. That was said in context to Margaret Salter when she asked him what was the matter with his wife and he said 'oh it's a boner' in the sentence. He has used the phrase obeying orders and following orders before and his demeanour seems to be ex forces. He also opened the door for the first victim Helen Burk and saluted her as she got in, it sounds daft....but.'

'You may have a point there George and the guy seems to be very precise in what he does, he is almost regimental in his approach to his work, if you can call it that, killing people I mean. Anyway what's been happening with the Police, how far have they got with it?'

The police are waiting for a DNA sample from his hat babe. It was a wide brimmed trilby hat and perhaps he has his DNA on record. You know, they should make a law that everyone born has their DNA taken at birth, it would help solve a lot of crimes,' said George.

Alan Reed, alias the Primrose killer rang Simon Lovett and told him all the details of how he was almost caught but he managed to get away. So now he was going to cause bloody havoc.

'Hang on' said Lovett, 'look slow down a little tell me again what you have in mind.'

'Maybe you can print that in your paper, I feel much better when I send another bitch on her way, you know all you have to do is take a walk around the West End on a weekend night. These bitches are everywhere and they wear almost nothing at all. They roll about in a drunken frenzy then puke in doorways. They fall over showing their Fannies and lay there semi naked, and then they have the cheek to moan if they are raped. You can see them in shop doorways getting screwed by anyone who passes them by, it should be stopped and you know what? That's exactly what I am going to do, there's going to be a lot more put away before they catch me Mr Lovett, a lot more. I'm on a mission to get rid of these obscene hideous harlot's.'

Lovett wanted to laugh 'Harlot's' he thought that's Shakespeare. Lovett asked him 'why are you doing this, there has to be a reason? There is always a reason because you're acting like a man completely out of control. If you tell me, I can get your story in all the nationals. You are probably going to become the most famous serial killer since the Yorkshire Ripper and earn a lot of money. You will need an agent, plus a ghost writer. There could well be film rights as well. Good god you're on the road to becoming big, very big, and also very rich.'

'Mr Lovett, listen to me very carefully. I know what I'm doing and I'm not out of control. If you do print that you will make me very unhappy, and you wouldn't want to meet me when I'm like that Mr Lovett, that's something I can promise you.'

'Can we possible meet up?' Asked Lovett 'I promise you I won't tell anyone of our meeting, why not have a think about it? I can guarantee everyone will be interested in your story. The Lovett Column is read by thousands. Just have a think then call me back because I have contacts in the newspaper world and also the film world, if you stick with me you will do very nicely.'

'I would have to think about this first' said Alan 'the Police are a bit slow and I have considered giving myself up to the Police. I don't mind getting caught if I'm honest. I'm fed up with all of it now, but as I said I do have a lot more work to do, and I'm thinking of taking a holiday to relax and to come back fresh where I can start all over again.'

'Look' said Lovett, 'we can talk about this. If you hand yourself over to me, I will make damn sure they look after you, no one would get hurt and you will be looked after, I will promise you that much. If you tell me your story as a 100%

exclusive, you will also be paid a hell of a lot of money, and we all need that don't we? It's going to be at least £100,000 plus film the rights, we're talking silly money. My advice to you is not to waste this opportunity and to go for it. Think what you could do with a shed load of money and all the people you know and any good causes you could help with this money.'

'Hmm as I said let me think about it first Mr Lovett, I will be in touch later. My head hurts now, it's all been too much lately. Listen to me very; very carefully do not publish anything I have said to you. So I give you fair warning, if you do then you will have to face the consequences. They won't be good.'

'I won't and not without your approval first. So you just have a long think about what I have told you. Please don't go throwing money away. We can both do well out of this.'

The next day the headlines screamed.... **The Primrose killer man** is about to give himself up to the Echo. Police fail once again to capture this serial killer. Simon Lovett persuades the killer to come in.

When Alan saw this in the newspapers he was more than furious he was raging. He did not want Lovett to write anything at this moment in time, he told him not too. But only when he thought the time was right to do so. After all he'd said let me think about it, but now Lovett had betrayed him.

However, he would get his revenge. Alan found out the address of Lovett so he decided to pay him a visit. Another thing he also found out his favourite club 'Gingers' was a gay club but he decided he would leave it for the moment Lovett could wait a while. Now he had an urge to go to Bristol, the whole place needed cleaning up without delay. Feeling like a saviour he felt a certain purity running through his veins. He was going to clean up the city. He thought it was an open sewer of filth and rampant sexual disease. Someone had to deal with it, and that someone was him.

On the Friday evening, he drove down to Bristol. He got there at 12.30am and did a slow cruise around the night club area. He was flagged down several times yet he didn't stop. The taxi sign said NOT FOR HIRE. At 2.15am his luck was in when he saw two middle age women staggering down the Anchor Road obviously pissed as farts. They were wobbling about all over the pavement and one was constantly falling over. They saw him and tried to wave him down standing there with their hands in the air waving their handbags swinging from their elbows. One of them fell over on her arse laughing, but he just carried on. However he was checking out other cars and people in the area. Suddenly he decided to go back to pick them up and drew alongside of them. At this time one was still sitting on the pavement laughing, legs wide apart showing next week's washing. The other one helped to pick up her mate and managed to get into the taxi, or rather they fell into the back of it.

Alan asked them to settle down and he was appalled at the way they spoke to each other. They both had the shortest of dresses on and their breasts were virtually hanging out, and they reeked of booze. Both had lipstick smeared all over their faces, they had obviously had some sort of liaison with some men as they were both bragging about it. 'Hey yours couldn't get a hard on' shouted Shelly, 'and mine had a bloody big club between his thin legs, what a whopper he had, my god I can still feel it' she howled with laughter. 'But he must have been the last in the queue when looks were dished out' she laughed. 'Still who would look at his face with the size of that weapon,' she laughed.

'I know, it's alright for you Shell, but what's your old man going to say if he wants a shag when you get home because after that, he won't feel the sides.' They screamed out with laughter.

'Oh bollocks to him' she screamed out, 'anyway he's a twat, he can save his shag for another day. Bloody hell I'm still throbbing.'

'Would you do it again Shell, even though he's obviously hooked on ugly pills for the rest of his life, you can see he is.'

'Bloody right I would Gloria, I have his card. That was the best knee trembler I ever had. So anyway as I said who the hell looks at the face? I want a good shag not a bloody film star, unless they have a big whopper for an old shopper.'

Screaming with laughter, they had got in the taxi and started to settle down. Alan asked them 'and where to lovely ladies?'

'Ladies' they howled laughing.

'We're no ladies!' They shouted in thick Bristol accents and then sat in the back with their skirts almost around their waists saying 'I could do with a piss driver. Shelly here is busting for a slash as well' she laughed.

'Take us to the Bristol Marina there are plenty of places for a piss, look it's just down there driver, there's a good boy.' He barked back 'woof, woof.'

Alan drove slowly down to the Marina where they told him to stop by a container. Shelly managed to get out first and wobbled about until she had found a place out of sight behind a container to have a pee. By now he had opened the back door where he quickly grabbed Gloria, the other pissed up lady. Quickly he was injecting her in the arm. And then he hit her in the throat with his stun gun where she violently slipped off the back seat into a heap on the floor.

Shelly came wobbling back five minutes later to the taxi and slurred 'where's Gloria?' She was now laughing 'oh look she's fell off the seat, she's pissed again' and howled with laughter.

She bent down to help her friend sit up while laughing her face off. Creeping up behind her he used the stun gun on the back of her neck as well, she quickly passed out. Injecting Rohypnol into her arm too was a precaution as he had done the same to Gloria. No-one was walking about so now he had the time. Quickly he trussed them up separately. Their earrings were a priority so he pulled out a pair of gold studs and a pair of gold hoops. Not the best he'd had before, but he was still pleased at his find. They would join the other earrings in his collection.

They were both a little overweight and dressed like kids, they were both so bloody disgusting. Noticing Shelly's legs were wet because she had pissed herself down her left leg he was gagging. She had no knickers on either, they made him sick. He was determined he would rid Bristol of these loathsome creatures and very quickly. Oh god he wanted to get back to London; that was bad enough but this Bristol City was to him a far worse place.

The thought of married women getting pissed and stuffed by almost anyone made him feel ill. They would soon be out of their misery. Bristol should thank him for doing the city a big favour. Being given the freedom of the city would be a good idea.

Both women were now tied up with garden ties and neither of them was moving. So he decided to move quickly. Then he drove a little further then stopped where it was quiet. There were lots of boats moored up and lots of small cruisers, 4 and 6 berth cruisers all moored together. He would put both of them together in the water, but then he thought no why should he? They can drown separately. Scrubbers didn't deserve to die together, so to hell with them.

Having gaffer taped their mouths shut and tightly tying a supermarket bag with two railway bolts inside each bag around their fat necks, he was now making absolutely sure no-one else was about. Slipping Shelly into the water first, he held her by her feet as her dress slid down onto her large hips. She had no knickers on and he was revolted by her bush between her fat legs, she also smelt. Slowly he slid her head first into the murky oiled slicked water of the Marina. With her heavy weight she sank like a stone, but head first. Turning around he went back to get Gloria, he picked her up and thankfully she was half the weight of Shelly, but at least she had her knickers on. When he held her upside down head first she started to come round but she had no chance. Holding her there for a while he let her go into the filthy water. There was rubbish and oil on the water, not that he cared a toss. She also sank like a stone. He said a prayer for them 'good riddance to bad rubbish you pair of disgusting scrubbers.'

Thinking to himself he had a job to do down here, he was considering returning in the not too distant future. The whole place to be truthful did really need cleaning up. It was like being a sheriff going in to clean up an old western town.

Anyway he decided to wait around for a while until there were no more bubbles coming to the surface, and now satisfied Alan slowly drove off towards the M5. It was incredible; he was amazed at the gangs of slags wondering about the centre of Bristol. The blokes were all drunk and seemingly snogging anything they could without any difficulty.

Quickly he headed for the Junction to the M5 motorway back to the M4 leading straight to London. It had happened so quickly, he didn't get much of a thrill from it even though he had killed the two women. The trouble was it was too quick, he should have savoured it more.

Nevertheless he was out of his depth in Bristol. He didn't know the area very well which made his job a little precarious. But he'd got rid of these two bitches for good. And now he felt a little cleaner for it, and he reckoned Bristol owed him a favour for it.

When he arrived back at the lock up garage he took the cloned number plates off which were held on with Velcro strips and then he destroyed them. He was also pleased because now he had two more sets of earrings. One set was a pair of gold studs the other a pair of small hoops. The two women had £128 between them which he kept, along with their phones. Their bags were dumped into the Marina. The satisfaction he felt was amazing at what he'd done. There were no clues that he left, he was sure of that. He knew the Police would have access to all the CCTV cameras in the area and his taxi was back to its own number plate, so they could not connect him with the killings.

CHAPTER TWENTY ONE

On the Saturday morning Richard Newly was waking up in his new six berth motor cruiser with his latest girlfriend of seven weeks called Karla. They had been out on the town and had a great night, even though he didn't drink he woke up needing the toilet, he checked the time it was now 5.30am. After his visit to the loo he checked his new girlfriend out, and seeing her still asleep he fancied a cigarette. Now he was making his way to the stern of the 6 berth cruiser to have a smoke because his girlfriend Karla didn't really like the smell of cigarette smoke. Sitting at the stern, he pulled a long drag on his cigarette and blew out the smoke as he was looking at the rubbish in the water. There were fag ends, condoms, chip bags; coffee cups...all sorts of garbage. Something caught his eye as he saw something bobbing up and down in the water at first he thought it was a dead dog. Looking a little harder he saw a bottom moving up and down. Then again he stared at the sight and thought what the hell is it? Was it a tailor's dummy? Looking again, but harder this time after rubbing his eyes to get the sleep out of them, he was certain this was a woman's body. Then he saw another body. This one was lying on her back a little further away. She was taped up around her mouth. Immediately he rang the police who were not slow in appearing and were there by 5.47am. They pulled the two dead friends out of the Marina with the help of two fishermen and the harbour master and laid them on the ground. Within twenty five minutes the area was taped off and the forensic guys turned up. There were five of them in all.

DCI Andy Richardson knew what had happened. He had been reading the police Gazette about some lunatic called the Primrose Hill killer in London and this was either him or a copycat killer. He managed to get hold of the officer in charge, a DCI Eric Fletcher. The time was now 6.55am. Andy told him about the grizzly find and how disgusted he was.

Fletcher asked him 'were they wearing any earrings.'

'Earrings? I don't know.'
'Would you take a look please, it's very important.'
DCI Andy Richardson went to the two bodies and noticed they had no earrings, none at all. They quickly dragged the Marina but found nothing. Their bags must be somewhere else.
'No DCI Fletcher, no earrings at all. Does this mean something?'
'It's the same scene as up here. What the hell is he doing in Bristol? Look, I will send you details of what we have, transcripts and videos but we have no damn clues as to who this guy is. The man leaves no clues, we do know he wears surgical gloves though and he kills quickly and then disappears just as quickly. I mean seriously, he really kills them almost within the hour. You won't find they have been sexually molested or touched, he doesn't touch them sexually at all.'
'I haven't established this yet Inspector Fletcher and if they have I will let you know sir.'
'The car he uses, well actually we think he uses a London black cab. He's used one before so maybe he used one of those, I wish I could do more to help but it would be a good idea to check your street CCTV network. It sounds like he may have used a taxi cab. Anyway if you could check it out and then could you let me know please it's very important that we know.'
DCI Andy Richardson did check the CCTV's and there were several black cabs available but there was only one that went to the Marina. Then he saw one woman get out for some reason and she went behind a container but a few minutes later he slowly began to drive off. He must have stopped behind some more containers because it was a while before he came in view again. The light was good in the Marina and he did get the number plate. He posted it straight away to all the Police forces, especially the Metropolitan Police in London to stop and apprehend the taxi owner. Amazingly they had his address within minutes.
DCI Eric Fletcher had the details and rang DC Ron Buckley. 'We have an address Ron lets go, but it won't be him. He's cloned a taxi before, let's face it with over twenty one thousand black cab drivers he can pick any he wants for a couple of days,

then change them again. Anyway he's been down to Bristol and killed two middle age women who had been friends all their lives.'

'Two of them, two sir. What the hell's the matter with him? He's clearly taking the bloody piss now. Christ sake he's gone bloody nuclear, we're going to lose count at this rate, how many more is he going to kill? There must be a clue somewhere. Look he has to leave something behind sir.'

'Well Ron, he has done.'

'What, what's he left behind sir.'

'Several dead women Ron and no trace of who he is, and this new clue with the taxi number is just another cloned number plate, I know it. He's one cunning clever man, but we will nail him because everyone leaves a clue somewhere, everyone sooner or later does. But we do have his DNA from his hat he left behind after trying to kill Abigail.'

The time now was 8.23am. Brian Hitchers was trying to wake up and rubbing the cobwebs from his eyes while his wife Beverly was still asleep. He could suddenly hear cars pulling up and then voices, he thought oh not again hoping he hadn't left the TV on in the lounge. At that same minute his front door of no 118 Spring Grove, Camden Town came crashing in. His taxi was on the front drive and then five police officers rushed up the stairs shouting 'Police! Stay where you are. Do not move, I repeat do not move stay where you are.'

For one mad moment he thought it was an episode of the Sweeny, until a huge policeman crashed into his bedroom followed by two more and a WPC, while his wife was still happily asleep.

DCI Fletcher and DC Buckley walked in behind the wake of the burley Police officers to see one man in his late forties and a woman about the same age being dragged down the stairs, each with a Police officer either side of them. They sat them down in their living room and started to question them on where the taxi had been, but it soon became apparent the man was not the Primrose killer for one thing he was only 5ft 6in tall and was as bald as a coot. He also walked with a limp due to having half his right leg blown off by a land mine in Iraq when he was in the army. With the money he received from his injuries he bought his taxi after studying for three years to pass the knowledge test to become a London cabbie. It soon became obvious his taxi plates had been cloned by the Primrose killer, this was getting to be a nasty habit. The police brushed him down and apologised, they tried to explain it was a mistake and all damages would be taken care of immediately.

Two weeks later one warm evening the time was 9.13 pm when the doorbell rang. Lovett wondered who the hell it was at this hour, he was sitting watching a DVD dressed in his shorts and a T-shirt. Putting on his dressing gown he went to the door but not before first looking through the spy hole. Seeing a very handsome man standing there smiling he thought to himself well he seems OK and opened the door, still making sure the security chain was on. A security chain is a waste of time because one good kick and the person would be in your home in a second. Suspiciously looking out of the gap in his door he said 'Yes, how can I help you and do you know what time it is' as he looked at his Rolex watch.

'Ah yes look I'm so sorry Simon, but we did meet some time ago at Ginger's, you know the club? I'm Derrick Green, you were three sheets to the wind at the time but you gave me your address, so here I am in London at a loose end so to speak. Oh yes, I had a goatee beard back then.'

'I'm sorry I can't remember you at all' said Lovett.

'And you did mention if I'm back in town again to drop in and say hi, so hi! Look the thing is Simon, I have some information regarding all these Notting Hill murders and I think I know the man who is doing it, but I need to talk with you or someone before I lose my mind about it. I don't quite know what to do for the best and you told me you're a journalist. So if you're not interested I can go to another national newspaper. This information I have is pretty damning to be honest and I think it may be worth a few quid. If you would sooner I take the information to someone else, well that's ok. Enjoy the rest of the evening and I'm sorry to have disturbed you I even have seven clear photographs of him, and also his address, look it's up to you.' He was waving a large brown envelope at the door.

Lovett looked confused 'is this true because as I mentioned, I can't even remember you.'

'To be honest it was a while ago now, and you were to put it mildly, pissed' he laughed.

Lovett looked again and saw the envelope. You look okay so come in and we can have a chat and a coffee. I hope you're not going to waste my time on this. Foolishly opening his door, he invited Alan in. 'Oh what's your name again, you said it's Derrick, yes it does ring a bell, but it must have been a while ago now.'

As Lovett turned around he realised this man was wearing surgical gloves, but it was too late, far too late. His fate was sealed in that one stupid act of misjudgement. He fancied the man like mad and that distracted him from the real issues at hand.

Alan had taken his right hand out of his pocket and shot Lovett with the stun gun in the middle of his neck. Lovett fell forward onto a chair in the hallway next to the bathroom door leading in from the hallway. Alan quickly jabbed a syringe into him containing 15mg of Rohypnol and then he manoeuvred him into the bath head first, where he managed to tip him into his bath quickly managing to secure his hands behind his back and his ankles too with thick strong garden ties. Lovett was 6ft 4in tall and weighed about seventeen stone. Grabbing Lovett's arms he tied them again by the wrists and then his ankles. Lovett looked strong and he didn't want a confrontation with a guy this size.

Quickly he gaffer taped his mouth, and then pushed him hard into the bath where he proceeded to fill the bath with water. When it reached the desired level he plunged a syringe again into his neck, it was Rohypnol again. There was about 10mg left in the syringe, and then he lifted Lovett's feet in the air while keeping his head submerged. Managing to turn him around in the bath Lovett was now on his back he wanted him to see him killing him, after all he deserved it, because he double crossed him.

Lovett thought what the hell is going on, he could see and hear but was unable to do anything due to his feet being held high above the bath. He managed to struggle that's all he could do, and then he felt his lungs beginning to burst. He knew who it was now and he could hear him shouting at him. Then he began to feel dozy as the drug kicked in. Alan let his feet down to speak with him.

'Simon, I did tell you not to print anything, yet you did behind my back, well that was a death sentence. I have no choice but to kill you now because you totally betrayed me.
Let me tell you that's not a nice feeling, so now this is your penalty. Oh don't worry I will phone your editor to let him know what has happened to you. I will also send some pictures of your body so maybe they will print those as well. The trouble with people like you is you just don't listen do you? You think you know it all, but you don't and now it's too late for you.'

Lovett could hear his voice it was muffled and Alan could tell he could hear because his eyes were pleading with him to stop what he was doing. He wanted to talk, but Alan wanted to kill.

'The daft thing is I was going to hand myself over to you after having a good think about it because what you said to me made good sense and I could have used the money for good causes, now you have ruined it for me and also for yourself.'

Lovett could still hear the muffled talk, a strange sound but he could not answer back, he was drowning. He wanted all this to stop, but the harder he tried to move the more he drowned, and then he passed out where he died. Taking fifteen slow minutes to drown. Simon Lovett was a big man yet Alan found he was easy to handle and he didn't struggle much, except for the last minute now it was over. The feeling had been of pure pleasure. Lovett was a nasty man he had rid the world of him but he did have one earring in his left ear which he took along with his Rolex watch. He also found his wallet containing two hundred pounds and a further three thousand pounds in a drawer in his bedroom along with his passport and private papers. There were also photographs of Lovett with several men at what could only be described as a homosexual orgy. Alan looked at these and then went into the bathroom and shouted at Lovett's dead body, 'you dirty bastard he shouted. I'm glad I killed you. What a stinking pervert' he shouted!

Alan also shouted 'you pervert idiot, now you have spoiled it for me. I wasn't going to kill you but you made me do it.' He took several pictures of Lovett's body in the bath. They looked a bit gruesome. It was Lovett's own fault, because after all he did warn him. He shouldn't have let him down. The pictures were posted by Lovett's mobile to his editor saying 'he let me down. So he had to pay the price for his betrayal.'

Alan checked he hadn't left any clues behind him and then he left the apartment. It was time he went home to plan another murder. Killing Lovett didn't mean anything, it was far better to do another woman although the world would be a better place without the likes of Lovett and he did have one earring he took which doubly annoyed him, he wanted a pair. Still he had his Rolex watch and three thousand pounds in cash. He would enjoy spending that money in Paris.

CHAPTER TWENTY TWO

Alan Reed looked at his list when he got back home from killing Lovett. Suddenly on his list he came across a woman called Lucy Raymond who was a receptionist at the Houses of Parliament. She was aged 49, or so she said. She was a divorcee of some five years with no children but she did have a goldfish called Eddie who she claimed was the current love of her life. The next morning he would phone her.

Now he felt a little sad about killing Lovett, but he had let him down and he knew that Lovett was going to use him to make money out of him and he would ghost write a book and get the film rights to his life's story. How could he write that rubbish in the paper about him coming in giving himself up to the newspaper with Lovett in charge?

'The next day after a good night's sleep he reached for his phone. 'Hi is this Lucy, Lucy Raymond? It is, good, this is Doctor Paul Sinclair. We spoke some weeks ago now, but I had to go to France and I have only just arrived back. I had been thinking about you, in fact I only kept your number Lucy as I came off the site. I wonder if you would like to meet up for a drink or a meal, whatever you like. You choose if you like Lucy, sorry to get to the point, but you may have found someone by now, a nice looking lady such as yourself wouldn't be on her own for long I can tell.'

Lucy Raymond was thrilled, a Doctor, but she could hardly remember the conversation. She had wondered why he had gone off the site, but she had been seeing someone else for seven weeks. However, he was just a carpenter and this guy was a Doctor. So to her it was a no brainer. 'Yes a meal sounds lovely, when are you thinking of Paul?'

'Shall we say tomorrow evening, oh do you like Italian? You do that's great. I know of a nice place in Soho called Gino's. If I send a taxi for you say at 7.45 pm, he can pick you up and then pick me up on the way into town, so that way we can have a drink without either of us driving. You have to give me your address, 22, Slough Road, Bayswater, thanks for that. I live in Blenheim Crescent, Notting Hill. I have just bought it only last week so I need a decorator, if you know of anyone, let me know.' He laughed.'

'As a matter of fact I do know one or two' she said.

'The taxi man is called Jimmy and he will beep you three times when he arrives. He's a nice man and he will pick us up later and will take you back home, is this okay for you Lucy? I know it's a bit sudden but as I said I thought you may have found someone by now as it's been a long time, you haven't found anyone? That's great. I will see you tomorrow evening. I look forward to that'

Lucy Raymond was as pleased as you could be. This guy was a Doctor and a great looking guy he has money, lives in Notting Hill, what more does a girl need she thought. Terry the carpenter who had been taking her out was now going to become history well hopefully.

Anyway he lived in a crappy rented flat with a very old dog which was now on his last legs and it smelt bad. Then again he was always round his elderly mother's house doing odd jobs and things for her. However he did have one large asset and that was between his legs, but you get tired of someone with no intellectual stimulation. Having good sex is one thing, but there's more to a life than that. Half the time she had to pay as he never seemed to have any money. She would see how this panned out and it would make a change to have a meal out which was bought for her and also being picked up in a carriage too and being driven back in one, well it was a Hackney Carriage after all. Who wouldn't want to go out with a good looking Doctor with money?

George Penny was talking with DCI Eric Fletcher in George's office. Eric was passing as he has just seen his snout in the Red Bull about some information not twenty yards away from where George was situated. So he'd rang George who said pop in my office for a drink Eric, which he did do. Now both had a coffee supplied without asking by Julia who was also in on the conversation. She asked him 'so is there any more news about the latest developments on the Primrose killer Eric?'

Eric had nothing more to add, he was going mad with frustration at having no new clues to go on, but as he said to Julia, 'we have no further information on the man and his whereabouts,' it was driving everyone mad. 'Well we know he must be a local man' said Eric, 'because, he knew the area so well.'

Suddenly, Eric had a call from DC Buckley who said 'shit can you believe this sir? They have only found Lovett in his bath, he's been murdered the same as the rest of them by drowning. How the killer had got in was not hard to figure out. Lovett must have let him in, and then the Primrose killer drowned him. Lovett was a big man, he stood at six feet four inches tall and you could see he was a strong man. I heard he worked out five times a week at Step Ups, the local but very expensive gym, so the Killer must be a strong man to deal with Lovett.'

George was in on the conversation, 'hey look George I have to go, and this mad bastard has struck again for Christ sake. Let's hope the guy has left us a clue, even a tit bit will be a start but this shit is clever George, so here comes another bloody night without any sleep. Do I look knackered' said Eric. 'Don't answer that and don't give me any pitying looks Julia.' She laughed.

'Well it goes with the job Eric, we know that one don't we George?' said Julia.

When DCI Fletcher arrived at the apartment there were Police and newspaper reporters all over the place. When DC Buckley saw Eric he told him 'sir it's the same scene as the rest of them, the poor man must have known what was going on it was a terrible way to go. You know when I think of drowning through your nostrils it makes me feel ill sir. He's a cruel twisted bastard, but why did he kill Lovett? Usually its women, all I can think is Lovett was a gay man, maybe that's the clue, it's not his normal procedure is it sir.'

'Christ sake Ron what's bloody normal then, have you been drinking again.'

'Sir it is 11.35 pm and it's my night off, and yes to answer your question I have had two pints and a steak and chips down the White Lion. I was with a young lady who I was about to invite back to my flat who is now very pissed off. This guy makes this all look so easy, the more he kills the easier it seems to be for him. He sent his editor these pictures he took on Lovett's phone and told him to call the pathetic Police. You know what? I do feel pathetic now, really pathetic sir. Most of all I feel angry really angry.'

DCI Fletcher knew that the more annoyed you become the more it took you in the wrong direction. Editor Sam Elliot was distraught when he'd received the pictures on his phone showing Lovett dead in his bath. It didn't seem possible that anyone could do that to him and after all he was a very big man and strong too. Because as he knew only too well, he went to the gym most days and sometimes he went with him. You could plainly see he was very fit. After viewing the pictures again he had rang the police. DC Buckley had the call first then he rushed round to Lovett's flat but no one could do anything for him. DC Buckley managed to get hold of DCI Fletcher. Lovett was very dead and looked a mess. It was only in his final moments he started to struggle, sadly he had banged his head and face a few times on the rim of his bath in his desperate struggle to live, it hadn't worked. His left eye was swollen and closed. Also his nose looked as though it was broken and the tip of his tongue had been bitten in two. It was not a picture the paper could use. The police knew Lovett was a complete pain in the arse, but no-one deserved to die like that. So whoever killed him, must also be very fit and a very strong person.

DC Ron Buckley said 'Sir why did he kill Lovett, now I reckon he knew his killer how else did he gain entrance to his flat, there is clearly no struggle by the door or anywhere else apart from the bathroom and very little signs of a struggle there either. Somehow he must have known the killer that's how he managed to get in.'

'Well Ron we know he had phoned Lovett more than once. I reckon your spot on about that. It seemed to me he upset our killer and what about that statement Lovett made about the killer who according to him he was going to bring him in. That would have given him hero status and maybe also making him a lot of money too. Now we won't find out unless we apprehend the killer. Jesus this killer is clever, mean and more dangerous than ever. We have to get this man before he kills again. If you ask me this was about money the same old story the route of all evil. Gut instinct tells me it was a double cross in some way.'

CHAPTER TWENTY THREE

Lucy Raymond was sitting by the window she looked at her watch, the time said 7.50pm when around the corner came a London black cab. It stopped outside and sure enough he beeped three times. She excitedly stood up and went to the door after saying goodnight to her goldfish Eddie. She closed her front door and locked it. The Taxi was waiting for her she walked the ten yards to the taxi as she stepped inside the driver said good evening madam. She answered good evening back and closed the door. She put her seat belt on and the Taxi indicated and then it slowly drove away.

She asked him 'where are you going now?' The driver replied 'to Blenheim Crescent, Notting Hill to pick up Dr Sinclair.' She was pleased, but after five minutes the driver pulled into a lay-by and said 'I'm sorry miss, the seat belt light has come on again, I have to fix it but not to worry it won't take a moment.' He got out and opened the back door where she sat. He fiddled with the belt and said 'there you are its fixed'. He smiled at her then shot her with his stun gun. She collapsed in a heap and quickly he injected 10 mg of Rohypnol into her arm and bound her wrists behind her back with the garden ties. Then he did the same to her ankles he also speedily gaffer taped her mouth. He checked her earrings. Now they were nice, large gold hoops. Pleased, he pulled them out putting them in his pocket. He laid her on the floor of the cab. But this time he drove the Taxi back to his lock up, and then he injected her with the Rohypnol again which turned her into a sleeping Zombie. He used four times the dose, about 16gms this time. Waiting until 2.20am he set off again, this time she was going in the Camden Lock. By the time he arrived the time was now 2.48am. He made sure no one else was about then he slipped her into the canal with her bag where she quickly disappeared. This time he had put extra weights around her neck in a supermarket bag. She never made a sound and after a few bubbles all went quiet it was as though she never existed at all.

This spooked him a little it was just too quick for him, he hardly got any satisfaction from killing her. At the same time he could not hang around or he would be caught, and he was not ready to be caught yet. Turning one last time to where he put her in the canal there was no sign of her none at all, he felt weird about it.

Slowly turning back to his Taxi he simply drove home, locked his Taxi in his lock up garage under the railway arches and went home to his bed. He put the earrings in his jewellery box, sniffed his box and went to sleep. Job done he slept like a log.

In the very early hours of the morning a post office worker called Chris Andrews was on his way to work as always, going the same way past the Camden Lock only because it was a short cut to the post office. Chris was a post office sorter and the time was now four twenty two. Finishing his cigarette he flicked it into the canal watching it glow through the air until it landed in the water with a fizzing sound. It was then he saw what looked like the soles of two feet poking out of the water. Laughing, he thought what the hell is it, so he went to investigate. When he saw the feet he realised they were human feet. Quickly he rang the police who arrived within ten minutes and the forensic team fifty minutes later, along with DCI Eric Fletcher and DC Ron Buckley who both stepped into their forensic white plastic suits. It was obvious who did it. 'This guy has to be caught Ron, he's going to kill all the single women in this area if we can't stop him. Jesus we need a break on this, someone must know who he is. Mind you all of us Police investigator officers say that, always.'

DC Ronald Buckley noticed his boss was getting more and more upset because again no-one had seen or heard this lunatic putting this poor woman into the canal. Now it was the same scene as before. They searched the whole area and found nothing. The body of Lucy Raymond gave off no clues either, and anyway the water destroys most clues if there were any. She was a nice looking lady. They found her bag after dredging the water, there was nothing. It just had her wallet and her house keys but no phone and any money she had was missing.

She did have £65 but Alan had taken it. They had also noticed her earrings had gone or she was not wearing any at the time, which was doubtful. They went round to her house and searched it, but they found nothing, only her diary which had an entry saying 7.45pm Dr Paul Sinclair and a mobile phone number which belonged to one of the murdered girls as he now used their mobile phones all the time he would no doubt use hers too. They found details of Terry the carpenter who had been taking her out, he was shocked to hear she was going to see someone else and not best pleased about it either. Then he thought or kidded himself, well if he was a Doctor maybe she was seeing him about a health problem which she wanted to keep to herself. He was visibly upset about the way she died. He needed answers but they had no idea who killed her, along with all the other women and one man, Lovett.

Terry the carpenter asked if he could take away Eddie her goldfish. When he went to pick the bowl up Eddie was floating on the top of the water, he was dead. After all he was seven and a half years old. At least that's what she had told him.

When George Penny heard about the latest killing he was more determined than ever to try and help catch this mad man, but the Police still had very little to go on.

George said to DCI Fletcher, 'the trouble is he has no sex with any of the women so he leaves no DNA. All the time he wears surgical gloves and he picks them up in his cab, except the first one Helen Burk. He then kills them in a matter of a few minutes and dumps them the same, or almost the same in the water. This man must be a real hater of women and for some reason only known to him he collects their earrings.'

'I know George, and it's so frustrating,' said DCI Fletcher.

'Look Eric, let me go into the house of the first victim Helen Burk. I want to get the feel of this lady and let me see inside of her car and any possessions she had with her that night. I also want to talk with the neighbour. I'm going to ask anyway, but I feel it's best I run it through with you first Eric, are you ok with this?'

'Yes, George go and do it, what the bloody hell have we to lose and sometimes a fresh pair of eyes can see things others don't, so go along and try and find out if we have missed something and I really hope you do mate. As far as we know Helen was the only one who actually ate out in a restaurant with this man and saw him twice. With all the others, he sees them for what seems minutes, maybe we missed something so you go for it George.'

George called round to see Iris who was Helen Burk's neighbour. Introducing himself he asked her 'if she wouldn't mind going over the events again on that night Helen went missing, and what was this man like as she was the only person who had seen him. He told her not to worry, but sometimes going over the event even months can reveal new evidence when the mind has time to slow down.'

'Well he was a nice looking man, tall about six feet or perhaps a little higher. He had a nice modern dark blue jacket on and he was wearing, I think you call them Chinos. He had dark sort of wavy hair and it was greyish at the sides and he looked like an actor or a model, in fact he walked like a model would walk.'

'How do you mean Iris, like a model would walk?'

'Well he sort of marched up to her door very straight and with purpose, but when she opened her door he stepped back and sort of turned around like a model would do, holding on to the corner of his jacket as though he was showing it off to her. She was looking at him and he seemed to turn around for her approval. I know that sounds daft, but he did and I saw her laugh. And then she put her arm through his and she walked to his posh car. He opened the door for her like she was a star, he even saluted her and she laughed and then she got in. He walked round to his side and got in; they talked for a couple of minutes and then they drove off. That was the last time I saw her, god bless her.' Iris wiped away a tear and looked so sad but she was extremely helpful in what she had said. George had recorded the conversation on his mobile phone.

George thanked her and said 'look Iris, I'm just going to take another look in her house. You can come in with me as well if you wish to.' She declined.

Looking all over the house there was nothing to indicate any date she may have had or been on, but he had spoken earlier to Katie Parish, the Nurse Practise manager who was also Helen's friend and workmate. She had told him he wrote down his name and address also his car number plate, and gave it to Helen as a mark of his trust. If so where was the note unless somehow the killer had taken it back? He didn't believe that and there was no note in her handbag, but he decided to look in Helen's Mini Cooper car. The car was neat and tidy, the same as the rest of the house, there was nothing to see so he went back into her house to look again. Then he noticed her medical bag under the telephone table in the hallway. Opening up the bag he only found all sorts of pills, bandages, syringes and various medicines. Then he saw her appointment diary, he flipped through it for the day she met the killer and there was nothing written down, but there was a piece of the page for that day which had been torn off.

Going back to her car to take another look inside he used the car key to unlock the door and sat in to take another look but he found nothing. Now frustrated, he locked up her mini and went back into her house. He dropped the keys to her mini on the work top but the keys hit the top and fell onto the tiled floor. Then he noticed the small Mini car attached to her key ring which was a mini replica of her car. The small boot had popped open, in fact even the small doors opened too it was like a miniature toy. Inside the boot was a piece of paper which matched the ripped off portion and it had his name and address and a mobile phone number but he knew it was all going to lead to nothing now at least he did have a sample of his hand writing. Checking the writing against her own writing in her diary it was obvious it was not hers, so presumably it was the killers.

Iris had said he marched out of his car and up to Helen's front door. She had said he was also a good looking man as though he could be a male model. This made him think, perhaps he was? He also saluted Helen as she got into his car. Okay, maybe it was a funny gesture but many a true word and action has been seen and heard to be the truth? So was this man an ex army man? He seemed to fit the bill in action, words and mannerisms. Also using the term 'obey orders,' then the saying 'it's a boner,' which means in army terms a pointless action. Then there was his fitness, he seemed to be very strong.

'George, have you anything yet on this mad man' asked Julia.

'Honey I just have a feeling this guy is ex military, maybe a soldier.'

'Why do you think that George, you have mentioned that before? Have you found something out?'

'It's just a hunch babe, a feeling in the way this guy moves.'

'So tell me why you think so George. Let's see babe, write this down.'

1. 'He has used military terms a couple of times.'
2. 'Obeying orders.'
3. 'It's a boner, meaning pointless.'
4. 'He's a good six foot tall and stands straight, that may mean nothing.'
5. 'He now uses a Taxi, let's go back to when he first used the Taxi, and then check out the auction house to see who bought a used Taxi that day.'
6. 'A wheelchair I have no idea where he got that from.'
7. 'Dating site, but then he snatched one young WPC from the street.'
8. 'He goes for women between 40 and 60.'
9. 'He hates women of that age.'
10. 'He collects earrings as trophies.'

'Julia, why does he collect the earrings? There has to be a reason for that. Most serial killers collect things from their victims, almost as if they still control them. Also, he mostly keeps their mobile phones to use so no trace on him. You know babe, this guy operates as though he is on a mission and I reckon more than ever he is ex military. By the way he moves quickly he doesn't hang around, because he meets, greets and kills all within virtually the same hour. He seems to have nerves of steel because he plans it all out, well mostly. So far he's messed up a couple of times, so he has taken his eye off the ball. The thing is we can't tell every woman not to go on a dating site can we. DCI Eric Fletcher should have some DNA from the hat he dropped as he ran off after dumping Abigail into the canal, so maybe there will be something on the police records, let's hope so babe.'

'So where do we start George?' Asked Julia 'I reckon the car auctions is a good start. Do you want me to check out the dates, I mean they can't have Taxis for sale every week can they?'

'Yes babe, can you do that for me' said George 'and you're right, I think it's about once a month, remember I bought one too and it was once a month at that time. Another thing where does he keep it garaged? I bet he doesn't keep it at his house that would be too obvious.'

Julia found out the killer picked up her friend the hairdresser Lisa Davey in a Taxi about eight weeks ago. She rang up the car auctions and found they had an auction nine weeks ago. They had a list of 11 Taxis for sale and they had a list of 11 people who bought the taxis. She was given the name of Belinda Mann, but she was away on holiday for the next ten days, she was the one who could help her. 'At this moment we won't have the details but Belinda will as soon as she comes back and at this moment we are really short of staff. If you need a job pop in, we need another three girls' said the manager Mr Alex Bexley and laughed.

CHAPTER TWENTY FOUR

The next morning George rang DCI Fletcher. 'Eric, have you any DNA on this hat yet.'

'Yes George we have and the bastard is not on our list, not at all. However his DNA is on the cap from the second victim Lisa Davey and it matches the DNA from the Abigail case, so this puts him at two of the crime scenes, one a murder the other an attempted murder.'

'So where do we go from here Eric? I'm a bit stumped but I may have an idea. Do you guys, and this is a slim chance, do you guys get access to Military DNA?'

'Why George, have you found out something? Go on tell me, we are working this together remember, don't you dare leave me in the dark on this.'

'I just have a hunch this bastard is ex army and maybe, just maybe he may have a record in the army. This is a long shot probably nothing to go on it's a wild guess Eric.'

'No George, the army keeps its nut cases to itself and doesn't like to share their DNA base with anyone. Anyway you could try MI5 they may help to persuade them' he laughed.

George said 'you know what? I may just try that Eric.'

Eric laughed, 'well good luck with that one then mate, they just laugh at us. I have asked a couple of times before in the past and they never get back, which is a bit of a clue.'

When DCI Fletcher had gone, he made a phone call asking Julia to stop all calls to him as he wanted to speak with MI5.

'Hello how can we help you?'

'I would like to speak with Sir John Kingsley please as soon as possible.'

'Sir John is away until tomorrow. Who shall I say called sir?'

'George Penny PI. Can you please get him to call me, it's rather urgent.'

'Certainly sir is there any particular time?'

'Mornings as early as he likes will do fine. I know he likes to start early the same as me when the mind is the sharpest. Oh and thank you.' He put the phone down.

'What can he do babe, can he help you?' asked Julia.

'Honey he can do anything, he's the one who got me to Spain to see to you in that Jet plane.'

'God George, please don't remind me that was a bad day all round. Anyway so what can he do?'

'What can he do? What can't he do? He can get us the DNA we want, that's if of course he's on any forces database and I have a feeling he is, however he may not be. It's just a hunch babe, just a strong hunch. I think we may get a good result. I do have a positive feeling about this.'

'I thought you said the army keeps itself to itself George, so why would they help MI5.'

'The army needs MI5 babe and they do work hand in glove a lot of the time, they need each other for obvious reasons of security. All I can do is to ask.'

CHAPTER TWENTY FIVE

Alan Reed was thinking about the women on his list but there was one woman who he really wanted to kill, and that woman was Fiona Blackwood. She almost had him caught and he was not going to let it go without him killing her. There was no way he could let a woman get the better of him not now after all he had done. No she was going to be the next one on his list and he wanted to do it as soon as possible. So he rang Fiona's mobile number but it had been changed, which was not surprising in the past circumstances. That evening he decided to drive past her house and see if she was in. The time was now 7.10pm and he set off for a quick cruise around in his VW estate car. Finding Fiona's road again he parked a good way away so he could stroll past and get his bearings once more. As he came closer to her house he pulled his baseball cap a little lower but he suddenly saw her talking with a neighbour. They were in the front garden and it looked as though they were talking about gardening.

    Fiona was wearing old jeans and there were mud patches on her knees where she had been kneeling. You could see she was planting flowers in the border running under her window and she was also by the looks of it making up a couple of hanging baskets. Her neighbour was handing her a drink it looked like white wine. Walking by he was pretending to speak into his mobile as he passed them, it seemed obvious she was on her own. So he carried on walking past the house and on turning the corner he could see the house had a large back garden and there was a lane leading past all the back gardens. Walking along the lane he saw the numbers on the back gates, he found number 16, so thinking quickly he tried her back gate which was open. Stepping into the garden the French windows at the back of her house were half open and there were flowers in a tray ready to re-plant. The back garden had a border running down both sides with various flowers which needed to be sorted out. Quickly walking up to the French windows he let himself in. She still had her front door open and he could hear her talking to the neighbour they were laughing. But now he moved silently upstairs and found the back bedroom was more or less a store room. Finding the main bedroom, he found the bathroom next to the back bedroom. So he decided to wait for his moment in the back bedroom. There wasn't long to wait.

Fiona was now becoming impatient, she wanted to get on with her planting, but Mrs Denning from next door was droning on and on about nothing in particular as per usual.

'Look Gloria I really am sorry but I do have to get going. I've got an early start tomorrow and I need to get my plants in, so I'm sorry but I do have to get a move on.' She handed her wine glass back and said 'Thanks for the wine'

'Oh sorry Fiona, of course go on. Its okay for me as I don't work' she laughed 'anyway they will look lovely. But you do have such good taste you know.'

'Thanks Gloria but I have to go, it was lovely chatting though.'

Alan looked at his watch which now said 8.30pm now it was beginning to get dark. While he waited a while longer he heard her come up the stairs. She walked into the bathroom and started to fill the bath she needed a long soak after all that planting. She wasn't used to her body being put through its paces by gardening and was surprised by how tired and aching she felt. She poured herself a large glass of red wine and when the bath was half full she checked out the temperature making sure it was not too hot and then slipped into the water thinking oh yes this is bliss. Taking a long sip of her wine she closed her eyes to feel the effects and the warmth of the water and started to think of the long holiday she had booked. Suddenly she heard the bathroom door shut, she opened her eyes, she saw Alan standing there smiling at her.

'Who the hell are you, get out go on get out!' She suddenly sat bolt upright, but he hit her so hard on her head with a rock he found in the garden that she immediately slumped under the water semi conscious with blood now oozing from her head and turning the bath water red. Grabbing her arm he turned her halfway round. Quickly tying her wrists together behind her back with the garden ties and he did the same with her ankles. He gaffer taped her face after first drying it, then he covered her mouth but left her nostrils free and her eyes so she could see him. The water was still turning a crimson colour as the rock he hit her which had split the side of her head open near her temple the gash was open and bleeding badly. Turning on the tap until the bath was almost full, she came round to see and feel what he was doing to her. There was a look of triumph on his face as he spoke to her.

'You young lady should not have betrayed me, now I've had to work hard to come back and send you on your way. Oh yes you are going on a journey, but first dear, oh dear I almost forgot' he laughed 'let me see your earrings, yes these will do nicely, hey what lovely little crosses they are. I take it they are gold aren't they? Yes of course they are they will go towards my collection so thank you. Look, in my opinion its best you don't struggle, so Fiona please let the water do its thing. It won't take long, so you have a nice long enjoyable journey to the afterlife. The water is warm. All the others had cold murky water to die in. At least you won't be cold so you're very lucky indeed, let me tell you.'

She looked at him and her eyes were now filled with terror. Her head was moving frantically from side to side. Christ sake she didn't want to die, her head was killing her and the pain was severe. I'm not going to die said her eyes and then she started to struggle like mad. She remembered what George Penny had said to her 'it is best if you could take a couple of weeks off as this nut case could come back.' Why the hell didn't she bloody well listen to good advice, but she wished she had done now. She had booked her holiday two weeks too late. Now she was thrashing about and trying to stand up to get out of her bath, but she just couldn't manage it and kept slipping. The water had turned a muddy red colour due to the large gash in her head. It was pouring out her life blood and now she felt very dizzy, but she was so desperate to live. But he just watched her struggles and smiled back at her.

'Oh dear Fiona, will you please listen to me, let me help you out please.' Now he bent over the bath and lifted her ankles high above her head, making her sink under the water. Standing next to the bath he held her there for ten minutes. She tried to kick out and fought as hard as she could. She knew what was happening. It was certain she was going to drown as the water would not come back out of her nose. She was hurting now, her lungs hurt, she tried to yell out but she couldn't breathe. She was now in great pain and started to go dizzy again. There was a huge lump in her throat which would not go away and it hurt her so much. Then her nose seemed to burst, she felt her own blood gush out, she was suffocating, but then thankfully she passed out.

Alan now felt elated. He had rid the world of this woman who had betrayed him in his own mind. Looking around he was certain he left no clues. So he went through her bag and found out where she worked. He took her mobile and then her money, altogether there was £298. He also took her diary but he noticed she had written about some guy called George Penny who was a Private Investigator. It had his phone number and his address. In the local rag there had been a write up about what happened that night the Taxi driver was grabbed by George Penny and his assistant a woman called Julia. It had explained the part that George had played in trying to apprehend him, it was the Taxi driver he had sent who was grabbed. Well he thought the guy he saw was a big man but his assistant was a very attractive looking woman and he thought maybe she was his life partner. Either way one of them deserved to die for what they had tried to do to him. Now he decided it was going to be this woman called Julia and if he had the chance, the man as well.

Fiona had written down everything she had said to this George Penny, it was all there and he was glad he had killed her, very glad indeed, but now he wanted to get this Julia bitch. The next day he rang George Penny's number. Julia answered the phone. 'DCI enquiries how can we help you.'

'I would like to see if you could help to find my wife who has been gone now for seven weeks, she just upped and went. I'm very worried. So can I come in and see you please. Look I can't talk much on the phone, it's very difficult with people all around me, and it's very embarrassing.'

'Of course you can come in, look can you make it say tomorrow at 10am? I can take your details and pass them on to the boss, he won't be back until later in the evening, so can we say at 10am tomorrow, err its Mr?'

'Oh Sorry, it's Mr Wallace, John Wallace. Oh dear look I can't see you tomorrow at 10 am. But I can do say 5pm that's the only time I have, but all I have is an hour. Will this be okay with you, if so is there anywhere to park near you?'

'Yes John there is, ok look make it 5pm and you can park around the back. There are four car spaces so it's not a problem. If you give me all the details which are in strict confidence as you will have gathered, I'll make a start.'

'That's great; I will see you at 5pm. I will bring all my details of my wife I have two recent photographs of her and all relevant paperwork relating to her.'

Alan was pleased she would be on her own. And now he would teach this George Penny a lesson which was not to mess with things that don't concern him, and now his partner would pay the price for his meddling in somebody else's affairs. Why can't these people leave things alone?

CHAPTER TWENTY SIX

George woke up early, he wanted to get hold of Sir John Kingsley from MI5 and he knew he always started work at five thirty am. Ringing a number at MI5, 'yes how can I help you, Kingsley here?'

'John its George Penny, I desperately need to talk with you.'

'Good god George, how are you? I heard you were in China, how did that go, how very cultural for you, it's not that good over there is it old chap?'

'You can say that again, but how the hell did you know I was over there John.'

'George please that's a daft thing to say. Look I'm incredibly busy with this entire damn Jihadist running about these days, well it doesn't leave a lot of time, and it's virtually 24/7. So what do you want me to do for you, it must be something you can't deal with' he laughed 'and you still owe me some of your time George, do you remember?'

'Yes John, I can still remember and still intend to keep my word too, but look can you get hold of the army's DNA base? I need to check out a hunch of mine, it's to do with this Primrose killer chap. I have a feeling he's ex army and we do have some of his DNA, well we think we may have it, but the police say the army won't help them, they say each to their own which is bloody stupid.'

'So George, the local plod has nothing on this guy, no name, nothing and how many has he killed now, its six so far is it not?'

'Yes, so far, but this guy is out of control and he won't stop until he's stopped, so if I get this recent DNA we have over to you, could you please run it through for me and help me get his name? There might just as well be no name, he may not have been in the military at all it's just a hunch, which so far has been pretty good to me John.'

'Ok George, bring it to the Red Bull say at 2pm and we can go from there but if there is a name then it didn't come from us, you understand this don't you?'

'Perfectly, all I need is a name; I will take care of the rest myself we have to stop this maniac. Anyway I will see you later in the pub. Oh this conversation didn't take place' he laughed. George kissed Julia goodbye 'see you later babe.'

Alan Reed pulled into one of the car parking spaces at 4.55pm at the back of George Penny's office and walked around to the front office door, the time now said 5pm. He knocked on the door and walked into the office.

'Come in' shouted Julia. She was sat behind the large desk, looked up and said 'hi, Mr John Wallace is it, please take a seat.'

'Good afternoon yes, John Wallace we spoke earlier, is the boss back yet?' asked Alan.

Julia was struck by this man's good looks and he looked very fit, but what struck her first was the question why would a woman leave a nice looking man like him? There must be something odd here. Still she thought who am I to judge? 'No I'm sorry, he had to go out and won't be back until much later but you can fill me in on the details, so when you're ready?' She switched on the recorder and sat back.

'Oh something smells nice, the coffee I mean.'

'Oh I'm so sorry, would you like a coffee I have the percolator on the go.'

'You read my mind' he laughed 'yes please but only if you're having one or I will feel as though I have put on you.'

'Don't worry I have to have a coffee at this time of the day too. She brought over two coffee cups and set them down. How do you have your coffee milk, cream, black? I have black at this time, it helps me focus' she laughed.

'Oh cream for me please.' As she turned round to pick up the percolator, he quickly tipped about 15gm of Rohypnol into her cup. She brought the coffee over and poured it into both cups then she added the milk. So far he had touched the door handle and the chair but not the cup. He would wipe everything clean of prints afterwards.

'Right John, is it okay to call you John? That's good it makes it more comfortable to chat,' she put a sugar cube in her cup and then stirred it and took a sip. 'Oh this is good' she said, as he did the same.

She asked him various details of his wife, her name, height, hair colour, where she worked if at all, what car did she have? She took another drink of coffee and asked him if she has been seeing anyone else, then she started to see double. She put the coffee cup down and said 'oh wow I feel a bit woozy' and then she fell forward onto the desk. She saw everything in double but she couldn't move. She wanted to sleep so badly she had to let go, and then she passed out.

Quickly standing up he put on a pair of surgical gloves and went to work. Locking the office door he cleaned the office where he had been, then he tied Julia up and gaffer taped her, the same as the rest of the women. When she was secure he checked out the back where he had parked his VW Estate. It was parked near the back door and seeing it was clear he opened the back of the Estate and carried her out. Putting her into the back he covered her up, she was gaffer taped around her mouth and if she moved about he would deal with her with the stun gun. Now he decided he was going to leave her until much later. The plan was she was going in the Thames because he decided it would be a change and also a challenge, but he knew she would sleep for hours yet because she had about three times the dosage. He wanted this George Penny to realise that he, Alan Reed the Primrose killer, had got away with killing his partner. He wanted him to respect him. Seeing her earrings he removed them, he held Julia's gold hoops in his hand and thought these are really thick hoops, they must have cost a lot. They were a double pair and he was well pleased with his find.

The day before at Putney Wharf he had hired a small motor cruiser. Turning up at the wharf to collect his cruiser he'd been handed the keys. Then he was shown how to operate the boat which was easy it had a forward and backward gear and that was it, a simple manoeuvre. After stepping into the boat he got his bearings and then putting the boat into forward gear he set off. However, after five minutes he'd returned back to the wharf, telling the surprised owner he had to pop out for about an hour or probably a lot less and would be back. He had forgotten to post a valuable parcel he'd left in his car and should be no longer than that. Leaving the boat in a mooring he set off to post his parcel. What he did do was go to a key cutter in a shop called Safe Keys and Shoe repairs which was just a few minutes away in Kew. He managed to get a couple of keys cut for the motor cruiser for later the next day, because he had planned to kidnap Julia and throw her into the Thames after teasing her partner George Penny. This was a moment he was going to enjoy. Then he was going to steal the motor cruiser at night, after all he had the key it would be easy.

Having hired the boat for a period of three hours after a cruise around the Thames he brought the boat back to Putney Wharf and handed the keys back to the owner then he left. There was a large car park nearby yet he saw no CCTV cameras around anywhere. His idea was to come back at night about 10pm, and then he would steal the boat and dump Julia in the Thames near Battersea Bridge. But he would have to keep her quiet for a few hours so he took her back to his home. He placed a black hood over her face while she just slept; there was plenty of air to breathe so she would be okay until later. He had to leave her in the back of the Estate, she had no chance of escape and it would save him from being seen. His driveway was a long one big enough for four cars but he parked it next to his kitchen door. In doing so he could hear any noise from the car but she was tied and gagged so she had no chance. Putting her earrings in with the rest of his collection made him smile; they were lovely they smelt good too. He'd managed to pick up her bag with some perfume in and had her phone from her bag plus £137. So he decided to use this to taunt George, he felt pleased with himself. Happily he wanted to show this idiot man how easy it was to steal his woman. Now he laughed at how easy it had been. What he didn't realise was George had inserted a tracker device in Julia's phone so he could track her anytime. There was also one in her watch. That's because she had been abducted before which was a nightmare for them both and it was not something he wished to happen again to either of them.

At 10.33pm Alan decided to drive to Putney Wharf, steal the boat and taunt George before he tipped her into the Thames, he laughed and felt well pleased with himself.

George had to leave early that morning because he had to see DCI Eric Fletcher and get a DNA sample, then take it to Kingsley who would do his best to get a match from the military if there was indeed a match. After all it was only a hunch that he had and he may not have been in the army at all, it could mean nothing, but they did have two matches from two different men's hats.

George met with DCI Fletcher and his partner DC Ron Buckley, he saw DCI Fletcher in his office at Notting Hill Police station.

'George it's most inappropriate to give you this sample and I hope you realise this, I could be in deep shit if it ever got out. So take good care of it, or my pension will quickly disappear.'

'Eric, please, no-one will know it came from you I promise you, but you will be the first one to know. If we get a name and then an address I want you to smash this bastard's door in because find the missing earrings and you will have your man.'

Eric handed over the DNA he said 'I hope you're right George, now piss off and try and get a match. I seem to remember your hunches were legendry, let's hope they still are. Look for Christ sake we need a break on this George, because yesterday Fiona Blackwood was found dead in her bath, the same scene. He'd tipped off her office with the details and laughed, can you believe this bloody madman?'

'Oh no Eric, I told her to go away take a holiday, and always keep her eyes open I had a feeling he would come for her, and now he has.'

Sir John Kingsley was sat in the Red Bull with a large Irish. He was reading the Times and squinting as he'd forgotten his glasses again. But still, he thought his shares were doing okay.

'Every time I see you John you seem to have an Irish in front of you, have you got shares in that whiskey?' George laughed.

'As a matter of fact, yes I have, and according to this report in the Times they're going good at the moment up by 4 % so the dividends will pay for a very nice holiday this year.'
'Well it's okay for some,' laughed George.
'Now then George envy doesn't suit you. So then have you brought me the sample? If so let me have it and let's see if we can get you a match, that's of course if there is any. I may have a result in about six hours so all you need is a name and if possible an address. I think we can do that if we have a match, if there is you never got the information from MI5, is that understood and I'm bloody serious on this George. Anyway we may not be able to get you a match if he's not on the data base.'
'Yes John I understand perfectly and thank you, I owe you a favour on this one and if there is no DNA then it's back to the drawing board. Did you know this bastard killed a Lawyer yesterday called Fiona Blackwood? She had a date with this man about three weeks ago now, but she became suspicious of him and because I did some good work for her office a couple of years ago, she remembered and came to see me. She told me all about it and we set a trap for him, but the crafty bastard sent another Taxi to pick her up. I jumped on the man but it wasn't him and I told her to go away for a couple of weeks, you know take a holiday. I told her he had gone back and murdered another woman who had managed to get away from him, and he went back to her and he drowned her in a bath. He's just done the same at Fiona's home. He also did that shit reporter Simon Lovett, and killed him in his bath as well. Look this is a clever dude and I want him. He killed Julia's friend in the same manner in the canal, but the weirdo collects his victim's earrings and keeps and uses their mobile phones too, which is a nightmare to trace because he uses the phones then bins them. He certainly knows this area. He lives around here, makes out he's a Doctor on a dating site and has lost his wife, and of course he comes over as rich, good looking and available.'
'I don't like the sound of him myself George. Look I have to go as time is precious on this. I will phone you the minute I get any information, if there is any. Let's hope for some luck on this, I would very much like to see this creature snuffed out.

Have you any idea how someone suffers drowning like that through their nose? It's a terrible way to go for anyone and it defies belief he does it to a woman.'

'Yes it defies belief that another human can make someone suffer like that Kingsley' replied George. 'It's just sick.'

'This man must hate women George and I would say women of a certain age. It seems to me it may be mother linked somehow. Maybe his mother did something terrible to him but I can't understand the earring thing. Anyway please let me know how things are going and don't forget if you need any help I'll see what I can do.....oh yes this goes in the book George you owe me big time,' and laughed.

'You don't change John, you're all heart, but yes I do owe you and I'm certain you will remind me one of these days, but look let's get on with this ASAP, and thanks again John.'

The time was now 2pm and he had to go, and quickly. That's because he had to see a client about a missing daughter, but he had found her, she was living it up with an Australian idiot in Earls Court she was besotted with him. Well she was nineteen, well over the age of consent, but he had done his job and now he needed to tell his client and his wife. They owned a large shoe manufacturing company they were not short on money. George also needed paying.

CHAPTER TWENTY SEVEN

By the time he was finished and had been paid it was later than he thought. There was still an appointment at 4pm with his accountant and the time now was 4.15 pm so he phoned him to say he was on his way. It had been over a year and his tax returns were due. George didn't want to get into any trouble with the income tax office because he had always paid his tax on time, always had done. However, being stuck in China left him a couple of months short on time, but Mr Buxton his accountant had reassured him he would be able to put it right. However, there may be an extra £100 to pay as a late penalty for missing the deadline which is neither here nor there in the grand scale of things, but he never wanted any fuss with the tax man. He told Julia before he went out he wasn't sure what time he would get back and he'd get a bite to eat while he was out so don't cook anything for him. Anyway, he always had a drink with Mr Buxton and had done so for the last seven years or so. They may do a Chinese, but on second thoughts maybe the pub will get him a steak and chips, that would make a change. After all he had seen enough of the food in China for the last nine weeks and somehow the novelty had worn off.

When he did eventually arrive home there was no-one in and no lights on. The place felt wrong, it felt dead, and he knew something was very wrong. After he put the lights on Julia was not there. He rang her mobile and after three rings a man's voice said 'George Penny, Mr-Fancy-I'm-the-best-investigator, is that you?'

'Who the hell is this?'

'Oh it's just the Primrose killer, that's who. You had better listen to me. I have your woman here and I'm afraid she is going to have to go for a swim in the Thames. Julia is such a nice looking lady, but I'm afraid she still has to go. I'm sorry about all this. Then again you shouldn't have tried to stop me killing Fiona. You have really put me out to say the least, and now I'm a little behind schedule. I have this list you see, still

Julia will do nicely for now. Anyway look, I'm feeling a little generous so I'll let you say a last goodbye. Oh by the way she can't talk, because she's taped up. Bye George, you have a nice evening.'

George didn't panic; he never did because as he said that's when you lose control. But he immediately turned on his tracker device which could tell him within two feet where Julia was. She had it on her mobile phone and the killer now had it in his possession and was using it to ring him on. Yet she also had one in her watch. Big mistake on the killer's part thought George.

Pressing the on switch the screen lit up on his mobile, he could see where she was. They were on the Thames travelling towards Battersea Bridge and moving fast. So he couldn't hang about.

Rushing out he jumped into his BMW series three and took off. Finding himself in Pembridge Road and then at the bottom he turned right into Notting Hill Gate swiftly turning into Kensington Church Street. At the bottom he took a right into Kensington Road and then almost immediately turned right into Palace Gate. Continuing into Gloucester road then turning left at Cromwell Road where he took a right into Onslow Square. Taking another right into Fulham Road and then continuing until he took a left turn into Beaufont Street where he finally saw Battersea Bridge. Thank goodness for Satnavs!

Parking up in the middle left of the bridge with the tracker still going, he suddenly saw the small motor cruiser coming into view, it was heading towards the middle of the bridge and still moving fast. Luckily he had parked on the left hand side and the motor cruiser couldn't see him because he had killed his car lights. He quickly began climbing down onto the middle column and waited a few seconds until he saw the tracker indicating she was about twelve feet away and coming through the middle of the bridge. Now his phone was put in his pocket. As the motor cruiser came within range, he launched himself onto the back of the boat. George could have missed the boat completely, but in the circumstances what choice did he have? It was hit or miss but it was a hit! Managing to grab the back rail with one hand he started to pull himself aboard with both hands. He was looking at Alan Reed, not taking his eyes off him for a second. Julia was sat there tied up he screamed at her to get up.

Alan Reed was totally taken by surprise he turned quickly with the stun gun in his hand. Julia was lying in the back of the boat, but she was unable to do anything. She was confused and not sure what the hell was going on, it was then she heard George talking. She also heard a sound, a loud hooting sound coming from somewhere and it seemed it was getting closer and closer. She felt uncomfortable and she realised what had happened to her, now she was very scared.

'Put it down, put the gun down now.' She heard George yelling at someone.

'No way Penny.' Alan Reed went to use the stun gun on George, but he suddenly stumbled as a wave bumped into the small motor cruiser. George quickly lurched forward and grabbed Alan by his wrist and then he grabbed the other wrist. Now violently shaking both of Alan's wrists' the stun gun fell from his grip into the back of the boat. The two of them struggled in the back of the boat trampling over Julia who was now fully awake. The hooting sound was now a lot louder and was deafening.

The two of them were now trading punches and kicks, but both of them were very strong men, now it was a desperate fight to the end. George managed to break Alan's nose with his elbow and then hit him hard in the throat with his fist. Alan was a onetime tough Paratrooper and was still very fit. Quickly he rallied where he caught George with a left hook and then hit him with a straight right to his jaw, but George always had a granite chin. Coming back with a kick to Alan's balls, one hard kick sent Alan onto his knees.

Julia could see what was happening now but could do nothing. Alan simply picked up the stun gun next to his knees, and now he was smiling at George, his smile was bloody as his lip was split and blood trickled down his chin, he wiped the blood from his chin with the back of his left hand he looked at it then back at George, then he smiled as he took a step nearer with the stun gun in his right hand. The hooting was now deafening getting louder by the second!!

George having no chance of getting the gun quickly grabbed the wheel where he violently turned the boat to the right as the mad hooting sound was now even louder. Alan grabbed the hand rail at the back with one hand to hold on to steady him. George had nowhere to go as Alan came towards him again with the stun gun both men had completely forgotten about Julia.

Alan slowly came along the side of her as she lay in the back of the boat, but then she suddenly lifted her knees up to her chest as she remained lying there. Then very tightly like a coiled spring with her knees tight to her chest she let go and kicked Alan as hard as she possibly could in the side of his knees you could plainly hear a loud snapping sound. Screaming out loud, the force from her kick had broken one of his knees and sent him straight over the side of the boat into the dark swirling cold water of the Thames. Behind them came an even louder hooting sound. The huge Thames barge could not possibly manoeuvre out of the way. The huge barge always came through the middle of the bridge which was the deepest part, unfortunately right where the motor cruiser was. The barge's captain looked on in horror as he knew there was going to be a crash, but there was nothing he could do about it, he had no chance to stop. He'd continually hooted his presence and now his heart stopped, it was now in his mouth as he awaited the inevitable. The huge Thames Barge looked like a giant whale about to gobble up a smaller fish.

George however managed to pull the motor cruiser hard to the left, but the barge came straight on just as Alan Reed surfaced where it ran over him. The look on his face was something George would never forget. Then Alan was sucked under the barge where he became entangled in the huge propellers which had smashed into his once handsome face, taking out his right eye and half of his face including his lower jaw and all of his teeth. It also ripped out his tongue. Suddenly he was in great pain yet was unable to scream out. His right arm was torn off so was his left leg, and his right foot was completely ripped off as he was stuck in the prop shaft as the propeller was taking chunks out of him bit by painful bit.

Where he was once a handsome man, now he became jammed in the prop shaft after the propellers had finished with him and spat him out like a piece of rubbish. When they finally found him later there was nothing much left. They were all pleased because he must have died in great pain. But it was a fitting end to a cruel twisted evil man.

George managed to steady the boat and undid Julia who suddenly became like a spitting tomcat. She laid into him, cursed him and slapped him hard. She punched and kicked him 'you stupid fucking bastard. You almost had me killed again, what the hell is it with you? Are you some kind of moron? I'm going straight back to Spain you bloody idiot. So you Mr bloody Penny can sod off just like a bad penny.' On and on she went....

George took it all because he loved her. She punched and slapped him some more until she held onto him, because she was now utterly exhausted. Holding her close to him she was now sobbing.

He whispered 'I'm so sorry babe, but look it's all over now and it was all thanks to you. That mad man was going to kill us, but you sorted him out easily with one kick and it was you who were tied up at the time. Jesus girl, I'm so very proud of you. Hey you're one gutsy lady and I love you. Thanks for saving my miserable life honey, I owe you.'

'Oh so you owe me do you, then go and get me that bloody ring you promised me.'

'Okay babe, tomorrow I promise you. Come here.' He kissed her and held onto her.

'Listen, I'm never going to let you go, you saved my life. Julia will you marry me babe?'

'What? Marry you? Are you fucking insane do I look like I'm a desperate woman? No bloody way George Penny. You must be joking, you're just too dangerous to know so you can sod off, but I still want that diamond ring.'

CHAPTER TWENTY EIGHT

George's phone rang, it was Sir John Kingsley.
'The man you want is a guy called Alan Reed. Apparently he was discharged from the 16th Medical Regiment, the Parachute Regiment back ten years ago, and he was kicked out for assaulting a senior officer. After being interviewed by the Army's top shrinks over a few days, they found out this guy had one hell of a shitty childhood. It seemed this officer he assaulted was gay and had tried to seduce him and then Reed just lost it. Unfortunately he put the guy in hospital and if it wasn't for two passing corporals, he would have killed the officer who was his captain. As it is the officer was discharged and took early retirement due to his injuries. Under hypnosis everything that happened to Alan came out it all stacked up, but George, it was a very desperate very sad story. We have no reason not to believe the shrinks, yet they were very upset about his childhood and It's a wonder he came this far. His army record was exemplary. The reason he became unstable was due to his terrible upbringing. Apparently it crept up on him over the years and at some time he would lose control, which he has done.'

'Well John, it must have been bad for him to turn the way he has done. Look at the women he killed, and one man. None of them deserved to be killed in that horrible way. He almost killed Julia the same way' said George.

'Every day he was in misery because of the pain, and the beatings George, plus his sexual abuse as a child while his mother had looked on after selling him for an hour at a time to paedophiles while they filmed his pain, especially while half drowning him at the same time. They used to put their hands around his face and over his mouth to stop him screaming but left his nostrils free to breathe, that way he made no noise. One man in particular called uncle Peter liked to press his head with the help of his mother into a large wash basin full of water and while he struggled to breathe the vile man was being satisfied by his mother's hands, also while she was on her knees. They both enjoyed the pain they inflicted on him as a small boy which started from the age of seven until he was eleven years old. Peter paid his mother a large sum of money for his sickening pleasure. For Alan's pain, he always had two Mars bars, and sometimes three tubes of Smarty's and a comic of his choice from the local newsagents. His mother was a hopeless druggie and a prostitute. His father had walked out on them when he was three years old and no one knew where he had gone.

His mother was a feckless one time prostitute who knew all the angles about sex and the sick trade she sold him into, but she needed the money for her habit.'

'Good god John what a terrible life he had' said George.

Apparently he could clearly remember the pain from what his mother and her friend uncle Peter did to him and the horrible moment when he thought he was dead, drowned in a large aluminium bowl of water. Being only eight years old and he remembered how sick he was and the pain from the retching into the bowl really hurt him. His mother told him not to say anything to anyone, or the Police would take her away from him forever. She told him he would be forced to live in a metal box full of worms in a hole in the garden because it was a well known fact if little boys told tales about their mothers that would be his fate, and he would never see anyone again because the worms would slowly eat him to death.

'OMG she was some sick woman John it's hard to know what to say.'

'Sometimes George when she had been on medication she was fine, but then she returned to her old sick ways. He grew up not trusting women, yet all he got for his abuse was a few bars of chocolate from his mother who should have been protecting him, not selling and abusing him. Then when he was eleven years old he found his mother dead in the kitchen with a needle in her arm. She had overdosed on Heroin or so he was told, but he had no idea what that meant, only that she was now dead he was glad about that and now hopefully he thought his tortuous pain would be stopped. However, he was not shocked or even upset; he was in fact happy that she was dead. He felt so free and felt elated that she had overdosed on her Heroin habit. Noticing her gold horseshoe shaped earrings, he decided he wanted them and that's all he ever had from her. He still has them to this day I shouldn't wonder, and he was then taken into care, but there he was abused again and again by the care staff. Finally when he was 17 he joined the army and signed up for the Parachute Regiment. He joined 3 Para where he eventually became a medic in the 16th Med Regt. Alan had served all over the world saving many lives. He was very highly thought of and was mentioned several times in despatches, but he was compulsorily retired as a sergeant when he was aged 38. Since then he had worked as a Paramedic in Exeter but he finally left when he was reported to have stolen drugs and then sold them on the internet, turning him into a prolific thief. Apparently his flat was crammed full of various drugs, he had lots of the date rape drugs which he sold on the internet. Finally he was caught because he was grassed on by a woman, a middle age friend. She was the only woman he had ever trusted. That incident turned on a switch which was just waiting to be tripped and turned him into a murderous killer. The sad thing was he was blessed with movie star looks and would use them to find his prey and eventually wreak terrible havoc. His main weapon now was to disable his victims using the date rape drug Rohypnol. There was plenty in his possession, also having two stun guns handy.'

'Well' said George, 'I suppose being a paramedic it was easy for him to get hold of the drugs.'

'Yes your right. So maybe that may go a long way to explain about his fixation with women's earrings George, and of course the drowning. It enabled him to keep control over them.'

'That sounds horrible John, how the hell could a mother do that to a small child. Yet it's a curious thing that the women he killed were all aged between forty and sixty years old, and his mother was forty seven when she died? It does seem to add up now, but who would have known that? So the mother would have a lot to answer for if she was still alive, but what a crazy bitch, she's ruined lots of lives. You have to lay the blame squarely on her, because she was responsible for this make no mistake.'

The guy was well thought of by his mates and he saved many lives. I wish this had turned out better, we all do, it's so very sad but that's it in a nut shell really. What a sad messy end and a waste of all those lives, seven in all and eight including him and I'm certain there would have been many more until he was caught, so well done George and a well done to Julia too.'

'I felt elated we got him John but now I feel sad, bloody sad. Oh and don't forget it was Julia who saved the day she saved my life as well as her own.'

'Oh yes George, and his last known address is 93, Lenox Street, West Kilburn. That sixth sense you have which you call a hunch should be bottled. Yes you were correct, he had been in the military and he also had a record. Oh and try and remember we will be requiring your services one of these days.'

'John you don't need to remind me of that, but being a man of my word I have made a mental note. So listen John he's dead, very dead, so we thank you for your help. Can I pop round to see you say 11am tomorrow in the Red Bull? I will tell you the full story tomorrow, at the moment I have the Police with me. We are going to go over all this again while it's still fresh. Remember as I said he almost killed Julia, and believe me she is now one very pissed off lady. She's just beat the crap out of me and now I'm in the bloody dog house without a roof!'

Sir John Kingsley laughed 'serves you right George. I'll see you tomorrow.'

George had rung DCI Eric Fletcher who came straight out with his sidekick DC Ron Buckley. Fletcher had the Police dive team recovered the body of the Primrose killer. There was not a lot left as his legs were missing because they had been wrenched off and also one of his arms. His once handsome face had been pulverized to skin and bone, but there was plenty of DNA left and later it did match the DNA in the two hats the killer wore. They were 100% certain he was the Primrose killer. They didn't celebrate, it would have seemed wrong in the circumstances.

They were all glad he was dead and out of the way, but later the newspapers had a field day and dug around until they found all about Alan Reed. They printed his life story which went on for months.

Eric thanked George for his help but he really wasn't bothered about the glory of catching the killer. He was just pleased he was dead and would not be killing anybody else.

DCI Fletcher asked George how he had been able to get the DNA from the Army.

George said to DCI Fletcher, 'look this is in strict confidence Eric. He had worked with MI5 on a couple of occasions in the past. In fact it was not that long ago, but he could not, and would not disclose any details or he would be slung into the Tower of London where they would throw the key away,' he laughed. 'Anyway it was all down to a favour and now he owed them a favour in return, and that's about it really' he told Fletcher.

When they searched Alan Reeds house they found all the evidence they needed. There were all the garden ties, lots of the Rohypnol drug, and another stun gun. They found the taxi keys and the address where he garaged it. They searched the garage and found all the evidence they needed, including the DNA of the women he killed still inside of the taxi, plus lots of heavy railway sleeper bolts used to weigh the heads down and supermarket bags.

They also found some of the mobile phones. They had a sample of his handwriting which matched the writing on the torn piece of paper from Helen Burk's diary and the rip also fitted like a piece of jigsaw found by George in the boot of the toy car which was on her key ring. Last but not least, there were all the earrings in a small jewellery box by his bedside including other items such as bracelets and a few rings, in a drawer below there was a few bottles etc of perfume. When it was opened it smelt of various perfumes from all the women. Julia refused to have hers back and told George to get her some more.

That concluded to everyone 100% that he had been the Primrose Killer. There was also a book of photographs when he was in the Parachute Regiment from the age of seventeen to when he had been discharged out of the 16th Medical Regiment aged 38 on medical grounds.

At this moment in time George and Julia, are still together, but as yet still not married.

THE END